ERIC THE ROMANTIC

PETER CHILD

Benbow Publications

© Copyright 2006 by Peter Child

Peter Child has asserted his right under the Copyright, Designs and Patents Act, 1988 to be identified as the author of this work.

All rights reserved. No part of this publication may be reproduced, stored in a retrieval system, or transmitted in any form or by any means, electronic, mechanical photocopying, recording or otherwise without the prior permission of the copyright owner.

Published in 2006 by Benbow Publications

British Library
Cataloguing in Publication Data.

ISBN: 0–9540910–6–X

Printed by Lightning Source UK Limited,
6 Precedent Drive, Rooksley,
Milton Keynes, MK13 8PR

First Edition

OTHER TITLES BY THE AUTHOR

MARSEILLE TAXI

AUGUST IN GRAMBOIS

CHRISTMAS IN MARSEILLE

CATASTROPHE IN LE TOUQUET

NON FICTION

VEHICLE PAINTER'S NOTES

VEHICLE FINE FINISHING

VEHICLE FABRICATIONS IN G.R.P.

NOTES FOR GOOD DRIVERS

NOTES FOR COMPANY DRIVERS

Characters and events portrayed in this book are fictional.

ACKNOWLEDGEMENTS

Once again, I wish to gratefully acknowledge the help and assistance given to me by Sue Gresham, who edited and set out the book, and Wendy Tobitt for the splendid cover presentation. Without these talented and patient ladies this book would not have been possible.

Peter Child

PREFACE

Love………..

A life without love is no life at all.

You can't stop loving someone because they've stopped loving you.

You may fall in love once and believe that every other relationship may be a compromise.

To love is to burn… to be on fire.

You can't be wise and in love at the same time.

Disappointment in love must be embraced and treated with indifference.

The essence of romance is uncertainty.

Love can arrive unexpectedly so be ready to grasp it, otherwise it may pass you by.

True love will always win in the end.

Each and everyone of us has a guardian Angel to look after us to ensure that we are protected, as much as possible, from the trials and tribulations of this life and guide us towards a life time of love with one person. However, slight problems can arise if the Angel is on his first mission with no previous operational experience….

CHAPTER 1

PETER MEETS ERIC

Childe Eric Bloodaxe told me that he was born in Trondheim, Norway, but moved soon after to a little village called Storvigga, of course I have no way of proving that, or indeed anything else that he told me. All I do know is that he did have quite an effect on my life and I am still unsure whether to thank him or not. You alone know if you have made all the right decisions when you can look back sometime later using the accurate science of hindsight. Guidance from a sincere person like Eric is a wonderful thing, providing it is in the right direction. Unfortunately for me, Eric was much more of a 'hands on' Viking warrior with a very poor sense of direction, and I think Helen's experience was similar to mine.

Eric Bloodaxe is a Viking, or I should say, was a Viking. He was thirty two years old, about six feet six inches tall with a mop of blonde hair and the most piercing light blue eyes you have ever seen. With his tanned face, glinting white teeth and striking physique you might say he was or still is very handsome. He had that way about him, the gentle toss of the head, the smile, the melting look in his blue eyes that would, and apparently did, attract women of any age.

I first became aware of him as I strolled along the Ridgeway near the old hill fort above the White Horse at Uffington, on the Berkshire Downs. I was trying to gather my thoughts and praying for some sort of guidance out of the mess that was my life He was standing to the side of the path and I was more than a little anxious as I passed him by. I had never seen such a large man dressed up as a Viking carrying a huge double bladed axe and assumed he was part of one of these re-enactment clubs that put on shows of historic fighting and daring exploits for the public. Two walkers came in the opposite direction and they wished me 'good morning' as they passed by me but took no notice whatever of the Viking. I became more concerned as I looked back over my shoulder and saw that he was following me. 'Oh, God' I thought, 'trust me to meet a mugger that big and with an axe!' and I started to walk much faster, praying that I would meet more walkers coming towards me. The sun shone, the gently drifting clouds rolled by and there was no one in sight. I thought 'typical, when you need help there is no one around'. Perhaps I could outrun him, but gave that idea up straight away as I was conscious of his presence right behind me. Perhaps, with one mighty blow from his axe, he would kill me and that would put an end to all my troubles. No more letters from the Bank manager, no more credit card bills, and no more rows with my stupid wife. I would laugh like a drain as they cremated me. I could see them all now, gathered together in the chapel at the crematorium, crying and... suddenly a deep voice behind me called my name "Peter" and I stopped dead in my tracks and turned to face the Viking.

"Hello, I'm Eric" he said with a smile, as he looked down at me.

"How do you know my name?" I demanded, but not too aggressively, aware of his size and of his axe.

"It's a long story" he replied.

"Really" I said, unsure whether I was ready for a long story from this handsome giant.

"Shall we rest awhile so we can talk?" he asked gently.

"What about?"

"You" he said.

"Me?"

"Yes."

"I don't think so...."

"It is important" he persisted.

I thought 'well, I am my favourite subject' and replied "okay", being very curious and not wishing to upset his plans for me in any way. He indicated towards a small mound in the green grass of the Down, some distance away from the path and said "over there then."

"Why not" I replied, trying to sound manly and totally unconcerned whilst wondering who the bloody hell he was. I felt sure that if he planned to mug me or even murder me, there could not be a nicer place, the mound even looked like an ancient burial chamber; a sort of murderer's one stop shop. We reached the grassy top and he lowered himself gently and placed his axe to one side. Then he rested back on his elbows, his huge tanned forearms rippling as he relaxed. He tossed his head and his long blonde hair fell away from his shoulders. I sat down, sort of half opposite, not too close and waited for him to speak. He fixed his blue eyes in a distant gaze over the gently rolling countryside and said, very slowly "I'm here on a very important mission...."

"Really" I interrupted, hoping that I could soon resume my walk so that I could worry about my various predicaments in peace.

"I've come to give you some help and guidance, but I've never done anything like this before, you understand?"

"Perfectly" I replied, now certain that he was a nutter as well as an axe murderer; well I suppose they are one and the same. We sat for a while and admired the view before I decided to break the silence.

"Well, I'd be happy to have any help that would settle some of my problems, for a start there's my Bank overdraft...." I began.

"That is of no interest to me" he replied looking at me for an instant before returning his gaze to the countryside.

"It is to me!" I replied and added "I thought you said you were here to help me?"

"I am, but not in unimportant matters."

"Goodbye then, Eric" I said and stood up. I had no more time to spend with this strange bloke talking about 'help' and 'guidance', he was obviously a dead loss and probably just wanted someone to talk to about his problems. 'A lucky escape from a boring conversation' I thought as I hurried away. I had just reached the path and was retracing my steps towards my parked car when his voice boomed out "Peter, I need to talk to you!"

"Oh, do you" I replied and added "I'm not interested...."

"It's all about your future" he said.

"Really" I replied in a disinterested tone.

"Yes, you and your wife...." That stopped me and thought perhaps I had just better listen for a while.

"So, come back and sit with me" he called.

"I can't stay long, I'll be late for lunch, I've got business to attend to and my wife...."

"Never mind about lunch, this is important" he interrupted.

"It had better be, Janet gets awfully cross if I...."

"Peter!" There are times in life when you know that to disobey someone can land you in very hot water and this was one of those times. I made my way back to the burial mound and sat down, well away from the axe. I decided to go onto the offensive.

"Are you one of these re-enactment characters putting on a show up at the fort?" I asked.

"No, I'm a Viking."

"Yes, I can see that"

"And I'm far from my home" he replied wistfully.

"Where's home then?"

"A village near Trondheim."

"What's it called?"

"Do you care?"

"Not really, I'm just curious" I said with a shrug.

"It's called Storvigga."

"That's nice."

"Have you ever been to Norway?"

"Yes, twice to Oslo, in the winter" I replied.

"Ah, Oslo, the women are very beautiful there" he sighed.

"And it snows a lot" I added helpfully.

"That doesn't matter when you're in the long house beside the fire, covered with furs and a strong, warm woman underneath you" he laughed.

"I suppose not" I replied as my mind conjured up the scene, all hot and sweaty.

"But Valhalla is different" he said cheerfully.

"Valhalla, isn't that where Vikings go after they are dead?" I asked a little anxiously.

"Yes, it is" he replied looking me straight in the eye. The enormity of what he had just said struck me like one of Thor's thunderbolts. 'Was this man dead? A ghost? O, my God' I thought as my imagination went into a spiral dive followed by the rest of my numb mind.

"So, if you've been to Valhalla" and I gulped at this point "why are you here?" I asked, then wishing I hadn't.

"In Valhalla I was told I was there too soon for my age and experience and I would not be allowed to stay there."

"Really?" I asked, open mouthed.

"Yes."

"So, I take it then, that you think you're dead?" I paused, dreading the implications.

"Only my body is."

"You look as if you're all there to me" I replied, thinking this bloke was just a joker.

"Well, it seemed a like a dream" he replied.

"Tell me then" I said, my curiosity beginning to overcome my fear.

He returned his gaze to the view before us and we sat for a while in silence whilst he gathered his thoughts and memories. I confess I did pinch myself a couple of times just to make sure I wasn't dreaming.

"When I left Storvigga in our long boat with the others, I was looking forward to the adventures that Gunther had planned." I listened and was mesmerised, was this true or some mighty send up? A sort of candid camera or new TV spoof? Would I see myself on television some months later as the 'idiot on the Downs'?

"We rowed hard for several days, until we picked up a gentle wind and hoisted our sail. The sea became calmer and the air was warmer as we sailed towards the south, it was very pleasant for us. We passed the time by telling tales of Childe Harold and Beowulf and wondered what Thor would do to us if we failed in our raid on the coast."

"You must have been concerned" I said helpfully and he nodded.

"Gunther had been with the warriors who raided Lindisfarne, and was very successful."

"Good for Gunther" I replied and Eric looked at me for a moment. The murderous bastards had slain the monks at Lindisfarne and made the place desolate. I was right to be suspicious of this teller of tales. Eric continued with his story, all the while praising Gunther for his powerful leadership and going into great detail about their voyage down the east coast of England. I waited with interest to find out where they landed to begin their raid upon the poor English peasants who were quietly going about their business of just trying to survive.

"After we landed we made our way to a small village and

found the men waiting for us, but they couldn't fight and we overcame them quickly."

"Good for you" I said encouragingly.

"And then we had some of the women who didn't run off and hide......."

"I'm glad it all went well" I interrupted and stood up.

"The woman I had was very lovely and she gave into me without a struggle" he said wistfully.

"I'm not surprised" I replied.

"It was a good adventure......."

"I'm sure it was....."

"And only a few days later I met my death...." And he paused and looked wistful.

"Go on" I said.

"We were attacking another village and the men there put up a good fight, three of them surrounded me and whilst I slew one with my axe the other two came close and stabbed me with swords, I fell but managed to strike a blow at one of them and brought him down, then I saw Langfred kill the other as I lay dying......."

"Very interesting if I may so, but you'll have to excuse me, I have a customer to see and an angry wife at home who is getting angrier by the minute" I said firmly.

He looked up at me, smiled and said "very well, go to your business and your wife but aren't you curious to know how I can help you?"

"No, not really" I replied, I was not interested and just wanted to get away from this overpowering and frightening person.

"You are a strange man and I think you will be difficult to guide" he said.

"I'm strange?"

"Yes, and I will have to meet you again to try and make you understand what I am trying to do" he replied in a firm tone.

"Then I look forward to seeing you sometime, goodbye" I replied, hoping I had humoured him enough to make my escape.

I walked as fast as I could towards the car park, glancing back only once to see if he was following me. He was still where I had left him, sitting on the grassy mound and I began to breathe a little easier. When I reached my car I fumbled nervously with the key before at last opening the door and swinging in behind the wheel. I tried to compose myself before starting up and driving off towards Reading, where I was due to see an irate customer with a paint problem before going home to face Janet and her moods. I must admit, I had the shakes and only by concentrating on the driving did I manage to put Eric to the back of my mind.

I arrived at Marparts vehicle repair shop in Caversham, parked and went into see the paint shop manager, Geoff Davies. Normally quite a reasonable person but when he was under a lot of pressure from his boss, Tony Gardner, Geoff could be very difficult.

"I'm glad you're here, come and see this bloody awful colour match!" he said as soon as I entered his untidy office. I followed him to the spray booth where a Ford Mondeo stood with a re-sprayed door that was an entirely different colour to the rest of the car.

"Just bloody look at it!" he commanded.

"Did you check the colour before you sprayed it?" I asked meekly, sensing his growing anger.

"Charlie said he did" replied Geoff testily.

"But did he?" I persisted.

"Look, Peter, that's the third mis-match we've had this week and I reckon some of your formulations on the colour scheme are way off."

"I promise you, they are all carefully checked in the lab before........."

"Bloody hell, Peter, I don't care! Just look at it!" he shouted. I was stuck for words.

"We've got to re-spray the bloody thing again, more cost and Anne on reception told the customer he could pick it up tonight!"

"Oh."

"Tony's going mad and has told me to chuck your mixing scheme out and go over to ICI Autocolor!" That struck terror into my heart because vehicle refinishers would change paint suppliers at the toss of a coin and the loss of such a big account would ensure that I was on the end of a tongue lashing from my manager, Freddie Martin, who could be really unpleasant when the occasion arose, as I knew from past experience.

"No need for that, Geoff, I'll arrange for one of our technical reps to come down tomorrow and colour match the paint so that the owner will never know it's been re-sprayed" I said, hoping that one of our tech boys was free. Oh, God, I seemed to fly through life on a wing and a prayer. Geoff smiled and relaxed.

"Okay, I'll let Tony know what's happening and we'll put the owner off until tomorrow evening" he said and I managed a sickly grin hoping that the company could meet the commitment I had just made.

I had started work in the sales office of Beauclare Paints four years ago and two years later had been promoted to sales representative covering outer London and home counties. I enjoyed the freedom of being out on the road but the complaints from customers and the pressure from Freddie made me feel like a plum in a vice, and sometimes it seemed as if everything was getting unbearably tight.

I left Marparts and settled down for a quiet drive home, fully meaning to 'phone the lab to see if either Jimmy or Frank were free to come down to Reading, colour match the Mondeo and save the day. Events, however, often take over and one's best intentions get forgotten.

As I drove down the Oxford Road and out towards Pangbourne I saw two young women standing by the roadside thumbing a lift. As I drew closer I noticed that they were both very attractive and foolishly, I stopped.

"Where are you going to?" I asked the petite one.

"To Oxford" she replied in an Italian accent accompanied by a big smile. She was gorgeous with a flawless olive skin, a mop of thick black hair and deep brown eyes.

"You're in luck, so am I, jump in!"

The petite one clambered in beside me while her taller and statuesque friend sat in the back and I had a big smile on my face as we drove off.

"We've been awaiting ages for a lift you know" said the petite one in her Italian accent. The Italians sing their language and it is a delight to listen to them.

"I find that hard to believe" I murmured.

"So, I thanker you for a stopping, we both thanker you."

"That's okay, now tell me your names, please" I smiled.

"I'ma Sophia and my friend is Nicole, her English is nota too good at the momenta, but she gets a better everyday and she will try something on you later, I'm a sure."

"Anytime she likes" I replied as I looked at the attractive girl in my rear view mirror. She had the same flawless skin, shoulder length black hair and brown eyes with amazing eyelashes.

"And whatsa your name?"

"Peter."

"Peter" Sophia repeated.

"Are you on holiday?" I asked as we approached the centre of Pangbourne.

"No, we are au pair in London" replied Sophia.

"Have you been here long?"

"Justa three months" she replied.

"And where in Italy do you come from?"

"Milan."

"That's a lovely city" I said.

"You've been there?"

"Yes, several times" I replied.

"Dida you like it?" she asked.

"Certainly did, and the one thing I noticed was that, whilst some English girls are beautiful all the Italian girls are very beautiful" I said as I turned to look at her and she laughed.

"I thinka you could be a naughty man" she replied.

"Me? No, never, I'm a straight laced Englishman, far too shy to be naughty."

"Whatsa 'straight laced'?" enquired Nicole from the back seat.

"Proper, er, dignified" I replied unsure of how to explain it.

"Okay" said Nicole.

"So, why are you going to Oxford?" I asked.

"We've never been and we want to see it on our day off" replied Sophia.

"And are you staying in Oxford?"

"No, we go back to London tonight" Sophia replied.

"You're not going to hitch hike at night I hope?"

"Of course, it will be a okay" she replied.

"No it won't, look, how about I drive you around Oxford, show you the sights and then drive you back to London" I said, not missing an opportunity to spend time with lovely young women.

"You woulda do that for us?"

"I'd be delighted" I replied.

"Oh, you are so gooda for a naughty man" she replied. I smiled and felt all warm and comfortable, I quite liked being a 'good naughty man'.

"Have you eaten at lunch time?" I asked.

"No, nota much, justa sandwich" she replied.

"Okay, on the way back tonight I'll take you for a meal in a Berni that I know at Maidenhead."

"You take us for dinner tonight?"

"Why not?"

"You must be a rich, naughty man" she laughed.

"No, it'll be all taken care of" I replied whilst wondering if I could put the bill on my expenses and get it passed Freddie's beady eyes for approval.

"Okay, that'sa very good and thanker you."

"My pleasure." We motored on up through Wallingford and onto Oxford. I drove around the city slowly, pointing out the various colleges that I knew and the girls asked me to stop several times to take photos. They were both as delightful as they were beautiful and I was quite enchanted by them both. In my enchanted state I completely forgot about 'phoning the lab and my permanently angry wife, Janet.

It was still quite bright when we left Oxford in the rush hour and headed for Maidenhead where I planned to take them to a steak dinner with all the trimmings.

"Whata do you do for a living?" asked Sophia.

"I'm a vehicle paint rep" I replied.

"Whatsa 'rep'?" asked Nicole.

"I represent the company, I sell car paint."

"You're a salesman?" asked Sophia.

"Yes."

"Is it harda to sell paint?" she asked.

"Very" I replied.

"Why?"

"Because we have so many technical problems with it" I replied.

"Like a what?"

"The colours don't always match and the owners can spot the difference" I replied as suddenly I remembered that I had to phone the lab for Jimmy or Frank. I glanced at my watch, it was almost six. The lab was closed and everyone would have gone home by now. Bloody hell! I made a mental note to phone first thing in the morning and then relaxed into easy conversation with the two Italian beauties.

We eventually arrived at the Berni Inn at Maidenhead where we enjoyed steaks followed by ice cream and several drinks. The girls were quite relaxed and giggly when we climbed back in the car and set off for London.

"Where do you live?" I asked as we joined the M4 motorway and I accelerated to keep up with the traffic.

"Highgate" replied Sophia and then after a pause "do you know it?"

"Certainly do" I replied.

"Good, but whena we get home, there's no coming in for coffee" she replied and they both started to giggle. I laughed and replied "that's okay, I don't like coffee." They laughed out loud at that.

"So, whata do you go in for?" asked Nicole between giggles.

"There's no answer to that" I replied and more laughter followed

"Come on, you naughty man, tell us" demanded Sophia.

"I never get asked, so I never go in" I replied honestly. More laughter and silly banter followed and the journey to Highgate was over all to soon for me. When I pulled up outside the imposing house I looked at Sophia and asked "am I going to see you again?"

"Why nota?" she smiled and then opened her handbag and produced a little card with her name, Sophia Portovecchio and phone number.

"Call me" she smiled.

"I will, Ms Pinocchio" I replied and she laughed.

"Portovecchio" she corrected firmly as I lunged at her for a quick kiss but she dodged away and got out of the car laughing. I waved and drove off, glancing in my rear view mirror at the two of them.

I drove quickly home to my little semi-detached house in Wantage and with a heavy heart opened the front door.

"Well, where have you been?" demanded my angry wife from

her place on the settee opposite the television.

"With customers" I replied as I made my way through and into the kitchen.

"Liar" she shouted. I shrugged my shoulders and filled the kettle.

"Want a coffee?" I called.

"Your dinner's in the oven."

"Thanks, but I'm not hungry."

"Not surprised" she replied, her voice full of contempt.

Janet and I had been at each others throats for more than six months now and the situation was getting noticeably worse. I could not stand it much more and had made up my mind to leave the angry, argumentative woman. An evening with Sophia and Nicole brought everything into focus and their light hearted, lovely attitude to life contrasted vividly with Janet's sour outpourings.

I made coffee for myself and wandered into the lounge and sat at the opposite end of the settee.

"Busy day?" I enquired.

"Shh, I'm watching" she replied whilst gazing intently at the television. I let my mind wander back to the pleasant afternoon and evening that I had spent with the hitch hikers and never said another word until the silly programme finished.

"Oh, I almost forgot, your manager, whatisname phoned earlier and wanted to talk to you, he said it was urgent and to call him as soon as you got in" she smirked.

"Oh, thanks a bunch, why couldn't you have told me when I first came in?" I demanded.

"I forgot" she smirked again and then put a large piece of chocolate into her mouth and returned her gaze to the television. I glanced at my watch, it was almost eleven and too late to call Freddie, I'd have to do it first thing.

"I'm going up, you coming?" I asked.

"In a minute" she replied.

"Please your bloody self" I muttered and went upstairs to bed knowing there would be no chance of any romance of any kind. I was just plain trapped in a marriage that didn't work and a job that squeezed the very life out of me and I had debts that would make a merchant banker weep. I lay in bed and thought of Sophia and I was sure that I would call her tomorrow, immediately after

Freddie and the lab. Sophia was my ray of sunshine in a gloomy world. Then Eric popped into my mind and I began to feel very uneasy. He was shaking his head at me and I wanted to ask 'why?' but I couldn't, it was a strange experience and I did my best to forget him. Then I heard Janet's heavy footsteps on the stairs, God, if only she'd lose some weight, and then I forgot all about Eric.

CHAPTER 2

HELEN GOES SAILING

I had driven from my home in Atlantic City on that bright April morning to Cape May where I moored my little boat, 'Indian Princess'. Actually the 'Princess' belonged to Dad, he bought her some years ago when his auto repair business made a decent profit for the first time, and he knew how I loved to sail her, so, when business got even better, he gave her to me. She is just the cutest little thirty foot yacht in the harbour and I love her to bits. Dad then treated himself to 'Atlantic Dreamer' a very nice forty footer with the most beautiful and luxurious cabin. Mom and Dad are weekend sailors who don't venture far along the coast but, like me, they enjoy the freedom of just getting away from it all with a touch of luxury. My only regret was that my daughter, Melodie, had decided that she was not going to go sailing after all, well eight year olds can be difficult, and I had deposited her with Mom for the day. They were both okay about that.

I parked my Chevrolet in the area close to the jetty where all the smaller boats were moored. The big boys with the sixty foot plus beauty's have got a large park where they draw up in their big, fancy Mercedes and BMW's at the weekend, before setting off to face the roaring Atlantic, returning to their offices in Baltimore on Monday, ruddy faced and exhausted.

I first saw Eric as I got close to the 'Princess', he was leaning back on one of the large wooden jetty supports, and I was struck first of all by his height. He was a very big guy and as I got nearer to my yacht I could not stop looking at him. He had a most handsome face, a mop of blonde hair and a pair of blue eyes that penetrated the deepest part of a woman's soul. Oh my God! He moved, straightened up and I realised he was going to speak.

"Hello" he smiled. I couldn't answer so I just nodded and mumbled something. Well it's not every day that a tall, very good looking, tanned, blue eyed stranger says 'hello'. I gazed into his eyes with a thousand yard stare normally associated with rabbits about to be run over on the Freeway.

"Hello" he repeated.

"Hi" I managed.

"Are you going sailing, Helen?"

"Yes" I replied, forgetting to ask how he knew my name.

"It's a good day for it, the wind is calm and the sea is gentle" he nodded.

"Sure is" I replied with a little more confidence. Was this guy trying to hit on me or did he just want to go sailing?

"Do I know you?" I said in a firm tone.

"My name is Eric Bloodaxe, but please just call me Eric." Well, I was glad we got the 'Bloodaxe' out of the way. I mean, why couldn't we have been introduced properly at one of Dad's auto trade functions? Eric would look fabulous in a white Tuxedo with that tan and blonde hair and I could look pretty cute in that little black dress that Reece bought me for my birthday, although it does make my bum look a bit big.

"Are you a yachtsman, Eric?" I ventured nervously, realising that I was all alone on the jetty with this gorgeous creature.

"No, not really, I'm a Viking, more use to rowing than sailing" he smiled.

"Of course you are" I replied, attempting to humour this giant.

"So, if you're going sailing, I'll come with you and we can talk" he said firmly.

"I don't think so, Eric."

"Why not?"

"I don't know who you are" I replied.

"I've told you, I'm Eric Bloodaxe."

"It's the Bloodaxe that makes me nervous" I replied, now certain I was dealing with a psycho and I glanced back along the jetty hoping I might see someone. There was nobody in sight. Suddenly he took several giant strides across the jetty and stepped aboard the 'Princess'.

"You have nothing to fear from me, I assure you, I've come to help and guide you" he smiled and held out his large hand. I couldn't resist him and suddenly I felt quite calm, I mean, if he was going to rape me before throwing me overboard, I might enjoy it. I hadn't been laid for almost a year and was forgetting how good it could be with the right guy. Eric might be the right guy, as long as he was gentle. On the other hand, a little rough stuff might be quite enjoyable, so I grasped his hand which was warm and surprisingly soft and stepped aboard my 'Princess'.

"There, that wasn't too difficult, was it?" he asked as his blue eyes danced and twinkled at me. I somehow felt his presence go right down into my soul.

"No."

"So relax, you're in command and I'll do anything you want me to" he smiled.

My mind raced with a thousand thoughts of what I'd like to do with this hunk. Have a quick sail along the coast and back, then get him cleaned up and out of his strange, sleeveless fur jacket and leather trousers, show him off to my friends Rachel and Karen, take him to dinner at Rolfe's cosy restaurant and then back to my place for late night coffee and a relaxing brandy or two. Melodie would have to stay over at Mom and Dads' for the night, I might make a noise and disturb her as I finally gave into him on the fur rug in front of my open log fire. I imagined my legs wrapped around that slim, tight waist... Oh my God, I felt myself getting hot and randy just at the thought of it and then common sense kicked in, I mean, who in the hell was this guy? I must be stupid having such thoughts about a complete stranger. I tried to concentrate as I released the 'Princess' from her moorings and started the little auxiliary motor to get the yacht clear of the harbour entrance. As soon as we reached the open sea I set the mainsail and a gentle breeze caught the 'Princess'. She started to make way and the gentle slapping of the waves was the only sound as she bobbed with the swell of the Atlantic.

"This is lovely" he said as he glanced up at me standing behind the helm holding on tight to the wheel.

"Sure is" I agreed and tried to look away from his piercing eyes.

"Do you always sail alone?" he asked.

"Sometimes I bring my daughter" I replied.

"What's her name?"

"Melodie."

"Melodie? That's a strange name for a girl."

"Not as strange as Eric Bloodaxe for a boy" I countered and he laughed out loud at that.

"You are very brave" he said.

"You think so?"

"I do, any woman who goes sailing on her own and calls her child, Melodie, has to be fearless."

"Right."

"But perhaps her father was responsible for the name" he smiled. As soon as he mentioned her father, I saw before me the face of that unreliable, unfaithful, bastard, Reece Jackman, who asked me to marry him, got me pregnant and then a month before the wedding, broke up with me. He wandered off to Paris and humped some French bitch that he met at a trade convention in New York. It was all very 'parlez-vous Francais, while I get my knickers off'. It is the accent that does it, the English are the same, we just get hopelessly sucked in by them. When he was all puffed out and broke in France he crept back home and thought I'd be okay about it all. We started to get back together but as soon as Melodie was born, he disappeared again. This time it was with a Mexican bitch, a waitress at some honky tonk bar in downtown Dallas. She was all big tits and long, jet black hair, but as soon as the first rush of horizontal hump dancing was over he was back in Atlantic City telling me how much he missed me and wasn't our baby beautiful? I was not impressed at the time and neither were Mom and Dad, but against their advice I gave the son of a bitch another shot at our relationship.

"No, I named her" I replied firmly as I tried to erase Reece from my mind for the moment. Eric caught the tone of my voice, nodded and looked forward, out over the grey green ocean.

"Sometimes I bring my best friend, Rachel, when she's up to it" I said, thinking of the lovely woman trapped in a wheelchair after her accident.

"Does she enjoy it?"

"Yes, she does, and I do too, she's great and we laugh a lot, we're just as silly as we were in High School together."

"It is good to have friends, they are very precious, because we choose them and they choose us."

"Not like relatives, eh?"

"Exactly!"

"Have you any relatives, children for instance?" I enquired, trying not to sound too curious.

"No, I'm not even married" he said in an offhand way whilst shaking his head. Yes! There is a God!

"Shame" I replied with a grin and swung the wheel to bring the 'Princess' more into wind and gather speed. Perhaps dinner at Rolfe's followed by late night coffee in front of the fire was a distinct possibility. I hoped I had brought enough logs in from the backyard.

"So, tell me about your friend, Rachel" he said as he stretched out his long legs across the cockpit.

"We were at High School, as I said, and we just went everywhere and did everything together until her riding accident a few years ago" I replied sadly.

"What happened?" he asked gently.

"She was riding her horse, Magenta, and she attempted to jump a hedge but there was a low wall beyond it and Rachel didn't see it until it was too late. Magenta caught the wall and stumbled and rolled on top of Rachel. The horse broke her leg and had to be destroyed and Rachel fractured her spine."

"That is very sad" he replied.

"Now Rachel's in a damned wheelchair for ever, she's very brave but sometimes she cries and says 'you have to be disabled to know what it is like'." There was a long silence whilst we both slipped into our thoughts.

"Is she married?"

"No, she was engaged to a nice guy called Mike, but after the accident, well, he couldn't handle her disability and they broke up" I sighed and swung the wheel in frustration at life in general whilst wondering why men always have to mess women up.

"That is shameful" he replied as he fixed me with his blue eyes that looked a little sad.

"Rachel says she's got no hope of getting married now."

"There's always hope."

"Perhaps."

"You never know what Fate has in store for us" he said with conviction.

"True" I replied vaguely.

"For instance, you didn't expect to meet me today, did you?" he smiled.

"No, I didn't, and what the hell do you..." I started angrily and then thought of coffee with Eric in front of the log fire and calmed down, well a girl has got to hope, before I continued "want with someone like me?" I smiled.

"Ah, you're a very special person to me" he replied nodding his head gently and I liked the sound of that.

"Go on" I smiled, intrigued and very curious, just at that moment a gust of wind caught the 'Princess' and she heeled over, I swung the wheel to compensate whilst Eric, realising the imminent danger, leaned his tall frame over the side to help balance her. I only just managed to get her back on an even keel and then decided that I did not want any more interruptions to our interesting conversation, so began a slow turn to head back towards the harbour.

"Are you alright?" he asked.

"Yes, thanks."

"We nearly tipped over" he nodded.

"I know."

"Are we going back?"

"Yes."

"So soon?"

"Yes."

"Shame, I was just beginning to really enjoy our voyage" he smiled.

"I'm not in the mood for two dangerous moments today" I replied.

"Two?"

"Yes, you're the first and the near capsize of my boat was the second!" He laughed out loud at that and shook his blonde head.

"I'm a dangerous moment, am I?" he was still laughing.

"You are to me" I replied with a smile.

"Really?"

"Yes."

"Why?"

"Well, for a start, I don't know who the goddam hell you are...."

"I'm Eric Bloodaxe...."

"I know that, but who are you really and what do you want with me?" I demanded.

"If you stop interrupting, I'll tell you...."

"And you're too good looking to be alone on my boat with me!" I interrupted boldly and he laughed out once again at that.

"Oh, no, Helen, you must not think of me as a man for lovemaking!" Well that shattered me and I nearly lost control of the 'Princess' for a moment.

"I'm not available for you, although, you are very attractive and in other circumstances I would like to have you naked underneath me in front of a roaring fire!" he smiled.

"Sounds good to me" I replied under my breath.

"No, Helen, it cannot be." Well 'fuck my old riding boots' I thought, what is he playing at?

"What are these circumstances I should know about?" I queried as I felt the unashamed, absolute desire for this man who was 'unavailable.' There is nothing so attractive to a woman than a man who, for whatever reason, is momentarily out of reach, I stress 'momentarily'.

"I have come to help and guide you" he smiled.

"That's fine, we'll moor up, get cleaned up and you can tell me over dinner tonight exactly how you're going to help...."

"No, Helen, I have to leave you as soon as we reach the jetty" he smiled.

"Why?"

"I'll explain everything to you later."

"Later? When?" I was so damned curious about this guy. He was so disarming, I felt foolish throwing myself at him, well, for God's sake, what was the matter with me? I hate being rejected, just hate it. I mean, I think I'm attractive for a woman of thirty, I've got a good figure, although I would like a slightly larger bust and a slightly smaller bum, I've got long legs and my dark hair is pretty neat, I've blue eyes, not the piercing type like Eric's, but big and hopefully, appealing. My nose needs a little straightening but other than that I'm in pretty good shape. And I know I could turn Eric on and give him a night to remember in front of the fire.

"So, when's 'later'?" I asked again.

"I'll meet you at some convenient moment" he replied.

"I guess I'll never see you again" I replied as I swung the wheel to bring the 'Princess' about a few more degrees as she headed towards the harbour entrance.

"You'll see me occasionally for the rest of your life" he said in a solemn tone.

"What?"

"You heard me" he replied.

I really did not understand this guy and I guessed it was the beginning of another frustrating relationship with a man. After Reece left me the third time for a black Creole lap dancer that he met in Louisville and attempted to come back after the shine had worn off her butt, thinking all would be forgiven, I had buried myself in Dad's business to try and forget. Although Reece kept on at me, I did not want to know the geek and a while later met Bobby. He was an auto accident assessor for City Insurance and often came to the autobody repair shop that Dad owned in Atlantic City. He would come and chat in the accounts office where I looked after some of the finances. He was a nice, amiable guy and we started dating. Nothing too serious because I was still unsure about men after Reece and I did not want to get involved too soon. However, Bobby lost interest after a few dinner dates when he realised that I wasn't going to slip my panties off for him as quickly as he hoped. Some men have no patience and I guess that I really didn't fit his idea of a prospective wife.

I buried my thoughts and concentrated on bringing the 'Princess' safely into the harbour with her little motor running, after furling the mainsail with Eric's help; my God he was so tall and he turned me on. I put that down to desperation on my part. I was in need of a man and this one said he was un-available! The irony of it all! I vowed to myself to nail this blonde baby down tight as soon as humanly possible, he was unmarried with no children. This was a barn door opportunity and I had both shotgun barrels emotionally loaded and was I ready to fire? You bet, and I did not intend to miss!

The 'Princess' bumped against the jetty and Eric stepped over the side and quickly made fast the mooring. I fiddled about with a few ropes to make everything secure and then picked up my sport bag before joining him.

"Well, I guess this is goodbye" I said as I fumbled for my car keys.

"Only for the moment" he replied.

"Oh, yeah" I said, not knowing what to say next to keep him talking.

"I will see you again, quite soon, I promise."

"I'll believe that when it happens, meantime I won't be doing any breath holding" I replied.

"You have my word as a Viking."

"I just don't understand this 'Viking' business" I replied slightly irritated.

"You know who the Vikings were don't you?"

"Yeah, but they are all dead" I said firmly.

"Precisely."

"What?" I queried.

"I'll see you soon, goodbye." With that he turned and strode away along the jetty towards the car park.

"Don't you want my number?" I called out in desperation but he didn't reply, so that's the end of that, I thought.

As he reached the end of the walkway, Terry, who moored his boat next to the 'Princess' came out of his cabin and said "Hi, Helen." I replied "Hi" and then he asked "who are you talking to out there on your lonesome?"

"Him" and I pointed at Eric as he stepped off the jetty.

"Who?"

"Him" I repeated.

"I don't see anybody" replied Terry as his gaze followed my finger and I shivered in the warm sunlight.

My mind was in a total whirl as I drove home to my little house in Jackson Street on the west side of the city. As I pulled up in the drive, Mrs Dawson, my nosey neighbour, a sixty something widow, saw me and came over to the picket fence that separated our homes.

"Been sailing that boat of yours this morning?"

"Sure have" I replied. She smiled and before she could ask another obvious question I made for the safety of my front porch.

"Melodie didn't go with you then?" she called.

"Nope" I replied as I rattled the key in the latch and swung the door open. I was glad to be alone and I slumped down in my chair opposite the television and sighed. What was this morning all about?

After a strong, black coffee I called Rachel.

"You in for visitors?" I asked.

"I'm always in" she replied.

"See you in a while."

"I'll put some coffee on" she said.

"With you soon, kid."

Rachel lived only about ten minutes away from me in a neat, ground floor apartment in a new block. Her parents had bought it for her and she lived quite comfortably with her tortoise shell cat, Honey, on whom she doted. She was all smiles when she saw me and as I followed her into her kitchen diner she asked "I thought you were going sailing today?"

"I've been."

"Hey, that was quick."

"Sure was."

"What happened?"

"I'll pour the coffee whilst you sit still and prepare to listen up like you've never listened up before."

She spun her wheelchair round and faced me with a big smile and said "sounds exciting!" Honey looked up from her comfortable place on the couch at that.

"You'll never believe it!"

"You've met some handsome guy!" she exclaimed.

"Hell Rachel! You must be able to read my mind" I replied.

"Couldn't I ever?" I handed her coffee to her and slumped into the easy chair by the window.

"I'll begin at the beginning" I said.

"Best place" she nodded.

"When I got down to the jetty this morning, a guy was waiting by the 'Princess'....."

"Had you seen him before?" she interrupted.

"Nope, it was a first time encounter."

"What did he look like?"

"In a word – 'breathtaking'...."

"Oh, my God!"

"Yup" I replied and paused to sip my coffee.

"Go on" she said impatiently.

"He's so tall...."

"How tall?"

"Six feet and a half, give an inch or two."

"Oh, my God."

"Blonde hair, tanned face with the bluest eyes you ever did see and...."

"Is he handsome?" she interrupted.

"Fabulous...."

"What's his name?"

"Eric."

"Eric?"

"Eric Bloodaxe."

"What?"

"I can't believe it either...."

"Eric Bloodaxe?"

"He says he's a Viking...."

"But they are all dead" she screwed her face up.

"I know."

"What did he say to you?"

"He said he was there to help and guide me."

"Straight into bed no doubt" she said firmly.

"No, he said he was un-available....."

"Married to a wife in Baltimore with two kids then" Rachel looked prim.

"No, he said he wasn't married."

"That's what they all say."

"Honestly, Rachel, I believed him."

"Like you did Reece?"

She scored a point with that one and I kinda smirked.

"This guy is different, he really is, I mean he's so, so..." I was stuck for words.

"I think you're getting desperate and your clock is ticking" she said before sipping her coffee.

"Eric seems so relaxed and I felt great being with him, I'm talking 'extraordinary experience' here..."

"You probably imagined him, baby" she interrupted firmly and a shiver went down my spine as I remembered that Terry didn't see Eric at the end of the jetty. Now I was worried and perhaps Rachel was right, but no, I hadn't imagined seeing him.

"We went out in the 'Princess' together...."

"You let this guy on your boat and then took him out sailing... alone?" She asked, her eyes shining with surprise and a little anger.

"Uh-huh"

"Helen Milton, you're just plain crazy!"

"Seems so."

"He might have been a psycho, what did he say his name was, Bleeding axe or something?"

"Blood axe" I corrected.

"There you are, he's an axe man, it seems you've had a lucky escape."

"Rachel, you don't understand" I said.

"You're right first time baby, I don't understand."

"Look…"

"Now you listen up, you're my best friend, my only friend, and I love you truly, and if anything ever happened to you, well, " she faltered and her eyes became moist "I'd just die, you're the only person who keeps me alive and sane in this poor, mad life of mine!" She started to cry and even Honey looked concerned at that. I put my coffee down, went close to her and put my arms around her whilst gently kissing the top of her head.

"You've will always have me with you" I said softly.

"I hope so, I really hope so" she mumbled.

"Always" I whispered and decided to change the subject.

"Let's forget all about it and tell me if you've…"

"Are you going to see this guy again?" she interrupted.

"I guess not" I replied.

"Good."

"Although he did say we'd meet up again sometime…"

"Oh, Helen, this is so wrong, I just know it is" and the tears rolled down her pale cheeks once again.

"In fact, he said, the rest of my life."

"Oh, my God!" I realised she was really upset so I decided to put her mind at rest.

"Listen, I promise you, if ever he shows up again, which I doubt, I'll tell him that it's no deal and to stop hustling me, okay?"

"Promise?"

"Promise."

"Even Reece is better than a psycho with an axe" she said firmly, I just smiled and half nodded.

"I guess you're right" I replied whilst wondering if Rachel was just a touch jealous of me. I knew what she had often said that after Mike left her nobody would want her, was probably true.

"Okay, now get me another coffee, baby, this one's going cold" she held out her cup and smiled as Honey curled up again and closed her big brown eyes.

It was late afternoon when I eventually arrived at Mom and Dad's spacious house on Lennox Avenue to pick up Melodie.

"You're back early" said Mom as I wandered through the back door and smelt the coffee.

"Yup" I replied.

"Wasn't it good today?"

"Oh, yeah, the sea was pretty calm" I replied as Melodie came through to see me.

"Hi, Mom" said my daughter and she put her arm round my waist and swung around like kids do.

"Hi, babe" I smiled.

"You okay, Helen?" asked Mom as she started to pour coffee for us all.

"Yeah, fine," I replied, all Mom's have a sixth sense where their kids are concerned.

"Oh."

"Why?"

"Nothing" she replied and then said to Melodie "tell Granpops his coffee's out and his favourite cookies are on the table."

"Okay" replied Melodie as she skipped off to find Dad.

"Something's happened, want to tell me about it?" asked Mom in a gentle way when we were alone.

"I met a man…"

"Didn't I just know it" she interrupted.

"Yup."

"What's he like?"

"Just simply gorgeous" I replied with a sigh.

"My, my, sounds as if he's really hooked you and is reeling in fast." she smiled.

"Doubt it, Mom, I'll probably never see him again."

"Why?"

"It was a kinda strange meeting" I replied as I sat at the kitchen table.

"Tell me about it" she said as she put the coffee cups down and moved the plate of cookies towards Dad's place. I told her all about Eric, leaving out the 'Bloodaxe' and 'Viking' bits in case she became worried, and she listened with a smile.

"He sounds nice" she said as Dad and Melodie came in.

"Who's nice?" asked Dad as he sat down.

"Helen's met a nice man, called Eric" said Mom.

"Good for you, baby, anybody's better than that Reece" said Dad firmly.

"Now, Joe, he is Melodie's father……"

"Yup, I know, Rose, and I'd rather you didn't remind me" interrupted Dad as he picked up a cookie.

I retold the events of the morning and my Dad just smiled. He was a happy, easy going person, it had been very tough in early days but he had always looked after Mom and me and now had come shining through at a time in life when folks can spend a little and enjoy themselves. I loved him and Mom very much and respected both of them for their care and kindness. I seemed to be the daughter who disappointed them by not getting married and being the model of a middle class all American woman. Still, they didn't blame me and they loved Melodie to pieces. We stayed for dinner and it was almost ten when we got home to our little house. I packed my daughter off to bed and sat thinking for a long while about Eric. It was almost midnight before I went to bed and then spent a restless night wondering if I'd dreamed the whole damned thing.

Next morning, I felt a little tired at first, but after several cups of coffee at the office and a chat with Dad over some overdue accounts with City Insurance, I was beginning to feel a whole lot better and Eric slipped to the back of my mind. Naomi, my accounts assistant, was bright and bubbly as usual and her chatter about her date last night made me smile as it brought back some memories of mine. It was a lovely bright day and when it came to lunchtime I decided to go out and buy some rolls and sit and eat in a small park, just across the road from the office. There's a neat little deli, just up the way and I bought myself some cheese and salad rolls. I was almost tempted to buy several chocolate bars but remained firm and good to my diet and stayed just with the rolls. I sat on a bench, in sight of the office and began to enjoy lunch alone with my thoughts. I never heard anyone approach me until suddenly his voice made me jump right out of my skin!

"Helen." I turned to see Eric standing there.

"Oh, my God" I said with a mouth full of salad roll and mayonnaise dribbling down my chin.

"May I sit with you for a while?"

"Why not" I replied, feeling all excited and shaky inside. He sat down, not too close, then smiled at me and I just melted.

"You're dribbling" he said and I blushed and struggled to find a tissue in my bag. I dropped my roll in the process and he laughed.

"Another dangerous moment?" he asked.

"Seems so" I replied as I at last found a tissue and tried to clean myself up a little.

"And you've lost your lunch" he said gazing at the half eaten roll lying on the ground, which was now being eyed up by a couple of small birds hopping about some distance away.

"I've another one here" I replied pointing at the bag by my side.

"Good" he smiled.

"Would you like to share it?" I asked him.

"You're very kind, but no thank you." I melted a bit more at hearing that.

"So, what brings you to Atlantic City?" I asked hoping for the right answer.

"You, Helen" he replied. Right answer.

"That's nice" I smiled.

"I'm sorry I left you in a hurry after our short voyage…"

"That's okay" I interrupted.

"But I had to look after someone else." 'And what's her name?' I wondered.

"Good for her" I nodded.

"It was a man" his eyes looked very blue as he said it and I felt warm with relief.

"Oh, really" I replied hoping that my face did not show too much concern.

"Really, but I shouldn't have told you that" he said and looked away.

"Why not?"

"Well, you're just not supposed to know."

"Why?"

"Because only you are supposed to be the centre of my attention" he replied firmly and boy, did I like that!

"Sure you wouldn't like to share my cheese roll?" I asked, hoping that the way to a man's heart was through his stomach.

"No thank you, Helen." I just loved the way he said my name with his strange but fascinating accent. I was sure his English had a Scandinavian lilt to it and he spoke with some of the words clipped and very proper.

"I'm listening, Eric" I said with a smug grin on my face.

"This is the first time I've had to do this…"

"What's 'this'?" I interrupted.

"Helen, will you be quiet until I've told you all I have to tell you?" he looked a little angry and I tried a faint smile as I nodded.

"As a mouse" I whispered as he paused for breath and to gather his thoughts.

"I can't tell you much…" 'well, there's a good start' I thought.

"But you must believe me when I tell you that everything I say and do is for your future happiness." Oh, boy, dinner at Rolfe's was back on the table!

"Don't stop now, Eric" I said with my heart full of hope as he paused.

"Be silent, woman!" At that I closed my mouth tight and drew my hand across my lips as if to zip it up.

"What are you doing?" he asked quizzically.

"Zipping up" I replied and he looked confused.

"Just let me tell you about your future happiness" he said.

"My favourite subject" I replied and he sighed. Suddenly realising I could be as annoying as Melodie I decided to really quieten down and listen.

"What you have to do is think of me sometime during the day or night, perhaps when you're in bed…" I liked the sound of that.

"And I will send you your first thought after you have imagined me with you…" Imagined? I wanted the real thing! "Do you understand?" I nodded but I didn't really. "And that's how I will guide you to happiness" he smiled.

"Is that it?" I queried.

"Yes, Helen."

"Well, I had in mind, a dinner date and back to my place for coffee."

"It doesn't work like that."

"Well maybe it ought to!"

"You obviously don't understand."

"You're dead right, so let's have dinner together and you can tell me again, so slowly that I'll understand, then we can...."

"No, Helen" he said firmly.

"Oh, boy, are you becoming a slight disappointment" I said.

"I'm sorry..."

"Not as sorry as me!"

"Look, I'm trying hard to explain things and I need you to help me a little."

"How?"

"It's the first time I've been told to help someone..."

"Told? Told? Who told you, the United Nations? I thought you were interested in me not somebody else who told you to be!"

"I am, I really am!"

"Like man and woman in love? Making love? Even getting married? Although I don't know you I'm willing to take a chance at this point in my life!"

"Helen, we can never be together like that..."

"Why not?"

"Because I'm not..."

"Not what?"

"I knew this would end up in a mess, I told Gunther" he shook his head.

"Gunther? Who's he? Another furry, leather clad nut?" I said angrily. Well, this guy kept winding me up and then letting me go off in circles and it was more than I could stand. He was really messing with my mind!

"He's my friend" he replied slowly.

"Fine, well, it's been nice to know you, Eric... and Gunther" I said as I stood up and threw my cheese roll at the gaggle of birds that had now gathered on the grass. I strode away back towards the office in an angry mood with my eyes beginning to moisten as I thought 'another damned relationship going nowhere, why do I always pick them?' I never looked back and had to go straight to the powder room to tidy myself up. I didn't want Dad or Naomi seeing me in any kind of state. As I checked my makeup in the mirror I began to feel even more angry at Eric, I mean, I hadn't even finished my lunch because of him! Men!

"Hey, who was that guy you were talking to in the park?" enquired Naomi as I sat at my desk opposite her.

"You saw him?"

"Sure did, he looked pretty handsome to me, and so tall too" she smiled. I felt relieved, I hadn't imagined Eric.

"Some guy I met when I went sailing the other day" I replied looking at my computer screen.

"Lucky you" she replied.

"Not really" I said.

"Is he a secret lover?"

"No, he's not" I replied but thought 'I wish he was.'

"Is he free?"

"No, he's not available" I replied still staring at my computer.

"Married then?"

"Nope."

"Gay?"

"Possibly" I replied thinking of Gunther and then I saw Eric's handsome face in my mind and he said to me "I'm not interested in men!"

"No man that good looking is un-available, believe me Helen, some woman will keep trying until she nails him down" and I looked up at Miss Experienced of Atlantic City and smiled.

"Sure" I replied, but it wasn't going to be me.

"What's his name?"

"Naomi, we've got a lot to do, we'd better get on with it" I said slightly irritated.

"Just tell me his name, please."

"Eric."

"What's his other name, I think I might know him from…."

"Bloodaxe."

"Oh, my God!"

"Precisely" I replied and she then started tapping into her computer the figures for the month so far.

The afternoon dragged although I tried to concentrate on work, Eric's face just kept on appearing in my mind. Had I been too hasty? Perhaps I'd not paid enough attention to what he was saying. My only excuse was that I was too busy thinking about a

31

dinner date and what was likely to follow after to take it all in. Who was this someone who 'told' him to make me the centre of his attention? Was it Gunther? I was hopelessly confused but decided if ever I saw him again, I'd apologise for walking off and give him another chance to explain what it was all about.

At last it was time to go and I said goodnight to Dad, leaving him still working in his office, then picked Melodie up from Mom's and went home. As we pulled up in the drive I could see Mrs Dawson hovering by her front door. I hoped we could get indoors in double quick time but we were just not fast enough. She was down her porch steps and by the fence at a speed that Superman would have been proud of.

"Hi, Helen, hi, Melodie."

"Hi, Mrs Dawson."

"Finished for the day?" was her obvious question.

"Sure am" I replied.

"That's good."

"Yup."

"Now, I don't want to worry you, but, a little while ago a tall stranger came to your place and peered through the window and then he went away" she said.

"Really?" I asked, sure in my mind it was Eric and I began to feel a little excited. He wasn't giving up on me so there was still hope.

"Yes, do you think we should call the Police?" she asked.

"No, we need not bother them."

"I'm a little concerned myself" she said.

"Nothing for you to worry about, in fact, I think I know him" I said.

"You know him?"

"Yes, I think it's probably a guy I've been sailing with" I replied.

"Oh, well that's okay then, and come to think of it, he was dressed a bit rough, like a sailor" she smiled.

"Yup, now time to get some dinner started" I said as I put one arm around Melodie's shoulder.

"What's his name?"

"Eric."

"Nice name."

"Yup, he's a nice guy."

"Chance of getting hooked up then?"

"Nope, I don't think so."

"Well, you never know the future" she said and waved her hand as she turned away and headed for her porch.

Once inside, I put some coffee on whilst Melodie turned on the TV. I called her and we sat at our breakfast bar and waited for the coffee to cool down.

"Who's this guy, Eric, Mom?"

"Someone I met when I went sailing."

"Is he nice?"

"Certainly is."

"You gonna invite him for dinner soon?"

"I don't think he'd come."

"Why not?"

"He's a very busy guy."

"What does he do?"

"He helps people."

"To do what?"

"I'm not really sure, baby" and I really wasn't.

We had pizza for dinner and some ice cream afterwards. Melodie didn't ask any more questions about Eric and settled down in front of the TV whilst I decided to call Rachel and have a long chat.

"Hi, Rachel here."

"Hi, it's me."

"I know why you're calling me" she said with excitement.

"Oh, yeah."

"You've seen him again today!"

"Are you sure you're not spying on me from the top of your apartment block?"

"As if I could get up there, but I'm right, I just know I am!"

"Sure you're right."

"And what did he say?"

"Oh, lots I didn't understand."

"Like what?"

"He's only here for my happiness."

"Wow! When's the wedding?"

"No, no wedding...."

"Just shack up together then, you've plenty of room for a big guy at your place, and it could do with a little fixing up!" I laughed at that because it was true.

"I don't think so."

"Helen, you're confusing me."

"You're confused?"

"He must be gay?"

"Certainly not."

"How can you be so sure?"

"Believe me, I am."

"Well, get him hooked, baby!"

"It's not going to happen."

"Why not?"

"I don't really know."

"How long have you spent today discussing nothing with him?"

"Not long."

"I believe you."

"But he's been to the house this afternoon."

"Did you make out?"

"No, I was at work, but Mrs Dawson saw him peeking through a window."

"He's a strange guy."

"He sure is."

"And I thought you were going to tell him to get lost?"

"Well, I was, but in the end I couldn't."

"I'd better meet this guy soon and give him the once over" and I laughed at that.

"Then what?" I asked.

"If he's okay, I'll take him off your hands!" And we both laughed.

"You told me to tell him to back off if he showed up again" I said.

"I know, but I've changed my mind, I guess any man is better than no man at all" she replied.

"Damned right, and if I don't want him you'll snatch him...."

"If he's as good as you say, I sure will!"

"Oh, he's hot, believe me" I replied.

"I'm sure, now, hey, why don't you bring Melodie over for dinner tomorrow night?"

"Okay."

"I'll cook up my famous speciality, spaghetti bolognaise, with all the trimmings!"

"Great."

"And we'll open a bottle of something to drown our sorrows."

"Sounds good."

"Then you can tell me all about Eric, in every detail."

"Okay, Rache, see you about seven, tomorrow."

"Bye, Babe."

I sat for a while thinking about Rachel and she was right, she needed me in her life for some light relief and to give her hope. I then decided to call Karen and gossip a little with her. I'd known Karen Foster since we both started working for Jeeves and Butterworth, Attorneys at Law, with a spacious office on York Street in Baltimore. We were both silly teenagers, certain that we would become senior partners in the business once we had finished law school and then reality kicked in after a couple of years and I left to return to Atlantic City to help Dad. Karen opted for staying with the law firm to see how far she could get without going on to law school and getting over loaded mentally with all the book work and never ending exams. We had shared a small apartment in downtown Baltimore and it had been great, just two girls having a good time and we'd stayed friends ever since. Karen has worked her way up to some management position in the firm, I'm never quite sure what she actually does, but she seems happy and well paid, so I guess that's alright. She hadn't married and had turned into a career girl, all smart pin stripe business suits, designer shoes, handbags and neat BMW convertible's traded in every year for newer models. She still lived in Baltimore but had moved to a much bigger apartment and had someone come in and clean twice a week. Of the three of us she had been the one who had definitely 'made it'. I dialled her number and waited.

"Hello, Karen Foster."

"Hi, Karen, it's me!"

"Oh, hi, Helen, how are you?"

"Fine, just fine, you okay?"

"Sure, how's Melodie?"

"She's fine, thanks."

"Are you still seeing Reece?" She knew my weak points.

"Off and on."

"What exactly does that mean?"

"He bothers me from time to time…"

"And you keep on giving the jerk another chance" she interrupted.

"Yup."

"You're a real patsy, why that guy has two timed you with so many women……"

"I know, I know, I promise you, everybody tells me something I already know, but he is Melodie's Dad and that kinda binds us together, don't you think?" I countered.

"I'd give him the short and sweet goodbye."

"Okay, but …"

"No 'buts' Helen, you should just dump the no good, son of a bitch, I tell you…"

"I might quite soon, because I've met a really nice guy…"

"Best news today, what's his name?"

"Eric."

"I like him already, how did you meet him?"

"Down at Cape May and we went sailing together…"

"And what's he like? Tall? Handsome? Single?"

"He's all of those with deep blue eyes and blonde hair."

"Oh my God, have you fallen in the swamp and come up with a gold necklace or what?"

"I think so…."

"You only 'think so'? Hell, babe, get him nailed down tight as soon as you can before some other woman gets hold of him!"

"Karen, it's not that easy…."

"Explain why, and slowly so I can take it all in."

"He says he's not available…."

"They're all available…."

"He's not."

"What? Is he gay?"

"Nope, but he says I'm the centre of his attention and my future happiness is all he cares about."

"That sounds like a proposal to me, I hope you said 'yes'?"

"He didn't propos…."

"I'd better come over to Atlantic City and give this guy the once over, it sounds as if you're about to get involved with another loser who'll mess you up, hell, where do keep finding these guy's?"

"I don't know."

"You're like a goddam menopausal fridge magnet...." and we both laughed at that.

"Sure, come over sometime and save me" I said.

"I'll drive over next Saturday afternoon, and make sure this guy is around."

"Okay, I'll try and pin him down."

"You'd better, see you Babe" and with that she was gone. I looked forward to seeing her, she was great, pushy and self assured, a real contrast to Rachel but a good friend. I sat for a while thinking about Eric and was just about to tell Melodie to switch off the TV and get ready for bed when the 'phone rang, it was Reece.

CHAPTER 3

PETER IN TROUBLE

I was already awake when the alarm went off. The 'phone calls I had to make were uppermost in my mind. I dreaded calling Freddie and the lab but looked forward to hearing Sophia's lilting, musical tones. I left Janet dozing and got ready for work. She had a part time job as a dentist's receptionist and was paid a hopelessly low wage. We were in so much debt I often wondered why she bothered to go to work, still, it bought some food and chocolate. She could spend money but she was incapable of earning it and I knew I had to get out the marriage or face bankruptcy.

I called Freddie first.

"Morning boss, Janet told me you wanted to talk to me about something urgent."

"I did last night, where the hell were you?"

"With customers."

"Oh, yeah?"

"I've got the dinner bill to prove it" I replied as I crossed my fingers.

"I'll see that later, now then, there's been an almighty cock up…….."

"That's unusual" I interrupted in a sarcastic tone.

"Just listen, will you?"

"Okay."

"I can't go into detail over the 'phone but I want you to come to my office in Berkeley Square as soon as you can."

"What, today?"

"Yes, you should have been here first thing, I'm already late for a meeting."

"Oh."

"If you'd 'phoned me last night…….."

"I'm sorry boss, I'm on my way now" I interrupted.

"Okay, get here as soon as." He hung up and with a thousand thoughts rushing through my head I shouted to Janet upstairs 'I've got to go to a meeting with Freddie in town, goodbye' and left the house. I wondered if I might make a date with Sophia as I would

38

be in London and the meeting at head office would cover me from Janet's inquisition later.

I hurried up the motorway once more, thinking only of Sophia and hoping against hope that she would see me.

Freddie sat behind his glass topped desk in the palatial office that was the centre of the southern area's sales operations in Berkeley Square. As I closed the door behind me he glanced up only momentarily from the papers he was studying and said "better sit down, this could be a bit of a long do." I did as I was told whilst he phoned his secretary, Paula, and ordered coffee for both of us.

"This is an almighty cock up" he said aloud whilst glaring at the paperwork.

"Really?"

"Yes, really, the Paint Federation has organised a great big shindig in Paris and only forgot to invite JB."

"Blimey." JB as he was affectionately known by us all, was James Browning, our very popular Chairman, who was also a senior figure in the Federation and had been elected to Hon Secretary only last year.

"So, where's the problem, boss?" I enquired.

"Because we've only just been notified, it's too late for JB, he can't go, he's off to a meeting in the US with the Bradley Ponting consortium."

"Oh."

"Exactly, and he has to go, the Yanks get so uptight about these things and JB dare not cancel his trip to the US to go to Paris instead, God, no, the Yanks hate the French and they would regard it as an unforgivable snub, could damage our plans in the States for years." He shook his head whilst I wondered what I should say to ease Freddie's stress.

"How can I help?" I ventured at last as he started to write in the margins of the paper on his desk.

"Well, it comes down to this, fate has landed her fat arse squarely on our shoulders" he said.

"How unpleasant" I replied and at that moment Paula entered with the coffee, nodded to me and then made a hasty exit.

"George can't go because he's going with JB to the States" said Freddie as he slowly shook his head. George Paton is our sales

Director and Freddie's boss, a very energetic and larger than life person who we all looked up to.

"So, I'm afraid it's come down to me, accompanied by you" and with that he looked up and stared at me squarely in the face.

"Me?" I spluttered.

"Yup, we're going to Paris for a three day junket, I hope your passport's up to date and you can manage something in French, even if it's only 'where's the toilet?'"

"But…………"

"No 'buts' Peter, George has said we have to go and as you've got the worst sales figures of all the boys this month the trip might give me an excuse to cover your poor record." I managed a sickly grin.

"Besides that, you're good company and you occasionally make me laugh" he smiled and I felt considerably better at hearing that.

"And I'm going to need all the laughs I can get, dealing with those bloody fools that'll be at the meeting."

"Is it something special?" I asked.

"Yes, apparently, Benoir Paints in Paris and the Italian lot, what's their name, er, Milan AutoFinish, have been working together on a completely new system of vehicle painting and they want to show it off whilst having meaningful discussions with the paint industry, so the invitation says" he said as he tapped the papers in front of him.

"Sounds good" I said with not much enthusiasm.

"It's only an excuse for back slapping and secretary screwing accompanied by rich food and champagne" he replied with some disdain.

"No change there, then."

"The way of the world these days."

"When do we go?"

He glanced down and replied "fly out of Heathrow, next Wednesday at six thirty, the meeting is fixed for Thursday morning at Benoir's place and return Saturday night, sometime, oh, er, Charles de Gaulle, flight back, er, departure at nine."

"Okay, now can you help me out, boss?"

"If I can."

"I've got a serious problem with Marparts in Reading…."

"Not again" he interrupted.

"Afraid so."

"Well?"

"Could you see if Frank or Jimmy are free to go down there today to match a Mondeo door that's badly off colour?" He sighed and nodded as he picked up his 'phone and dialled through to the lab at the works in Stratford. After a short conversation it was agreed that Jimmy would go down to Reading and save my bacon. I sipped my coffee and was more than relieved, I then gave my full attention to Freddie as he went over the details of our planned visit to Paris.

It was almost lunch time when the meeting with Freddie was over and I was anxious to call Sophia. Paula had gone to lunch so I didn't hesitate to pick up the 'phone on her desk and dial the number on Sophia's card. A woman's voice answered in an abrupt tone.

"Hello."

"Oh, hello, is Sophia there please?"

"No, she's not, she's out at the moment, who is this?"

"I'm Peter, a friend of Sophia's."

"Really, she's not mentioned you before" she replied.

"We've only recently met" I replied.

"Well, she'll be back later."

"What time?"

"Ring after three" and with that the abrupt woman hung up.

I left Berkeley Square and drove round Hyde Park and found a rare, vacant parking space near the lake. It was almost two and I decided to walk for a while. The time dragged and my thoughts constantly wandered back to Sophia no matter how hard I tried to concentrate on my marriage problems, my finances and now the bloody trip to Paris. At last it was three and I found a telephone kiosk up near the Park Lane entrance and dialled the number.

"Hello" said the abrupt woman.

"Hello, may I speak to Sophia please?"

"Who is it?"

"Peter."

"Just a minute." I heard the woman call her name and then 'it's Peter.' I waited for what seemed an age.

"Hello" said Sophia in her lilting tone.

"Hello, do you remember me?" I teased.

"Si, you're the rich, naughty man" she laughed.

"I am."

"So?"

"I'd like to see you again."

"When?"

"Tonight."

"Tonight?"

"Yes."

"Okay" she hesitated as my heart leapt with excitement "pick me up about eighta clock."

"I'll be there" I replied.

"And where are youa taking me?"

"Just for a drink somewhere nice" I replied.

"Gooda, I'll see you a later then."

"Yes, bye." I hung up and I felt nervous and excited at the same time. I had five hours to kill and decided to wander around the Science Museum before getting something to eat and driving up to Highgate. The hours passed relatively quickly and after a reasonable meal in a Pizza Hut I drove at a leisurely pace and parked outside the imposing house where Sophia lived. I waited impatiently until nearly half past eight before the front door opened and out came the beautiful, petite, Italian. She looked fabulous in a red dress with matching shoes and handbag. Her hair and makeup were just so and I caught the scent of her perfume as I opened the car door for her.

"Hello, Peter" she smiled.

"Sophia" I half mumbled.

"Thanker you" she said as she slid elegantly onto the seat.

We drove off and as I turned the car at the end of the road she asked "where are youa taking me tonighta?"

"To a lovely riverside pub I know in Richmond" I replied

"Where is Richmond?" she asked.

"Not far, it's where Henry the Eighth used to hunt and chase his wives" I replied and laughed.

"I hope youa are not going to cut offa my heada like he dida" she replied.

"Only if you're naughty" I said firmly.

"Oh, dear, thatsa a shame because I like a being naughty" she giggled. I smiled to myself as I was absolutely captivated by this beautiful, young, extrovert woman. We chatted non stop all the way to Richmond and I was feeling very relaxed and at ease with her when we arrived at the pub. It was fairly quiet and we found a small table for two on the riverside terrace where she sat whilst I attended to the drinks. She had a red wine whilst I had a modest half of bitter and we settled down together.

"This is a lovely spota" she said as she gazed at the river flowing gently by.

"Yes, it is."

"Do you a bring all your girlfriends here?"

"No, you're the very first one" I replied truthfully.

"Thatsa good, I like a that" she smiled at me and the sparkle in her eyes just bewitched me.

"You are very beautiful, Sophia" I half whispered.

"Why, thanker you." She replied before sipping her wine.

"I expect many men tell you that" I said.

"Some have" she replied coyly and smiled.

"I'm sure."

"Anda you are very English, and elegant" she replied.

"I'm glad you approve" I smiled and my heart leapt.

"I like an elegant man, thatsa my French side coming outa."

"I thought you are Italian."

"Half, my father is Italian, my mother French" she smiled.

"How very lovely" I murmured.

"Si, I like elegance but I like a the passion too" she smiled.

"I like the passion as well" I said and she laughed.

"Thatsa good."

"Do you believe in love at first sight?" I asked before realising what I was saying.

"Si, I'm a sure it happens all the time" she replied as she sipped her wine and looked deep into me with her big, beautiful brown eyes. God, I felt my very being just melting in front of her and I realised I was falling in love with this woman I hardly knew.

"I'm married" I blurted out and then hated myself for spoiling the moment.

"I guessed you were" she replied with a smile.

"But I'm getting a divorce" I said firmly.

"Nota on my account, I hope" she smiled.

"No, it's all been going on for some while, it's all over between us" I replied.

"I'ma sorry, but itsa not very romantic when you're outa with someone having a nice drinka to talk about their broken marriage" she said firmly.

"I'm sorry, I just wanted you to know, that's all."

"You're very English" she smiled.

"And you're very understanding as well as beautiful" I replied and she smiled.

"Do youa thinka there's just one man for every woman in the world?" she asked.

"Possibly."

"I like to thinka so."

"It's a lovely thought, but I wonder what are the chances that they'll meet?"

"I don'ta know, it's a mystery" she smiled.

"It is."

"But we've met by chance" she smiled again. She was just totally captivating me, she was now in complete control of my emotions and I was under her spell. I knew there was no escape, ever, not ever. It hits you like a thunderbolt when it happens and you just know it. I was shaking inwardly as I asked her if she would like another drink.

"Si." I stumbled to the bar and ordered the same drinks again. I thought of Janet and realised how I had come to despise her. Compared with Sophia, well, I know comparisons are odious but it's the only way you set the criteria. I did not want to go home and decided to find a small hotel or something for the night. I wondered if Sophia would spend the night with me, but I felt too nervous to ask. I returned to Sophia and we sat, drinking slowly whilst she told me all about her parents and Milan. At last the barman called time and rang the bell. I drove her home as slowly as I could and when we arrived outside the house I took her in my arms and kissed her gently and then as she responded, more passionately. My God, she was gorgeous. We kissed and kissed until we were both breathless.

"I'm in love with you, Sophia" I whispered.

"I know, and I feel something very special for you, Peter."

"When can I see you again?"

"When ever you wanta" she replied before kissing me once more.

"Tomorrow" I whispered.

"Okay."

"I'll be here at seven and we'll go for a meal together" I said firmly.

"Okay" she replied and she kissed me again before getting out of the car. I leapt out and ran round to sweep her up in my arms and kiss her passionately once more.

"Until tomorrow" I whispered and she nodded as I let her go. I watched her as she approached the front door of the house where she turned and waved briefly before going inside.

I sat in the car for a few moments trying to compose myself before driving off when to my astonishment I saw a tall figure approaching under the street lights. I could not believe it, but it was him, the tall nutter that had stopped me on the downs and frightened me witless. I began to shake as he reached the car and opened the door but was relieved to see that he had left his axe behind.

"Hello, Peter."

"Hello, what are you doing here?" I mumbled.

"I've come to see you."

"Oh, why?"

"Let's go for a little walk together."

"No, 'fraid not, it's late and I'm going home to...."

"Peter, I need to talk to you" he interrupted.

"Okay. Okay" I replied and left the car, irritated by this strange and compelling person's easy manipulation of me. We walked along the pavement in step and he began.

"I'm here because I'm trying to save you from difficult situations and guide you in the right direction for your future happiness and well being...."

"You're not a life insurance salesman are you?"

"No, I'm a Viking....."

"Yes, we've been all over that nonsense before!"

"So, we shouldn't be meeting like this...."

"Shouldn't be meeting like this?" I repeated "you've been watching too many old films on television...."

"Will you shut up and listen?" he demanded angrily.

"Go on."

"You are bound to suffer sadness and setbacks but I've got to try and help you…."

"Good, I could do with some help" I rejoined enthusiastically.

"Firstly, this woman you've been with tonight."

"Sophia" I sighed.

"I know she is very lovely but she is dangerous for you…."

"I like a bit of danger where Sophia's concerned!" I interrupted.

"You don't understand" he replied.

"No, I don't."

"Sometime in the future she will let you down" he said in a serious tone.

"I doubt it" I replied.

"She is not for you."

"Let me be the judge of that, besides who are you to tell me what's good for me?"

"I'm trying to guide you……."

"How about minding your own bloody business!" I shouted.

"Peter, she will leave you emotionally crippled, which is worse than being emotionally dead because you'll have feelings for other women but the memory of Sophia and what she's done to you will for ever cloud your feelings and you'll never be free to love completely again" he said with concern.

"Well, we all bring old baggage to every new relationship and the older we are the more we bring, so if you don't mind I'll take my chances while I can" and with that I turned away and walked back to the car. Eric was standing where I had left him as I drove passed and I saw him shaking his head as I roared by. I thought 'how dare this bloke tell me whose right or wrong for me? He wasn't damned well about when I married Janet was he?' As usual in life, good advice, or any kind of help, often comes when it is too late.

In my troubled and clouded mind I decided that if I was going to see Sophia tomorrow night I had better go home and face the music and dance to Janet's unpleasant tune. It began to rain as I headed out of Highgate and towards the motorway. What an end to a very pleasant evening, everything had been fine until Eric had appeared and upset me. God, what a pain he is. I joined the motorway and speeded up as the rain became heavier and the traffic slowed. I was almost back to Maidenhead when dreaming of Sophia, I didn't realise the car in front was braking hard, I saw the rear lights brighten but it didn't seem to register in my mind somehow. Too late, I jumped on the brake pedal and then skidded smoothly and gently on the wet road into the car in front. The noise of the impact was horrendous and I bounced forward in my seat and then back as the seatbelt held me. God almighty! I was shaking as I switched on my hazard lights and hoped that no one would slam into my car stuck in the fast lane of the motorway. I got out to face the other driver as the rain lashed down.

"Bloody hell, mate, couldn't you see my lights?" he shouted angrily as other traffic slowed to gaze at the wreckage of my misfortune.

"Look, I'm sorry…."

"Sorry! Sorry! You should be, mate, just look at the back of my car!" he shouted louder and I thought for a moment that he was going to take a swing at me. In the light of the overhead lamps I could see that his Vauxhall was badly damaged and I was amazed at the amount of broken glass that was scattered over the road. The whole front of my Mondeo was well crushed and the steam from the broken radiator added to the Orwellian nightmare.

"This is a company car, mate" he said tapping his Vauxhall.

"So is mine" I replied.

"I should be at home now, instead of here with this bloody mess to sort out!" he shouted.

"Me too."

"I'll have to call the Police, it's company policy" he nodded as he came menacingly close to me. He was quite a well built man of about forty and again I thought he would resort to violence.

"You been drinking?" he asked with a glare.

"Well, I've only had a pint or so…."

"Over the limit I expect."

"No, not at all" I replied lamely. Oh, God it all seemed to be getting worse as I thought of Janet waiting for me, explaining to Freddie that I'd had an accident late at night and now unsure whether I could meet Sophia tomorrow night. Just then the wail of the Police siren concentrated my mind, apparently they did not need to be summoned, they turned up all on their own. The Police car pulled up someway behind us with its blue flashing lights illuminating the whole area and two officers approached with resigned expressions. They must have seen it all a hundred times before.

"It's his bloody fault, he crashed into the back of me, he's drunk, he's admitted it!" shouted the irate man.

"Alright, sir, let's just stay calm and get both vehicles onto the hard shoulder and clear the motorway first of all" said the older of the two officers.

"Okay, but I want to press charges…."

"All in good time, sir" replied the officer calmly.

"I mean it…."

"Right, sir, now is your car still driveable?"

"I expect so."

"We'll stop the traffic whilst you get your car on to the hard shoulder." The large man slipped behind the wheel of his car whilst the two Policeman waved the passing traffic down to a halt. He then drove across two lanes and parked.

"Your vehicle looks a bit of a mess, sir, so I think we'd better push it" said the officer to me and I gazed into his resigned face as the rain fell down harder, adding to the nightmare.

"Right" I mumbled before going to the car and opening the drivers door. I grabbed the steering wheel and began to push and steer across the road. The whole thing speeded up as the two Policemen lent their considerable weight to the operation. When we were safely off the motorway, one officer swept up the glass before the other drove the Police car off the road and parked behind my wreck. I was then summoned to the Police car with the older officer whilst Mr Irate sat in his Vauxhall with the other Policeman.

"Have you been drinking, sir?"

"Well, yes, but I've only had a pint or so…."

"How long ago, sir?"

"About a couple of hours."

"Right, I'm going to ask you to take a breathalyser test" he said calmly and produced the unit for me to blow into. I was shaking by now with the cold and wet coupled with a touch of fear. I blew and blew into the gadget and was relieved when the reading showed I was just under the limit. Having passed the test I settled down to the questions the officer put to me. It all dragged on and I wondered how I was going to get home and worried about the eventual fall out from this little misadventure The recovery trucks arrived and having completed all the formalities with the Traffic Police I climbed aboard the truck with my car and headed off towards Maidenhead in the relentless pouring rain. Once I was at the recovery garage I was able to call a mini cab with a Romanian driver whose English was limited and he constantly told me how happy he was to be in England and that he couldn't wait for all his family to join him.

It was nearly two in the morning when I arrived home and crept into my darkened bedroom, I got undressed listening to my snoring wife as I did so and then slipped in to bed.

Next thing I heard was the alarm ringing and Janet asking grumpily "well, what time did you arrive home last night then?"

"About two" I mumbled.

"And where were you until that time of night?"

"Stuck on the motorway..."

"Liar" she interrupted.

"I've had an accident."

"What sort of accident?"

"What do you mean 'what sort of accident?' The accidental kind, you stupid woman!" I replied.

"Liar" she replied as she dragged her corpulent body from the bed.

"The car's stuck in a recovery garage in Maidenhead." With that she turned and looked down at me.

"Really?"

"Yes, really" I mumbled.

"Oh, your boss, whatsisname, will be glad about that" she replied sarcastically.

"Yes, he will won't he?" I replied

"You'll end up getting the bullet" she said as she made her way to the bathroom.

"Not before I go to Paris next Wednesday" I called and she re-appeared at the bedroom door.

"What?"

"You heard, and I'll be late tonight, I've another meeting in town." I said in a truculent tone.

"I don't care anymore what you do."

"Really?"

"Yes, really, you're such a lying bastard, as far as I'm concerned you can piss off anytime you like to wherever with whoever; at least I'll know not to expect you home!" and with that she made her way once more to the bathroom. 'That went well' I thought as I laid in bed digesting what she had just said. It was now obvious that Janet and I had crossed the Rubicon and there was no going back. The marriage was over in all but name and I decided to get out as soon as humanly and legally possible. I felt that with a lovely woman like Sophia, happiness and contentment could be the way of life, each person spiritually and physically entwined together for ever.

As soon as I had finished breakfast I 'phoned Freddie at his office and told him the bad news about the company Mondeo.

"Are you alright?" he asked after I had described the accident in some detail.

"Yes, just a bit shaken."

"Understandable, so can you get up here today?"

"Yes."

"Okay, I'll arrange with transport to let you have a pool car until yours is repaired."

"Thanks, Freddie."

"So if you go straight to the works at Stratford, pick up a car and then call in here on your way back to fill in all the accident forms."

"Okay, see you this afternoon, some time."

"Right." That could not be better if I'd planned it all. I would be able to stay in London and take Sophia out to dinner as arranged. The day was looking up and I felt better already, when I told Janet what was happening she just shrugged and said "I'll see you sometime then, like whenever" and carried on getting ready for work.

After a long and tortuous journey from Wantage by bus, delayed train and finally Underground I arrived at Stratford. I walked from the Tube station to the works and was glad of the fresh air. The Transport Manager, Tom Barnes, was at lunch in the canteen and his assistant, a pale faced young man called Roger, would not sign the pool car out to me although he had the authorisation chitty on his desk. It was a 'jobsworth' situation so I decided not to argue but go along to the canteen instead and have something to eat. Not too much, as I was saving myself for dinner tonight with Sophia.

As I sat in the canteen munching a cheese roll I looked around at the women present and realised how beautiful Sophia was compared to anyone there. At that moment I truly knew that I was deeply in love with her. I felt warm and comfortable when suddenly Eric's face appeared in my thoughts, he looked serious and was slowly shaking his head. His comment about being 'emotionally crippled' came into my thoughts and worried me, my mood changed somewhat.

I arrived at Freddie's office about three and went in to face the music. Accidents in company cars were more than frowned upon because the accountants, who now run every business, complain bitterly when there is an increase in insurance premiums due to the actions of the stunt drivers employed as salesmen. I often wondered if this pin striped bunch of bores ever realised what it was like to face the risks and road madness which is part of British life today.

"How come you were on the motorway so late last night?" enquired Freddie. I hesitated and decided to tell him the truth.

"I'd been seeing someone." Freddie sighed and looked down at the completed accident form on his desk.

"It doesn't look good, Peter."

"I know, boss."

"George will have to know."

"Yes" I replied with a sigh.

"And you'd been drinking and were breathalysed by the Police" he said with a concerned tone.

"Yes, 'fraid so."

"Oh, Peter, what a mess."

"Yes."

"Was she worth it?" he asked with a grin as he looked up at me.

"She most certainly was "I replied with a smile.

"Does your wife know?"

"No, but she doesn't care, I'm afraid our marriage is over."

"Because of your new friend?"

"No, Janet and I have been struggling on the rocks for the last six months and it really is all over now" I replied.

"I'm sorry to hear it, so with one thing and another you're in quite a mess aren't you?" he asked firmly.

"Yes, I suppose so."

"A motorway crash, a wrecked marriage and the worst sales figures this month."

"Yes" I nodded.

"You'll be glad to get to Paris for a few days then won't you?"

"I will."

Freddie smiled and said "okay, the bollicking I was going to give you can wait for another time, and knowing you, there will certainly be another time!"

"Thanks, Freddie" I replied gratefully. We then discussed some aspects of the impending trip to Paris and he briefed me on various people he wanted me to contact at the functions planned by the Federation.

I left the office and drove to Hyde Park, found a vacant meter and slid the pool Mondeo into the space. I walked for an age thinking about what I should do next about my marriage and eventually gave up as my mind just could not cope with it all anymore. I decided to relax and enjoy the evening with Sophia. It was spot on seven when I pulled up outside the house in Highgate. She made me wait until twenty past before she appeared, but the wait was worth it. She looked stunning in a light green, high neck dress with dark green shoes and matching handbag. Her hair and makeup were perfect and her captivating smile made my heart melt. I was truly in love and I knew it deep down in my soul. She slipped into the car and said "hello, I see you've got another car to take me outa tonight."

"Yes, I'm afraid I had an accident in mine last night."

"You're nota hurt?"

"No, I'm fine, thanks." Then to my surprise and delight, she kissed me on my cheek.

"Thatsa good."

I took her to a very elegant restaurant at Harrow on the Hill where we enjoyed an excellent meal of smoked salmon, Tournedos Rossini followed by crepes Suzette, coffee and brandy. The house wine was perfect and complemented the meal. We talked endlessly about everything and nothing and I'm not sure which one of us was the most charmed at the end of it all.

I drove slowly back to Highgate and when I stopped outside the house I took her in my arms and kissed her passionately and she just melted into me.

"I'm in love with you, Sophia."

"Don'ta say that too soon" she whispered.

"I'm sorry, I shouldn't have said anything."

"Thatsa okay" she replied before kissing me again.

"Woulda you like to come in for coffee?" I laughed and replied "why not?"

"Gooda."

"Won't you get into trouble with your...."

"They're all gone away for a couple of days, I'm all alone here" she smiled and my heart leapt.

We sat, cuddled up on the settee, in the elegant and spacious lounge sipping coffee, chatting about life and love when suddenly she said "don'ta leave me tonight, Peter, stay here." I could not believe it and I just nodded as a shiver of excitement ran down my spine.

"Of course, my darling."

I eventually followed her to her bedroom and sat on the bed gazing at her. She undressed slowly and provocatively and eventually stood before me naked except for a beautiful gold crucifix mounted on a slim chain around her neck. I looked and was totally mesmerised by her beauty. Her skin was flawless, her breasts, firm and full with large nipples and her pubic hair was as dark as the hair on her head. She smiled, put her hands on her hips and asked "do you approve?"

"Oh, yes, I approve, my darling."

"Gooda."

"Come closer." She moved towards me and still sitting on the bed, I stroked her thighs so gently and felt her tremble.

"Your hands are so softa" she whispered.

"Yes" I replied and then I bent forward and kissed her pubic hair and then her discreet belly button. I heard her gasp. I stood up and enfolding her in my arms I kissed her again and again until we were both breathless.

"Peter" she whispered "I'ma so hungry for you."

"Okay, my darling" I replied as I placed her gently on the bed. I was in no hurry to penetrate her lovely body and I continued to stroke her, kiss her and gently massage her olive skin. At last she said, as we stopped kissing for a moment, "Peter, have me, have me now, I wanta you now!"

I struggled to undo my trousers before releasing myself and then gently rolling on top of her I slid easily into her moist, warm body. The pleasure for both of us at that moment was indescribable and I almost came as I reached right up to the top of her. She moaned with pleasure and pushed herself hard against me.

"Slowly, otherwise you'll make me come too soon" I whispered.

"I wanta you to come and then have me again."

"Let's make it last for as long as we can" I whispered as we settled down to a steady, gentle rhythm. To give her as much pleasure as I could, I withdrew myself as far as I dare before plunging back into her slowly.

"Oh, my God, thatsa wonderful, justa wonderful" she half whispered. I was now in a state of ecstasy that I had not experienced before in my life and I could not speak. I pushed gently and firmly into her yielding body and savoured every moment of every thrust. She was now so wet that the sensation each time I pushed became more silky smooth and I realised that very soon, no matter how hard I tried, nature would take over and I would be powerless to stop my orgasm.

It began deep down and I increased the rhythm and gasped "I'm coming, my darling, darling…" and I kissed her passionately as I arched up and with a mighty series of thrusts delivered every drop of sperm I had in my body. She pushed hard at me and cried out "Peter, Peter, oh, Peter!" as I wriggled uncontrollably on top of her petite body. At last I stopped and we lay gasping and sweating for a few moments before she said "that was a gooda one."

"Certainly was" I replied between gasps.

"Have a rest before we do it again" she smiled and I kissed her.

"Of course." We cuddled and kissed for a while before I needed to go to the bathroom. She escorted me there and watched with interest whilst I relieved myself. It was clear that she wanted to be so close and intimate with me and I was quite overwhelmed by her.

We made love once more before we both fell into a deep sleep with our arms entwined and our warm bodies as close together as possible. When we awoke in the morning I first kissed her gently before thinking that for the first time I had been unfaithful to Janet. I felt uncaring and guiltless about that and only looked forward to the future with Sophia. I knew that I had found my soul mate, my other half, the one person who I could be really happy with for the rest of my life.

CHAPTER 4

EVENTS OVERTAKE HELEN

I decided to take the afternoon off and go sailing. I thought it would help clear my mind and possibly I might bump into Eric on the jetty at Cape May. Dad was okay about it and, as most of the invoicing for the month had been cleared, he just smiled and nodded at my request. Naomi looked a little glum when I told her as she was getting ready to tell me all about a new guy in her life, David, an accountant with a promising future. Naomi believed that financial security was the most important factor in any relationship and possibly could lead on to a perfect marriage. Poor girl, I just smiled and told her I'd catch up with all her news about David tomorrow, when she could go into great detail. She smiled at that and wished me a nice day.

I arrived at the jetty and took my time in getting the 'Princess' ready for the voyage, hoping against hope that Eric would show up. Well, he didn't and at last I slipped the moorings, started the motor and chugged out beyond the harbour entrance. I hoisted the mainsail and the off shore breeze caught the 'Princess' and sent her spinning through the grey green sea. The wind was quite strong and my little yacht accelerated quickly, I was excited by the rush. I decided to be even more adventurous as I knew that if I raised the spinnaker in this wind I would drive forward even faster, probably dangerously so. The 'Princess' was now crashing through the wave tops and the spray hurtled back from the bow and drenched me. I just loved it and didn't hesitate to raise the spinnaker. The effect was exhilarating, and I hung on tight to the helm as the yacht ploughed on through the Atlantic at considerable speed. I grasped the wheel tightly as the 'Princess' shuddered with the impact of the waves and thought 'who needs men when you've got a sailboat as good as this?' I laughed out loud as I gently steered her round a few degrees to catch more of the wind. The sea was becoming rougher and looked more grey and I glanced back at the harbour entrance, fast disappearing in the afternoon sun. I wouldn't go too far as I would have to tack back into wind and I did not want to arrive at the harbour in the dark. I sailed on, enjoying every minute of the exhilarating experience and I wished it could go on for ever.

Sometime later, better judgement made me turn gently back towards Cape May and after reefing the spinnaker I began to tack the yacht back towards the harbour. The wind dropped a little but it still took me a lot longer than I had anticipated to get back and it was some time before I was able to start the motor and gently cruise into the harbour. I was dripping wet with tangled hair but feeling fresh and invigorated. As I got closer to the berth I saw Eric standing there. Wouldn't you just know it? Some guys pick exactly the wrong moment to turn up. I must have looked like a drowned racoon with a red face. I threw him a mooring rope and he smiled as he pulled the 'Princess' to the jetty with ease.

"Hi" I called. He nodded as he made the yacht fast.

"You've had an enjoyable trip?" he asked with a smile.

"You bet" I replied.

"Good."

"You should have come with me" I said firmly.

"I would have liked that, but I've been delayed elsewhere" he smiled.

"Was she nice?" I enquired and cursed myself for being so obvious but I couldn't help it. Hell, why should I be so jealous?

"There was no woman involved" he smiled and I knew as his eyes twinkled that he saw right through me. I thought 'God. I'm going to need some help in nailing this guy down because I'm not doing very well on my own'. We finished making the 'Princess' secure and then he said "let's talk for a while."

"Okay" I replied feeling delighted at the opportunity.

"In the cabin" he nodded and I lead the way into the snug interior of the 'Princess'.

"I'd better take this off otherwise I'll get too hot" I said as I began to struggle out of my waterproof jacket. I suddenly felt a little self conscious undressing in front of Mr Gorgeous but I soon got over it and would have stripped naked for the guy if he'd even mentioned that I should get out of the rest of my wet clothes.

"There" I said as I slumped down on the bench seat opposite and gazed at him.

"I hope you're not in a hurry?" he asked.

"No, not at all, take all the time you want" I replied with anticipation.

"Good, now, I haven't been able to tell you the whole story…." he began and I thought 'here comes the bit about the wife and two kids in Baltimore' "and I don't want to alarm you…." he continued 'I'm alarmed at that already don't you know?' I thought, "but you are the centre of my concern" he concluded in a firm tone.

"I'm pleased to hear it" I replied whilst wondering what was coming next.

"My only purpose is to guide you through a difficult emotional time ahead" he said.

"Does that mean we are, or we are not, having dinner together tonight at Rolfe's?" I enquired in a confused tone. He smiled and replied "I'm afraid not."

"Shame."

"I've come to realise that I might be slightly attractive to you…." he began.

"Slightly" I interrupted whilst my only thought was how to get him to put those bronzed arms about me, kiss me until I was giddy and then have me all night long on the fur rug in front of the fire. My God, was I hungry for this guy, and the hungry must be fed.

He looked at me quizzically "are you alright?" he asked.

"I'm fine" I replied in a strangled tone "just fine." I always say that when I'm not.

"Right, now then, I'm not supposed to tell you this, but you'll soon be going abroad…."

"Where?"

"That doesn't matter for the moment…."

"It matters to me" I interrupted.

"Will you please just listen?"

"Okay."

"Now you're going to travel to Europe and…."

"Whereabouts?" I interrupted, well I wanted to know.

"What do I have to do to make you be quiet and listen?" he asked a little angrily. I thought 'well, here goes' and replied "kiss me!"

"Helen!"

"That's me."

"I'm not supposed to."

"Who told you that you couldn't? The United Nations or Gunther?"

"Look, it's not allowed" he half whispered.

"Who doesn't allow it, the Boy Scouts?" I whispered back.

"No, listen….."

"I'm listening" I interrupted eagerly.

"I can't kiss you, it'll only lead on to other things…."

"You can bet your sweet bibby on that" I murmured.

"I'm not supposed to get involved with…." he started but I interrupted.

"Just one kiss and I promise I'll be good for the time being and I won't tell Gunther!"

"Helen" he sighed and then in one easy move he arrived on the seat next to me, took me in his arms and kissed me like I'd never been kissed before. Oh, my God, I was in heaven! I did not want to let him go and sought eagerly to kiss him some more. He broke away and said "now, please keep your promise, and listen to me."

"Okay" I murmured whilst my mind spun out of control. I then decided that I really should get out of these wet clothes so he could kiss me some more… starting with my lips then down my neck and all over my damp, naked body.

"Are you listening?" he asked as I returned from my fantasy to the here and now.

"Yup."

"Good, now when you arrive in Europe, you'll meet a man who you won't like, but that doesn't matter for the moment, because he's in love with someone else…."

"What are you talking about? I'm not going anywhere and I don't care, I really don't care about some guy that I haven't met and won't like!"

"This is serious…."

"So am I, let's get cleaned up and have dinner at Rolfe's and, if it's that important, you can tell me all about this guy who's in love with someone else before we go back to my place for coffee, okay?"

"Helen, no, you've got to listen to me."

"At the moment I'd rather kiss you than listen to you, so lighten up, big boy and relax" I said with confidence.

"You're making this very difficult for me, I'm sorry, but I've told you too much and now I have to leave you...."

"Oh, no, you can't...."

"Goodbye for the moment." And with that he stood up and left the cabin. I just sat in amazement with my mouth open and couldn't even manage to shout 'goodbye' as I listened to the sound of his footsteps fading on the wooden jetty.

I eventually pulled myself together and made my way to the car park. As soon as I slipped into the drivers seat I glanced up into the rear view mirror and was horrified by the sight of my pink face and straggled hair. It was a miracle that Eric was persuaded to kiss me at all. Well, you couldn't blame me for taking the opportunity to let him know that I was just plain crazy for him.

I drove home and managed to get indoors before Mrs Dawson caught me. After a shower, a change of clothes and a coffee I was just about to call Rachel and update her on my failing romance with Eric, when the 'phone rang..

"Helen Milton here."

"Hi, darling, I'm glad you're back home...."

"What is it, Mom?" I interrupted anxiously, sensing something was wrong.

"It's Pops, he's had an accident at work...."

"Oh, my God! Is he hurt bad?"

"I don't know, dear, Naomi just called and said they've taken him to the hospital......"

"I'm on my way, I'll pick you up and we'll get straight on down!"

"Okay, dear, see you soon."

Mom and I arrived at the accident and emergency department and rushed straight in. The receptionist was very helpful and told us that Pops had been taken to the x-ray department and if we cared to wait, she would call the Doctor, who would let us know how he was. We sat for what seemed an age before a young and quite handsome Doctor approached.

"Mrs Milton?"

"Yes" Mom replied as we both stood up.

"I'm Doctor Williams, I'm pleased to tell you that your husband is not seriously injured...."

"Thank God!" interrupted Mom.

"But he will be out of action for a while…."

"What's happened to him?"

"He's suffered a broken ankle and some cuts and bruises…."

"Can we see him?" interrupted Mom again.

"Of course, as soon as we've plastered him up and got him comfortable, I'll come and get you."

"Thank you, Doctor."

"That's okay, now don't worry, he's going to be just fine." He smiled and left us both looking at each other.

"This is all we need" said Mom as we sat down again to wait.

At last the good Doctor arrived and showed us into a side ward. Pops looked his usual self propped up in bed and smiled when he saw us.

"Joe, what in God's name happened?" asked Mom in an anxious tone.

Pops smiled and replied "I fell over a damaged fender."

"What?"

"Mitch had taken the fender off the front of a Dodge and left it on the floor, then he called me from the office to take a look at some other damage he'd found, which I did, and then I stepped back onto the fender, caught my ankle and fell over."

"Oh, my God."

"And as I went down I heard it crack" he smiled.

"Oh, don't Pops" I said and kissed him on his cheek.

"But I'm fine, I just feel such a dumb fool…."

"Well it sounds as if it was Mitch's fault" said Mom.

"Now, now, Rose, it was nobody's fault, it was an accident, I should have looked where I was going."

"Okay, as long as you're going to be alright."

"I'm fine, the Doctor says I'm in pretty good shape for my age."

"Good, now when are they going to let you out?"

"The Doc says, tomorrow, if everything is okay."

"Right."

"Now, Helen, you'll have to run everything at the office for a day or so until I can get back…."

"A day or so? You're not going anywhere until the Doctor says you're okay" interrupted Mom firmly and Pops raised his eyes to the ceiling.

"Listen, Rose...."

"No, you listen, Joe, Helen can cope with the business until you are well enough to go back and that's final!" I nodded at that and Pops smiled.

"Okay, okay, I'll do as I'm told as usual."

"Joe, you know it always works best that way" Mom smiled.

An hour or so later we left the hospital and drove back home. Melodie had come in from school and was anxious to know what had been going on. Mom explained everything in detail before we all sat down for dinner. We were just finishing our ice cream and chocolate sauce when Mom dropped the bombshell.

"Of course, I guess you'll have to go to the Paris show next week in place of Pops" she said in a matter of fact tone.

"What?"

"Naomi can run things while your away and I'll go in to help, answer the phone...."

"What this about Paris?" I queried.

"Didn't Pops tell you?"

"No, he didn't!"

"It's a big auto paint trade do, and Pops was selected to go as one of the East Coast delegates and Jack Simmons has asked Pops to make a speech" she said proudly.

"Oh, my God" I murmured as Eric's handsome face appeared in my mind.

"You'll have to go, Pops would be very disappointed if you didn't" said Mom and I felt as mixed up as my melting ice cream and chocolate sauce.

"This has all been arranged and I didn't know about it?" I asked with a touch of anger.

"I'm sure Pops must have told you...."

"Well, he didn't" I interrupted.

"I expect he did, but you just plain forgot about it, I guess you probably had Eric on your mind!" and with that she got up from the table and started to clear the dishes. I looked at my ice cream in stunned silence.

The next morning at the office I first had to placate Mitch and

Naomi and give them the up to date information on Pops after listening to their account of the accident, reliving the event several times over. I put a call through to Jack Simmons, who is the secretary of the American East Coast Auto Federation, I told him all about Pops accident and confirmed that I would be taking his place on the Paris trip. Jack is a nice guy and a good friend of Pops.

"I'll call over later and see if Joe's back at home, check on how he is" said Jack.

"Thanks, he'd like that."

"And in case you can't lay your hands on things at the moment, I'll bring another set of details of the trip for you" he said.

"Thanks, Jack."

"Okay, now just to let you know we fly out next Tuesday, flight time is ten a.m."

"That's fine, Jack, I'll be there."

"And bring some posh frocks, you know what the French are like!" I thought 'don't remind me' as I imagined Reece with his French piece doing the 'hotel bedroom can-can' all night.

"Okay, see you later" I replied and hung up.

The rest of the day flashed passed as I was so busy and Naomi, bless her, didn't even try and tell me about David. Mom called sometime late afternoon and told me the good news that Pops had been brought home and was sitting in the front room asking for coffee and cookies. I laughed and knew that he was going to be okay.

It was later than usual when I got back to Mom's and Jack was already there. I was just glad to be home and wasn't looking forward to this goddamn Paris trip and it must have showed because both Pops and Jack were full of it. To encourage me, Pops offered to sport me to some new outfits to wear in Paris, just to show the 'Frenchies that we also have a touch of civilisation this side of the pond.'

I eventually went home with Melodie, tired and a bit depressed, deciding on the way to have a long soak in the tub before phoning Rachel for a good gossip. I lay in the tub for more than an hour and eventually got out refreshed and feeling a lot better. Melodie was in bed before I settled down in front of the fire, my bath robe wrapped round me and a towel on my head. I poured a large Jack Daniels and had a sip before I dialled up Rachel.

"Hi, it's me" I said.

"Well I wonder what you've been up to, calling me this late" she replied in a curious tone and I laughed.

"You'll never guess."

"Sure I can, you've seen Eric and you've made out with him!" I laughed and replied "nope, just a kiss!"

"Well, that's a start."

"Sure is."

"Now, what kind of kiss was it? Perhaps the type you give your aunt at Thanksgiving for the box of mauve hankies she's bought you or, the mouth watering 'take my body now!' kind?" she asked and giggled.

"Take my body...."

"Oh, you lucky, no good...."

"Hey, I haven't made him yet so I'm not too lucky...." I interrupted.

"I don't know why he didn't give in as soon as you first met him...."

"Well, I guess...."

"Don't all men know that we always win in the end?" she asked and I laughed.

"It seems not."

"If they gave in at the start it would save a whole lot of hassle" she said firmly and I laughed again.

"Stop making me laugh will you? I'm trying to drink a Jack Daniels here."

"Take a sip for me while I get ready to listen up, I want all the details."

"Okay" I replied before taking a good swig of the reviver and then began to recount the days events, ending up with Pops accident and my impending trip to Paris.

"Paris, France?" she asked excitedly.

"Yup."

"Helen, don't you ever tell me again that you don't have any luck!"

"Okay."

"I wish I could go" she said wistfully and her sad tone caught me.

"Hey, next best thing, come with me on Saturday down town and help me choose something to wear on this trip" I replied.

"Sure thing, sweetie pie" she said with enthusiasm.

"Great."

"We'll get you all fixed up so all those Frenchmen will be drooling over you....."

"Don't be disgusting, Rachel" I interrupted and she laughed, although I did find the thought appealing for a moment before Eric's face appeared in my mind.

"You know you love being the centre of attraction" she replied.

"Sure, who doesn't, and, hey, that reminds me, talking about centres of attraction, Karen said she'd drop by on Saturday to give Eric the once over...."

"Oh, that'll be great, I haven't seen her in a while and I bet she's keen to meet him" she interrupted.

"She is, but I don't know if I can get him to show" I said wistfully.

"Call him, tell him it's important."

"I can't."

"Haven't you got his number?"

"Nope."

"How do you meet him then?"

"He just shows up."

"D'you know his address?"

"Nope."

"Helen, this guy is a bit strange, you must admit."

"He sure is."

"Well, it'll be good to see Karen."

"Yup."

"I guess she's as smart as ever and still working at the law firm."

"Yup."

"Keep an eye on her, because if this Eric guy is really as good as you say, she'll have him away to her place in Baltimore quicker than you can finish your Jack Daniels....."

"I know."

"Well just never say I didn't warn you....."

"Okay, I won't" I replied before I took another sip.

"I'll leave you to fix a time when we can meet up then."

"Okay, I'll make it after we've been shopping."

We chatted on for a while about clothes and the sort of thing I should wear on the Paris trip and at last we said goodnight and I hung up. I just finished my drink and got up to go to bed when the phone rang.

"Hi, Helen Milton…."

"Hi, babe" said Reece.

"Oh, Reece, what time do you call this? I'm going to bed…."

"Hey, babe, I've been calling all evening, but your line's been engaged."

"Yup, I've been on the phone to Rachel."

"I might have guessed."

"So, okay, what do you want, Reece?"

"I'd like to see you, babe."

"Don't call me babe" I replied angrily.

"Okay, okay, you sound a little tired…."

"I am, Reece, it's been a bitch of a day!"

"Okay, don't bite my head off…."

"Sorry."

"Okay, now, when can we meet up?" he asked.

"Not for a while."

"Why?"

"Pops had an accident at work…."

"Is he okay?"

"Yup, he's at home now with a broken ankle…."

"Sorry, babe."

"Reece!"

"Sorry."

"And I'm running the business in the meantime, and I'm going to Paris next week on business."

"Paris, France?"

"That's the one…."

"Oh, you'll love it there…."

"Well you should know, that's where you went with Madame Pompadour…."

"Hey, that was nothing serious…."

"You could have fooled me…"

"I only care about you and Melodie…."

"Yeah, yeah, yeah, beside I'm not sure I want to see you again."

"Why not?"

"I've got someone new in my life...."

"What, another man?" he asked in a anxious tone.

"Yup, another man" I replied firmly.

"Oh, my God...."

"So, as he's the jealous type, six and a half feet tall, Scandinavian and passionate, I guess you're out of the picture."

"Helen" he sounded quite shocked.

"That's me," I paused for a moment to let the surprise news sink in and then said "so, goodbye and goodnight, Reece" and put the phone down and went to bed.

The next day at the office was made even more frantic by Pops constantly phoning to check on jobs in progress. Which meant I had to keep calling for Mitch, our bodyshop foreman, for an update, or running out into the repair shop looking for damaged autos. Mom arrived just before lunch and I was glad to see her. I needed a break and so I left her in charge and wandered along to the deli, bought some rolls, pepperoni and cheese, managed to avoid the chocolate and went and sat in the park.

I was just finishing the first roll when he showed up and looked down at me with those captivating blue eyes. He just smiled his gorgeous smile and said "and how are you today?"

I sighed and replied "I'm fine, just fine."

"Really?" he asked as he sat beside me.

"No, not really" and I began to cry a little. He moved closer and put his arm around me and I suddenly felt the warmth of his body.

"There, there, please don't cry."

"I can't help it" I replied as I struggled in my bag for a tissue.

"Let me hold your lunch in case you drop it, the birds round here are getting so fat.........."

"That's true" I laughed as I handed him the bag and retrieved something to wipe my eyes with. When I was all sorted out he handed me my lunch and said "now then..."

"Before you say a word" I interrupted.

"Yes?"

"I'm really sorry about what happened on the 'Princess' the other day, I really didn't mean to embarrass you and…."

"I wasn't embarrassed, Helen" he smiled.

"You weren't?"

"No, I thought it was very sweet of you to want to kiss me." I thought 'Oh, God, did I really hear that? Was this guy gorgeous or what?'

"Perhaps we can do it again sometime?" I asked.

"Possibly."

"Like now?" He laughed at that and replied "not at the moment, so just try and save yourself for a little longer." I thought 'oh, I will try, I will.'

"Now then, I have to go away for a few days but I'll meet you again in Paris." I was stunned and frightened at that.

"I remember you said I was going to Europe but how in the world did you know it was Paris?" I asked.

"Well, I just know and don't worry about it."

"I do worry, oh God, yes I do, I mean, who the hell are you, and what's this all about for Chrissake?" I asked in an agitated tone. I thought 'he's a wonderful guy and I'm sure that I love him to pieces but sometimes he says things and does things that are downright creepy and my Mom never told me about guys like this.'

"Helen, I promise that in time you'll be able to relax with me and be confident in everything I do and say, and remember that I'm with always with you."

"Okay" I replied.

"Now, I must go, enjoy your shopping with Rachel and I hope you have a good time with Karen." Well, I nearly dropped dead at that and then I guessed the truth. Yup, it hit me, I really guessed the whole thing. Eric worked for the phone company and had tapped into my line and was listening to every word I said. My God! Was I dumb or not?

"So, you work for the phone company then?" I asked.

"What?"

"You're a line man or something? All outdoors and rugged? Is that how you got your tan?" he looked as if I'd smacked him in the face with a custard pie.

"No, I'm a Viking…."

"Yeah, yeah, yeah, I've heard everything now...."

"I don't know what you mean, but I must go, I'll see you in Paris." And with that he gave me a quick kiss on the cheek and strode away towards the centre of the park. I sat, stunned again and totally mixed up. I was sure he'd tapped into my phone line, how else could he know so much? I took one bite of my pepperoni and cheese roll and tossed the rest to the fat birds.

It was bright on Saturday morning when Melodie and I drove round to Mom to see Pops and have a quick coffee before picking up Rachel. Pops was fine but getting a bit impatient with having to stay at home. He had been working on his speech and told me it would be all ready for me to take to Paris.

"You expect me to give a speech?" I asked.

"Sure, honey, you can do it" he smiled.

"Well, I'm not so certain...."

"Of course you can, you know the business and besides, it's all written out for you, you've only got to read it out loud."

"Thanks, Pops, just another thing for me to worry about."

"You can do it, I know you can" he smiled confidently and I just shrugged my shoulders. When we were ready to leave Pops said "buy something really special for yourself honey, something that'll knock'em dead!"

"Okay" I smiled.

"Put it all on your card and I'll give you a company cheque to cover it" he said.

"Steady, Joe, she might go a bit crazy" said Mom.

"No, she won't let me down" he replied and I lent over and kissed him.

"Thanks, Pops."

Rachel was all smiles and ready to go when Melodie and I got to her apartment. We had her in my Chevrolet and her wheelchair in the trunk as quick as lightning and then we were off to the down town shopping mall. On the way I told her all about the last time I saw Eric.

"So, I'm not going to meet this guy of yours" she said as I struggled to move across the traffic into the lane for parking.

"Nope."

"Well that's a damn pity" said Rachel.

"Yup, but he's a man you just can't tie down" I replied.

"Eventually you can tie 'em all down, they just like to struggle a bit first, it makes it all kinda exciting" she laughed.

"Anyhow, I've found out what he does" I said knowingly.

"Okay."

"He works for the phone company, he's a line man."

"You're kidding."

"Nope."

"Did he tell you that?"

"He didn't have to, I found out he's been listening to all my calls...."

"Oh, no!" she interrupted.

"Oh, yes, he knew about our shopping trip, our meet with Karen and my trip to Paris."

"Well, the low down sonofabitch!"

"Every time I get mixed up with some guy, he turns out to be nothing but a bum!" I said with feeling.

"Aren't they all just the same" she replied as I swung into the parking lot.

"Seems so" I replied glumly.

"So, let's forget about men, we're out shopping for us now!" exclaimed Rachel.

"Hey, what did Granpops say you could buy me?" asked Melodie.

"Something nice if your good" I replied.

"I'm always good, aren't I Rachel?"

"Always, sweetie."

"So, Mom, what are you going to get for me?" persisted my daughter.

"Anything you want within reason and the budget" I replied.

"That doesn't sound good" replied Melodie as I parked in a convenient slot near the mall entrance.

Like all good American women we started our retail therapy at one end of the mall and worked our way steadily through the place. We did not miss a single shop and had to stop twice for coffee and once for the ladies powder room. I managed to find a very nice evening dress in light blue with a low cut neckline and high heel shoes in matching colour. Rachel said I looked drop dead gorgeous in it and Melodie agreed, so I felt okay about that. I also found a smart jacket and skirt in black which fitted me exactly and a high neck, pink blouse, ideal for day wear at the meeting.

"Now what about underwear?" asked Rachel.

"I've got plenty" I replied.

"You need something new and sexy" she said.

"Why?"

"You're going to Paris, Helen, remember?"

"So?"

"Well, you never know who you might meet and you don't want to turn him off at the critical moment by letting him see you in some old flannel panties you go sailing in!" she replied. I laughed at that whilst Melodie smiled and said "Rachel's right, Mom."

"Okay, okay, but the only guy I'm likely to meet is Eric" I said without thinking.

"What?" asked Rachel as she looked up at me from her wheelchair, her eyes wide open with disbelief.

"Eric said he'd see me in Paris" I replied lamely.

"You kept that quiet, Helen."

"I've only just thought about it" I replied, my mind confused once again.

"He's going with you to Paris, the most romantic city on earth and you've only just remembered?"

"Well….."

"Helen, we need to get you booked into psychotherapy as soon as possible!"

"I guess so" I half whispered.

"Meanwhile, let's find the sexyiest, see through, lace underwear we can possibly find" said Rachel with conviction.

It was lunch time before we had finished shopping and I was more than pleased with everything I bought, including the black lace underwear with little red roses sewn on for extra sexual impact. I had managed to find a dress and top for Melodie, which she looked cute in, and some sexy underwear for Rachel as a little gift.

"Well, I guess I can put it on after I've had a bath and dream that some handsome guy is waiting somewhere to undress me and smother me in kisses" she said with a touch of sadness.

"One day, Rachel, one day" I said.

"Yeah, one day" she mumbled.

We had lunch in a pizza parlour and eventually made our way home. Luckily we have only a couple of steps up to the front porch and Pops had made a little ramp so that we could wheel Rachel up and into the house. When we were all in, surrounded by shopping bags and I had just put the coffee on, Karen arrived.

"Hi, you guys" she said as she breezed in and kissed us all.

"We've only just got in from shopping" I said.

"I've come at the right time then, so, can I smell the coffee?"

"In a moment."

"Okay, meantime, show me what you've bought and then you can tell me all about this fabulous guy you've met, and more importantly, when am I going to see him?"

"I'm sorry, but he's not going to show" I said.

"What?"

"She's only going to Paris with him" said Rachel.

"Hey, I've come all the way from Baltimore, dressed up like a woman on a mission, to see this guy for the once over...."

"Sorry, but it's Paris next stop" I interrupted with a grin.

"Get me that coffee, make it sweet and strong while I sit down and wrestle with my first disappointment of the day" said Karen.

"Okay" I replied with a smile.

"Well, what have you been buying?" asked Karen.

"Sexy underwear for the big occasion" replied Rachel.

"Good for you, guys just love it."

"Helen treated me to some as well" said Rachel.

"Hey, you've got a man in your life too?"

"Not yet, but I'm ready for him when ever he shows up" replied Rachel with a smile.

"Good for you, honey, you'll knock him dead, I know you will." Rachel smiled and was lifted up by Karen's positive attitude.

We only stopped talking to sip our coffee and only stopped sipping to talk. We went over everything repeatedly, with Eric the main topic of conversation. Karen was full of advice on how to get him hooked in Paris and carried on to the point where she was making broad brush arrangements for my marriage. Well, as she said, you've got to plan ahead in hope and Paris was certainly the place to get him hammered into the ground. It was early evening when Karen invited us all to go out to dinner as her treat. We couldn't say 'no' and got ready pretty quickly, before setting off in my car to Rolfe's.

It was almost midnight when I settled down with a Jack Daniels in front of the fire and reflected on the last few days. I suddenly felt quite excited by events and was now looking forward to the Paris trip. Even if Eric didn't show, and for the moment I couldn't imagine how he'd get time off work to be in Paris, I might meet someone who'd give me a little attention. I was just busting to show off my lingerie with the red roses and surely somebody would be pleased to see it?

CHAPTER 5

PETER IN PARIS

I called Sophia, told her all about my trip to Paris and asked her to come away to Bournemouth with me for the weekend, prior to the business jaunt. When she said 'yes' my heart lifted and I felt so excited about the prospect of having her all to myself for a couple of days. I thought 'hang the expense, I'm in so much debt now that a little more won't hurt'. I booked a double room at the Wessex Hotel with a sea view and looked forward to collecting Sophia from Highgate on Saturday morning. The only blot on the landscape was Janet but I was saved from having to make excuses that evening, when she announced in a truculent tone "I'm going to Mum's on Saturday and I won't be back until Sunday night, so you'll have to look after yourself."

"Okay" I replied with a glum expression whilst my heart raced.

"There's chicken and chips in the freezer and plenty of eggs."

"I'll survive."

"I dare say" she replied and disappeared into the kitchen. I sat gazing at the television with a sense of total relief and not caring if she never bothered to come back from her mothers. I wondered if I should tell her now that I wanted a divorce, it would certainly give Janet and her mother something to talk about over the weekend. I decided not to bother for the moment but leave it until I had returned from Bournemouth on Sunday.

From the moment I picked Sophia up from Highgate to the moment we returned on the Sunday night, was perfect bliss. I was totally enchanted with this beautiful young Italian woman and just wanted to be with her all the time and for the rest of my life.

The first thing we did when we arrived in our hotel room was to make love, passionate, yielding love on the huge bed before taking a shower together. Then, casually dressed, we went in search of afternoon tea.

"This is so nice, Peter, I justa love it here" she said, her eyes sparkling with excitement, as we were shown to a discreet table for two in the dining room, near a picture window overlooking the beach.

"It's a very good hotel, and the food is excellent" I replied.

"I'll tella you if I agree after we've had a meal" she laughed.

"Dinner tonight will be superb, I promise you and the dancing afterwards, well, you won't know yourself" I said.

"Who will I know thena?" she looked puzzled.

"It's an English saying" I laughed.

"I'ma sure I'll never completely understanda" she smiled and I thought how beautiful she was. After a pot of tea and cucumber sandwiches, followed by a selection of cakes, we wandered out into the afternoon sun. There were a few people about, some with dogs and others with children, all intent on enjoying the spring sunshine.

"We met on the twenty third of April" I said in a reflective tone.

"So?"

"It's a good omen" I replied.

"Why?"

"The twenty third is Saint George's day" I replied.

"Who isa Saint George?"

"He's the patron saint of England, he killed the dragon" I smiled at her.

"I'ma not a dragon" she smiled.

"No indeed, you most certainly are not" I laughed and put my arm around her before pulling her close and kissing her cheek.

"You are so a English" she smiled and I nodded as we continued our walk.

"We'll never forget the day we met though" I said.

"Si, dragon day."

"No, Saint George's day" I insisted and she laughed as I fell more in love with her.

It was just before eight when we were ready to go to dinner. Sophia stood before me looking more beautiful than any other woman I had ever seen. Her hair was done up in a French roll and her makeup was quite stunning. Her dress was a red satin creation that showed her firm breasts and small waist to glorious effect. She walked a few paces and turned for me in a graceful gyration.

"Do you approve?" she asked.

"You look wonderful and you move like a dancer" I said.

"I wanted to be a ballet dancer but my father stopped me" she replied sadly.

"Why?"

"Because he thoughta that any body who's in the theatre is no gooda" she replied.

"That's nonsense."

"I know, but never mind, thatsa all over now, so, let'sa go to dinner and dance!"

We wandered through the menu and took our time in ordering. I was conscious that all the other diners were constantly glancing in Sophia's direction. She was a magnet that no-one seemed to be able to resist. We settled on prawn cocktails followed by duck breasts in orange sauce and finished with crepe suzettes, all accompanied by a light French rose The dance band had played quietly in the background whilst we dined but as we settled back with coffee and brandy they increased the volume and tempo. I danced with Sophia almost every dance until the end of the evening and we both had aching feet when we finally made our way to our room. We then made the most gentle and fulfilling love that I had ever experienced and it was in the early hours before we fell asleep entwined in each others arms.

Next morning I enjoyed a full English breakfast but Sophia stayed with toast, marmalade and black coffee. After we had slowly pulled ourselves together we went for a long walk on the beach. The sea was quite calm and the wind light in the morning sun.

"It's a lovely day again" I said.

"You always talka about the weather in England" she laughed.

"Well, if we didn't have the weather to complain about we'd only have the legal system and banks to moan about" I replied and she laughed.

"It'sa the same in Italy" she smiled.

"But your weather is good."

"Nota all the time" she replied.

"I'd swap."

"What'sa 'swap'?"

"Exchange, you have our weather and we'll have yours" I replied and she laughed.

"What else a would you 'swap'?" she asked with a smile.

"Only you" I replied.

"What for you swap me?" I smiled as she tangled her words.

"I'd only swap you for all the diamonds in the world so I could cover you with them along with thousands of kisses" I replied.

"But if you swap me, you wouldn't have me" she smiled.

"True, so in that case, I'll never ever swap you for anything in the world" and I kissed her passionately.

"Peter, you are a wonderful person" she said as we broke apart.

"There's a little list of people who don't agree with you" I whispered.

"I don'ta care about them, I only care about you."

"And I only care about you, my beautiful princess…"

"I'ma falling in love with you" she interrupted.

"I've already fallen deeply in love with you" I replied.

"But it's all too fasta" she whispered.

"No, it's not."

"I'm afraid it will not lasta…"

"What I feel for you will last until I die" I interrupted.

"Oh, Peter" she replied and we kissed again.

We enjoyed a light salad lunch at the hotel before checking out, I winced at the bill and my hand shook as I presented my credit card to the attentive receptionist. Sophia talked and laughed all the way back to Highgate as I tried to put the worry of my mounting debt burden to the back of my mind whilst listening to her lovely voice. When we arrived at her house it was dark and in the warmth of the car I put my arms around her and we kissed passionately.

"Sophia, I don't want this to ever end."

"Neither do I."

"I've made up my mind…."

"About a what?"

"You, I want to marry you…."

"Oh, Peter, no, it'sa too fast…."

"I love you…."

"It'sa too much for me, no…."

"Sophia, I have never been so happy in my life since I met you and I must have you as my wife…."

"Oh, Peter, you ask too much…."

"Yes, I suppose I do, but you have to understand how I feel about you…."

"Give us some time, besides, you're married."

"Not for much longer, oh, please say 'yes' to me." She hesitated for a moment and kissed me before whispering "yes." I could not speak, overcome with joy at her reply, and just kissed her until we were both breathless.

"I'll phone you every night from now on" I said as she slipped from the car.

"Thatsa good."

"And I make sure I call you from Paris."

"You do, and watch out for those naughty French women" she smiled.

"Oh, I will, and I'll see you as soon as I get back, my princess." She smiled and blew me a kiss. I watched her enter the front door before giving a final wave and driving off. I was sure I saw Eric standing in the shadow of a tree as I accelerated up the road and felt a cold shiver run down my spine.

During the long drive back to Wantage I re-lived every moment of the weekend and sank into the emotional, warm soup that engulfs everyone who really is in love. As I pulled up outside my house and saw the upstairs lights on, I made the decision not to tell Janet I wanted a divorce. I reasoned that the un-pleasant confrontation could wait until I returned from Paris.

On the Wednesday, Freddie and I took a taxi from Berkeley Square to Terminal 1 at Heathrow where we queued at the check-in for our BA flight to Charles de Gaulle, Paris. Airports are busy places that get me down and I prefer to spend as little time as possible in the warm, stale air that appears to engulf everyone in the whole unpleasant process of waiting to fly. I'm not afraid of flying, I would just prefer to do it with nobody else around.

"Got your passport?" asked Freddie as we got closer to the check-in.

"Bit late to ask me now, but yes, and you?" I countered.

"Of course."

"Good, and have you been practising your French?" I enquired.

"No, I've left that to you" he replied.

"Oh, nice one."

"That's called 'management delegation', Peter" he grinned.

Once on board and seated, I watched with bemused interest as the air hostess, without laughing, managed to demonstrate the life jacket and escape drill if we crashed into the Channel. I regarded it all as a pointless exercise and smiled at the pretty young woman as she maintained a fixed thousand yard stare to the back of the aircraft, whilst pointing to the emergency exits 'situated on both sides of the cabin'. The eventual take off was smooth but the landing was a bit of a bump and the time in between was taken up with Freddie and I rushing several gin and tonics down before we both picked our way through a tray of inadequate and un-interesting food.

"Thank God we're down in one piece" said Freddie as we taxied to the terminal and I realised he was a little anxious when it came to flying.

"Safest form of travel, Freddie" I said.

"Yes, so they say, but I've got an open mind on that" he replied and I laughed.

The taxi driver raced at un-necessary speed from the airport to our Paris hotel, The Excelsior, where we booked in and went to our room on the third floor. The beds were soft and the bathroom was quite spacious with a huge selection of soaps, shampoos and God knows what else that the French deem necessary for every guest.

"Let's see if we can get anything to eat, I'm starving" said Freddie after unpacking his case and we set off towards the dining room. We were shown to a table for two in a corner close to a long table with six men, three on either side with a woman sitting at the head. She was quite attractive and caught my eye as Freddie and I sat down. From my position I could see her clearly by just looking slightly to my right, which I continued to do. She looked about thirty, with a very pleasant face, dark hair in a page boy style and blue eyes. The men were talking loudly and she just kept smiling at them.

"They're bloody Americans" whispered Freddie.

"Really, I hadn't noticed" I replied.

"Would you believe it, we come all the way to Paris and it's full of yanks" he hissed.

"There's only seven of them, that's hardly a city full" I replied.

"Can't stand 'em" said Freddie as he perused the menu.

"Why?"

"They're such loud mouthed pratts with little imagination and even less intelligence" he replied from behind the menu.

"I think you're being a bit harsh" I said.

"You haven't had to deal with them like I have and you want to hear what George says about 'em" he replied.

"The Bradley Ponting Consortium?" I asked.

"Yeah, George has to keep in contact with a bloke called Hector Flanagan, would you believe?"

"Hardly." I replied as I looked across at the woman again.

"Apparently, he's all mouth and trousers."

"Really?"

"I've only spoken to him a couple of times on the phone and that was bad enough, believe me, he's a complete arse" said Freddie.

"So, you're glad that you're here in Paris with me rather than with J.B. and George in the States" I said.

"Well, I'm glad I'm in Paris, but I'm not so sure about being with you!" he smiled.

"Thanks a bunch" I replied.

"That's okay, anytime."

"You reckon that all yanks are over the top?" I asked.

"Yes, just like this lot on the next table" he nodded his head in their general direction.

"The woman doesn't look if she's making much noise" I replied defensively.

"You wait 'til she opens her mouth! Now, never mind about them, what are you going to eat?" he asked as the waiter arrived.

"Monsieur, are you ready to order?"

"Not yet, a moment or two, s'il vous plait" replied Freddie and the waiter gave a little bow and vanished.

"Fruits du mer followed by scampi, for me" I said before glancing at the American woman again.

"Okay, I'll have the prawns followed by the lamb, agneau is lamb isn't it?" he asked.

"It is" I replied. The waiter returned and Freddie gave him the order and then started to peruse the wine list.

"I think we'll have a Beaujolais, okay?" asked Freddie but I didn't hear him as my mind was elsewhere with Sophia.

"Peter!"

"Sorry, what?"

"Beaujolais okay for you?"

"Er, yes, that's fine" I replied and Freddie ordered a full bottle. The waiter gave a little bow and vanished as I looked again at the woman. She had a sweet face, not beautiful, but open and kind, her blue eyes were large, her hair, dark and quite lustrous.

"Why do you keep looking at her?" asked Freddie.

"I'm not sure, she's just got something about her that I find attractive" I replied.

"God almighty, Peter, aren't you in enough trouble with women already without getting in any deeper?" he asked in a petulant tone.

"Yes, but it is Paris" I grinned.

"You know, you're a bright boy who could have a good future with the company, but sometimes you cock it all up by behaving like a complete arse!" he replied testily. 'Cock' and 'arse' were Freddie's favourite adjectives and were used to describe every situation and eventuality. He was always wonderfully predictable.

"We all have a blind spot" I replied.

"Spot? Yours is more like a bloody great smudge!" At that moment the waiter arrived with the Beaujolais, the Englishman's choice when he's unsure of the wine list.

Freddie and I discussed the probable outcome of the first meeting at Benoir Paints and we were both aware that the conversation and laughter from the American table was becoming louder in parallel with their intake of wine.

"For God's sake, I wish they'd quieten down a bit, I can't hear myself think" said Freddie.

"We can't fight them, so let's give in and enjoy the meal, we can discuss things later in our room" I replied.

"Okay."

The meal was up to full French standard and I enjoyed every mouthful whilst wishing that Sophia was with me rather than Freddie. He was putting on weight these days and his complexion was becoming a little ruddy with either blood pressure or too many gin and tonics. As we finished our meal the Americans got up and left the dining room. The woman gave me a long glance as she stood up and I fancied that she smiled at me, just a little.

"Thank God they've gone" said Freddie and I nodded whilst

wondering if I would ever see the woman again. We then settled down and discussed the events of tomorrow before Freddie announced that he had had enough and it was time for bed.

"You go on up whilst I order a paper and an early call" he said as we left the dining room and he headed for the reception.

"Okay" I nodded and made my way to the lift. As I arrived the doors opened and I was delighted to see that the only occupant was the American woman. I stepped in as she said "hi, are you going up or down?"

"Up, third floor" I smiled.

"So am I, but I've been up once already" she replied and pushed the button. The doors closed and we were suddenly on our way.

"You were in the restaurant tonight" she said.

"I was."

"I'm sorry if we got a little loud on our table" she said.

"That's okay."

"Not really, I guess we upset people sometimes, especially the British, you are British?" she enquired.

"I am indeed" I replied with a smile.

"I guessed you were, and I'm sorry, I could see that the guy with you was getting a little sore at us."

"I assure you, it's alright."

"This is my first time in Paris and you're the first English man I've ever met" she smiled.

"Really?"

"Yup."

"I really don't know what to say" I replied.

"Hey, I just love your accent, say something else."

"Something else" I replied and she laughed out loud then the bell dinged announcing our arrival at the third floor.

"Here we are" I said.

"Hey, as we might not see each other again and you're the first Englishman I've met, I wonder if you could buy me a drink at the bar downstairs and tell me all about old England?" she said with a smile.

"Why not indeed" I replied.

"Just let me get my purse from my room and I'll meet you back here in a moment and we can ride down in the elevator together" and with that she was gone. A few minutes later the lift descended and when it re-appeared Freddie stepped out.

"You waiting for me?" he asked quizzically.

"No, boss, the American woman" I replied truthfully as she arrived back clutching her purse.

"Hi" she said to Freddie. He looked stunned and glanced at me.

"Good God, you'll regret this" he mumbled and went off in the direction of our room.

"He's your boss?" she asked once we were descending in the lift.

"He is."

"Is he unhappy with his life?"

"I'm afraid so."

"Aren't we all" she said.

"Only some of us" I replied.

"Are you unhappy too?"

"Unhappily married I'm afraid." There was a silence whilst that fact sank in.

"I don't even know your name" she said.

"Peter."

"Hi, Peter, I'm Helen, from the USA" she smiled and held out her hand which I shook gently.

"Welcome to Europe, Helen" I replied.

"Thank you, kindly, sir" she smiled.

At the bar we ordered two Jack Daniels with plenty of ice and wandered off to a table in a cosy corner.

"Well, I'm just dying to hear about you and England" she said as soon as we sat down.

"Really, what do you want to know first?"

"Do you live in London?"

"No, but my boss, Freddie has an office in Berkeley Square…."

"Oh, how romantic it sounds" she interrupted.

"I live at a place called Wantage in Oxfordshire."

"Is that where Shakespeare lived?"

"No, he lived in Stratford on Avon, just a little further north of Oxford" I replied.

"That's just wonderful, do you get to go there often?"

"Not really, I travel about in my job around London and out to the west."

"And what's your job?"

"I'm a paint salesman."

"What kinda paint?"

"Car paint."

"The type used for repairs?"

"Yes."

"Well, you'll never believe it, but my Pops has his own business in Atlantic City, repairing auto wrecks" she smiled.

"It is a small world" I replied.

"Yup, and I'm over here with the East Coast Auto Federation visiting Benoir Paints...."

"I don't believe it" I interrupted.

"Yup."

"That's why I'm here."

"Well would you ever!" she smiled.

"We must compare notes after the visit" I said.

"Let's do it" she enthused.

"I must ask, why are you the only lady having dinner with those gentlemen, are you a secretary or something?"

"No, I'm not a secretary or something, whatever 'something' is" she replied testily.

"I'm sorry, I didn't mean to be...."

"But you said it" she interrupted.

"What I meant was...."

"Do I look like a hooker?" she interrupted and several people close by glanced up.

"No, good heavens, no....."

"You're sure about that?"

"Why, yes, what I meant by 'something' was, are you a delegate?"

"You bet your life I'm a delegate, a pretty important one too I might add, because I'm giving a speech on behalf of the A.E.C.A.F" she said firmly.

"Your delegation...."

"The American East Coast Automobile Federation" she announced loudly with pride. The bar went quiet as the occupants stared at her and Freddie's opinions regarding 'loud yanks' and his comment about 'regrets' swirled around my brain. Oh, if only

Sophia was with me.

"That's great" I replied nervously.

"I think I could do with another drink" she said just before she finished off her Jack Daniels with a large final gulp.

"Be my guest" I said hurriedly as I stood up and made my way to the bar, grateful for a few moments alone to compose my thoughts. This woman was too loud and aggressive for me to spend any time with and I vowed this drink would be the last before I joined Freddie for a good nights sleep. As I sat down at the table I thought that she looked attractive but when she opened her mouth, well, it was just too much.

"So, who d'you work for?" she demanded.

"Beauclare Paints" I replied.

"Never heard of them" she said as she took a sip of her drink.

"No, I don't suppose you have because we don't sell in the States yet" I replied.

"Does that mean that you plan to?"

"Yes, we're teaming up with the Bradley Ponting Consortium."

"Who? Oh, never mind, I haven't heard of them either" she said in an irritated tone.

"Well they are big in the States" I ventured.

"We use DuPont paint back in Atlantic City" she said, trying to impress.

"Oh, right."

"Hey, what are we doing talking business, we're in Paris, supposed to be the most romantic city in the world" she said with enthusiasm.

"Yes...."

"Are you romantic, Peter?" she interrupted.

"Well, I like to think...."

"That's what the whole world needs, more romance" she smiled.

"I agree and...."

"I'm in love with the most gorgeous hunk of a guy, he's called Eric..." I smiled and froze inwardly at the sound of the name as the face of Eric flashed into my mind.

"Oh, I'm pleased for you" I murmured.

"Yup, he's a tall, blonde haired, blue eyed Scandinavian" she whispered and Eric re-appeared again.

"Oh, nice….."

"Have you got anyone special?" she asked.

"I have, she's Italian and her name is Sophia……"

"Good for you, are you going to get married?"

"As soon as my divorce comes through……"

"That's what all the men in the States say too….."

"Well I mean it" I replied firmly.

"Hey, you really are hooked on your little Italian piece….."

"She's not a 'piece' I'll have you know!" At that Helen stared at me for a moment.

"Either we've had too much to drink or not enough" she said as she downed the last of her Jack Daniels.

"Enough, I think" I replied.

"Up to bed then…."

"It makes sense" I replied. I escorted her to the lift and up to the third floor. We only spoke once to say an un-emotional 'goodnight' as we went our separate ways.

"Blimey, you haven't been long" said Freddie from his bed.

"No."

"Not even a quick 'leg over' then?" he smirked.

"Certainly not."

"She didn't take long to cure you of yanks" he grinned.

"No, boss, you were right, she was loud and……"

"It's such fun being right" he interrupted with a grin. I slumped down on the bed and thought of Sophia. Then Eric appeared in my mind. 'Oh, bugger, bloody Eric' I thought.

"Busy day tomorrow, Peter, so put your worries behind you and get some sleep."

It was now late and I hadn't phoned Sophia as I had promised. Oh, damn that American woman.

Benoir Paints have a very smart head office, training school and small production facility at Evry just south of Paris on the N6. Freddie and I arrived by taxi outside the brushed aluminium and black tinted windows of the imposing façade by ten o'clock and made our way into the reception. We were greeted by an attractive young woman who welcomed us and asked for our names.

"Freddie Martin and Peter Coltman of Beauclare Paints" replied Freddie.

"Ah, one moment, s'il vous plait" she said as she hunted for our name tags before ticking us off a list on her desk. She handed our rather smart tags to us and said "if you would like to go through there" she waved at double doors behind her "coffee and refreshments are being served, monsieur." We thanked her and made our way in to a large room already half full of suited men in groups. A tall, grey haired man in glasses broke away from the group nearest the door and advanced towards us with a smile and outstretched hand. He shook hands as he read our tags and said "welcome to Benoir, Monsieur Martin and Monsieur Coltman, I'm Roger LeDuc, sales director at Benoir."

"Pleased to meet you, Monsieur LeDuc" said Freddie.

"Non, please call me Roger" he smiled "we are informal here."

"Bon" I said and Roger smiled.

"I hope we're not the last to arrive" said Freddie as he glanced around.

"Oh, non, all these gentlemen are Benoir and Milan Autofinish sales people with selected customers."

"Right."

"We are just waiting for the Germans, the Dutch and the Americans to arrive" smiled Roger.

"Oh, good" smiled Freddie. Roger looked at his watch and said "the Germans said they will be here at ten fifteen, and they will be, the Dutch soon after and then the Americans some time whenever."

"They're always late for everything…."

"Non, Freddie, Americans always say they are never late, just delayed" grinned Roger and we laughed and nodded as he continued "in other words, someone else's fault."

"So true" replied Freddie.

"Please, help yourself to coffee whilst I locate Jacques Montreaux, my assistant who will look after you whilst I meet our other guests" smiled Roger.

"He's full of Gallic charm" said Freddie when we were alone.

"I bet his 'broken biscuit' accent has the women down to their bra and pants in a flash" I replied.

"You can be sure of it" grinned Freddie as we made our way to the table offering coffee and biscuits served by two pretty young things wearing smart, identical uniforms in black, emblazoned with the Benoir logo. The Germans arrived promptly and entered with their usual Teutonic assertiveness as Jacques Montreaux introduced himself to us. He seemed an amiable person and enquired anxiously about our flight and hotel arrangements. When Freddie assured him all was well, he looked very relieved, the sign of a man under stress. He then made his excuses and hurried off to join another group. We drank more coffee and chatted on before the Dutch arrived all smiles and slightly reserved. Then we waited for the Americans, and we waited….we drank more coffee, consumed most of the biscuits and generally were becoming more than brassed off when our US cousins arrived. Helen was in the midst of the men and looked very smart in a neat suit with a pink blouse. They made a bee line for the coffee and Helen said "Hi" as she passed us by.

"Morning" I murmured in reply.

"More like afternoon" whispered Freddie. I was surprised when Helen joined us holding her coffee and accompanied by a tall, grey haired man with a ruddy complexion.

"Hi, Peter, let me introduce Jack Simmons, who's our secretary and delegation leader."

"How d'you do" I replied.

"Pleased to make you acquaintance" replied Jack as we shook hands.

"And let me introduce my manager, Freddie Martin……"

"Hi, Freddie" said Jack as they shook hands.

"And this lady is Helen, an important delegate" I said to Freddie with a touch sarcasm.

"I believe we've already met, by the lift last night if I remember" said Freddie with a fixed smile.

"Yup, we did for sure" replied Helen as Freddie's eyes flickered with half concealed irritation. Before another word was spoken a short, well built man in a silver grey suit joined us and announced himself.

"Good morning everybody, I'ma Roberto Gillani, sales director of Milan Autofinish, I just want to say welcome to you all to Paris, and have we gotta a show for you!"

"Glad to hear it" said Jack.

"Yup, it's a long way to come for nothing" said Helen and I saw Freddie wince.

"I promise you, this finish system will revolutionise the way we paint vehicles all over the world" said Roberto with enthusiasm.

"Glad to hear it" repeated Jack in a lame tone and I guessed he had yet to be convinced.

"Gentlemen, your attention, s'il vous plait" said Roger LeDuc in a loud voice. We all turned in his direction as he continued "if you will kindly follow me across to our training school we will be pleased to carry out our first demonstration of the new paint system developed by Benoir Paints."

"And Milan Autofinish" added Roberto in a loud voice but it seemed to go un-noticed. 'The French take all the credit as usual' I thought. We filed through various corridors and out into the sunshine before entering the training school equipped with two paint spray booths large enough to accommodate the average car. When we were all gathered by the large observation windows, Roger warbled on in French and then English, describing in detail what we were about to see, as two painters clothed in white overalls, prepared their sprayguns. When they were ready and on the nod from Roger they began to spray a grey primer over the bodyshell of a Renault. As I watched I became aware of Helen standing next to me.

"I'm sorry about last night, I guess we got of to a bad start" she whispered.

"Seems so" I replied.

"How about we try again tonight after dinner?"

"Possibly" I replied in a cool tone.

"Only 'possibly'?" she enquired with a touch of firmness. I looked at her and smiled, thinking that she was really quite attractive, so why not?

"Certainly" I replied.

"That's better!"

"Forgive me but my English reserve has been a bit too reserved lately......"

"You can say that again, so lighten up and we'll have an easy evening" she replied.

"I'd like that" I replied. Freddie was standing to the other side of me and became aware of my whispered conversation, so he leaned forward to see Helen and then raised his eyes to heaven before saying "pay attention, for God's sake, we're not on bloody holiday!"

The painters finished their work and stood back from the bodyshell as Roger announced in clear tones "and now, we will spray the colour followed by the clear lacquer without giving the primer a chance to dry, so you will see our new wet on wet procedure that will save time and money." He nodded at the men inside the booth who then, using two colour sprayguns proceeded to spray a deep blue metallic finish over the Renault.

"They're mad, this will never work" said Freddie and I also had my doubts.

"The colour will sink like lead into the primer" I said and Freddie nodded in agreement.

"It'll be a right French cock up" he replied and I just smiled.

After the demonstration had finished and the booth was set to apply heat to dry the paint, we were escorted back to the room where we had enjoyed coffee and biscuits. A large buffet lunch had been laid out and there were now four bright young women dressed in Benoir outfits to serve the guests. Freddie and I, each clutching a plate of appetising bits of pastry and a large glass of red wine, mingled and circulated around the assembled throng, gazing at name tags and saying all the right things between mouthfuls of food and sips of wine.

At last, we were summoned by Roger into another large room where the conference was due to take place. We all found our name boards on the table and sat in anticipation of the first event. The afternoon droned on with Roger, followed by Roberto Gillani, informing the assembled group of the benefits of the new system shown up on a big screen accompanied by cost figures and all types of computer generated graphics, so beloved of business everywhere. I was bored and kept glancing at Helen who looked a little mystified by it all, but managed a discreet smile when our eyes met. Freddie noticed and tut tutted under his breath.

Returning to the hotel much later, we went to our room where Freddie flopped down on his bed and sighed.

"What a complete waste of time" he said.

"Yes it was" I replied.

"No one's going to buy this idea of theirs, spraying everything on top of wet primer" he said.

"When we went back to the spray booth after the smoke and mirror show, I thought the finish looked pretty flat with no gloss" I said as I stretched out in a chair by the window.

"It's nothing but another French cock up" he said.

"Well, at least we're having a bit of a break on expenses" I smiled.

"Yes, and tonight I suppose you'll be sniffing round the American female?"

"We've arranged to have a drink after dinner" I replied.

"You must be mad, still, it's your life and I suppose you know what you're doing" he said as he closed his eyes.

We sat at the same dinner table as the previous night and began to peruse the menu when Helen, Jack and the others arrived. They all greeted us and Jack asked if we'd been impressed so far by Benoir and the Italians.

"Not really, but let's give it time" smiled Freddie diplomatically.

"I guess there's always hope" said Jack as he sat down.

"Always" replied Freddie as he returned his gaze to the menu in an effort to close down the conversation. I caught Helen's eye and she smiled before picking up her menu and I hoped we would have a better evening than previously.

When we had finished the meal and the Americans had become as loud as usual, with Freddie constantly pulling irritated faces at them, I saw Helen get up and leave, giving me a quick glance and encouraging smile.

"I'll be in the bar if you want me" I said to Freddie as I stood up.

"Alright, I'll see you later" he replied. Jack saw that Freddie was going to be alone and called across "hey, Freddie, come and join us."

"No thanks, early night for me" he replied with a false smile.

"Freddie, we're in Paris, live a little" replied Jack and the others in the party called some encouragement.

"No, honestly….."

"Freddie, come over here and have a drink whilst I tell you about my stay in London last year and all the cricket matches I went to….."

"Cricket matches?" piped Freddie.

"Yup, I can honestly say I'm one of the few Americans who understand the game of cricket....." said Jack.

"Well, in that case, it would be rude to refuse....."

"You betcha, now get on over here!"

I smiled as I left my boss in the tender hands of the yanks he so disliked, apparently until now, and went to the bar in search of Helen.

Seated at a discreet table in the corner of the bar with two Jack Daniels, Helen and I settled down for a relaxing chat.

"Let's not talk business" she began.

"Certainly not" I agreed.

"I think I've had it with Benoir Paints today and God, their coffee is the pits" she grimaced.

"So, what do you do when you're not working?" I asked.

"Try and look after my daughter, Melodie, spend time with friends and go sailing" she smiled.

"And what does your husband do?"

"I'm not married."

"Oh, I'm sorry, yes, I remember now, you've got a boy friend....."

"Yup, Eric." I felt cold on hearing the name.

"And what does he do?"

"He works for the phone company, he's a line man" she replied.

"What does that entail?"

"He travels up the highways repairing faulty lines."

"Right, very interesting...."

"Not really, but it keeps him fit and tanned so, I guess it's honest work."

"D'you plan to get married?"

"If only...."

"Isn't he keen?"

"He says he can't, but I don't know why, some guys are just plain peculiar" she said with feeling and I got the 'un-requited love' message.

"And some women are more than peculiar" I replied.

"If they are, it's guys who make them that way" she replied as she took a gulp of her drink. She was too touchy for my liking and quite abrupt when compared with Sophia, but she had a pleasant face with expressive eyes and she was certainly better company than Freddie. Any port in a storm.

"You go sailing with your boyfriend?"

"Sometimes, when he's not working."

"Otherwise, you go alone?"

"I take Melodie and my friend, Rachel, when I can."

"Do they like sailing?"

"Yup, they do, but when I take Rachel, it can be a bit of a hassle getting her on board because she's disabled."

"Sorry to hear it."

"A riding accident."

"What bad luck."

"You can say that again" she replied as she finished her Jack Daniels.

"Another one?"

"I thought you'd never ask" she smiled. Whilst at the bar I thought about Helen and I realised that I did not know what to think. She was quite attractive, touchy, loud and too assertive but I was drawn to her. Strange when I was so in love with Sophia.

"Cheers" I said as I raised my glass to her.

"Here's to Paris" she replied with a smile.

"Paris." We sipped and smiled at each other.

"Before we go on" she said "can we cut to the chase?"

"By all means" I replied.

"D'you want to get laid tonight?"

"Not particularly" I replied as I blushed.

"You're blushing, that's so English, say, that is cute" she smiled.

"Well, I find you a bit direct" I replied.

"It's no good beating about the bush, I always like to know where I stand" she replied as she took another mouthful of Jack's finest.

"Me too."

"Well now we've got that out of the way and the answer's 'no' we can relax" she said firmly.

"Good" I replied.

"Are you comfortable with that?"

"Yes, and you?" I asked.

"Sure" she replied but her eyes gave her away and showed her disappointment.

We talked about everything and anything for what seemed a brief moment in time. It was almost midnight before we left the bar and made our way to the third floor. She kissed me lightly on the cheek and whispered "goodnight" before disappearing off down the corridor, leaving me confused about life in general and women in particular.

Freddie arrived back in the room much later, after I was in bed and half asleep.

"You know, old Jack's a bloody good bloke, he's not your usual yankee arse" said Freddie in slurred tones.

"Really" I mumbled.

"He knows a helluva lot about cricket" he rambled on.

"Good, I hope you'll both be very happy" I replied.

"Oh, yes, I've invited them all back to London on Saturday and while I'm spending some time with him for a couple of days, you can take the woman and the others on a guided tour of London......"

"What?" I interrupted, now wide awake at the news.

"You're good at that and it's all been arranged" he said as he wriggled out of his trousers and half fell on his bed before farting.

The next day at Benoir Paints dragged on interminably and the only bright spots were the buffet lunch and Helen's speech at the end of the session. She gave it in a confident manner and it was short as well as being amusing. It was obvious that she made quite an impression on the assembled guests. Winding up the days events Roger made great play on what had been achieved and finished off by reminding us all that there would be a private dinner party that night with dancing until dawn. I was quite looking forward to it.

Freddie and I went to the bar first of all to have a quick 'snifter of gin and tonic' to steady ourselves before we made our way to the Rousseau suite where dinner was to be served at eight o'clock. The room was elegant and romantically lit by candles used as centre pieces amongst fresh flowers set on a number of round tables, in an arc around a small dance floor. The four piece ensemble were already playing some tinkling Gershwin from the low stage as we acknowledged some of the guests already seated whilst we searched for our places.

"Bloody hell, they've only gone and put us with the Germans!" exclaimed Freddie as he spotted our name tags on little Benoir flags amongst the German guests.

"Never mind, Freddie, we'll survive."

"Another French cock up!" he said as we sat at the empty table and waited for the others to arrive.

"I guess the yanks will be last as usual" said Freddie and he had hardly finished speaking when Helen entered followed by Jack and the others. She looked stunning in a light blue evening dress with a plunging neckline that raised my temperature by a few degrees. She saw me and smiled and then made her way over.

"Hi" she smiled as I stood up.

"Good evening, Miss Atlantic City delegate" I replied whilst Freddie peered at her cleavage.

"Am I okay tonight, Mister Reserved Englishman?"

"You look stunning" I replied.

"That's okay then" she smiled.

"Hi Freddie" said Jack and the others crowded around as Freddie stood up and back slapped before complaining about the seating arrangements.

"We're over here" said Jack pointing at the next table along "with some of the Italians"

"We're with the Germans" said Freddie not to be outdone.

"Pity" replied Jack.

"Yes, they don't have a clue about cricket" smiled Freddie. Helen smiled at me and said "hope you're going to dance with me later."

"You can be sure of it" I replied.

"Hey, and nothing heavy tonight, right?"

"Right" I smiled. At that moment the Germans arrived with their ladies, quickly found their places and with polite nods, sat down. I had to turn almost completely round to see Helen at her place and asked Freddie if he would change seats with me. He looked hard and said "if I must." When everyone had arrived and attentive waiters had poured both red and white wines on every table Roger stood up on the stage and welcomed us all as honoured guests of Benoir Paints. He rambled on whilst I watched Helen and smiled when our eyes met. As she was surrounded by her fellow Americans I wondered how many dances she could spare me. I looked around my table at the middle aged women with pudding faces and too much makeup, obviously, the wives! There were also two pretty young things with light makeup and dresses with deep cleavages just holding back heaving bosoms, obviously, the secretaries. The wives intolerant and disapproving glances aimed at the heaving two told the whole story. On Helen's table, Roberto Gillani was accompanied by a young dark haired beauty, but he kept gazing at Helen's neckline and I was sure that his attention to her was not going un-noticed.

The meal was excellent and we started with fruits du mer followed on by coq au vin. The sweet was pear belle Helene and we ended with cheeses followed by brandy and chocolates. I struggled with a limited conversation between a grey haired, serious looking German and his frau who seemed quite jolly after a few glasses of wine. The music grew louder, as did the conversation around the tables, as the wine loosened tongues and lowered inhibitions. Jack was the first to dance with Helen and I felt a tinge of something when I watched them on the dance floor. However, she came straight for me as Jack sat down looking a little hot and over taxed after the first dance.

"Now it's your turn to show me what you can do" she said as she held out her hand towards me.

"Let's do it" I replied, and we did, for the next three dances, after which, she needed the ladies powder room and I needed some cool air.

"I'll be out on the balcony" I said and she nodded as she left me. I stepped out through the large French window into the cool night air and gazed at the Parisian lights below me. What a magical, sensuous place it is. I wandered along towards the end of the balcony and suddenly I saw a tall figure in the shadow of an alcove.

"Hello, Peter" said Eric.

"Bloody hell, what are you doing here?"

"Trying to keep an eye on you" he replied.

"How did you get here?" I demanded.

"It's a mystery, so don't ask" he replied.

"You're beginning to be a bit of a nuisance" I said firmly.

"Never mind about that, how are you getting on with Helen?"

"Not very well."

"Oh?"

"I don't like her that much" I said.

"Really?"

"Yes, really, not that it's any of your business" I replied firmly.

"Oh, but it is....."

"No it's not....."

"Listen, you're the first two that I've to concentrate on and you're not making it easy for me....."

"So sorry, I'm sure........"

"Just try and open your heart to her......"

"I'm in love with Sophia and nothing you say will change that, so, you'd better bugger off and mind your own business!" and with that I turned and walked away thinking 'bloody cheek.' I returned to my table just as Helen arrived back from the powder room.

"Shall we dance?" she asked.

"Why not" I replied as I followed her on to the dance floor.

"Jack tells me that Freddie has invited us all to stop over in London for a few days before we go back to the States" she smiled.

"I know, he told me last night just before he fell into bed, worse for wear" I replied.

"Hey, that'll be great, so, I'll shop for something in Paris and then in London!"

"Absolutely terrific" I replied.

"And Freddie said you'd be pleased to take me shopping" she smiled and winked at me.

"Did he now."

"Yup."

"Great, that's just what I need." I hate shopping.

CHAPTER 6

HELEN MEETS PETER

On Tuesday I arrived at Atlantic City airport just in time and found Jack and the rest of our party in the departure lounge.

"I was getting worried about you" said Jack as he gave me a quick kiss on the cheek.

"Don't ever worry about me being late when there's a trip to Europe lined up" I smiled.

"Sure" he replied.

"What girl could resist April in Paris?" I asked with a smile and he laughed.

"Now you know Bob Lowther and Charlie Wiberg....." and I did, they both had bodyshops outside the city and were friends of Pops.

"Sure, how are you guys?" I asked and they nodded and smiled.

"But let me introduce you to Dave Jensen, Steve More and Mark Fletcher, all auto repairers" Jack said and I smiled and shook hands with them all. They seemed like nice guys but you can never tell and I was the only women with six of them on our way to the most romantic city on the planet. I wondered if their wives knew about me.

We boarded the plane, got settled all together and then eventually roared down the runway before lifting off into the blue sky. As we gained height I looked down from my window seat at the blue grey Atlantic below and thought of my last sailing trip on the 'Princess'. Then Eric drifted into my mind and I wondered if he really would show up in Paris. I doubted it because I could not see how he could get off work and over there in time. I had looked around for him at the airport in the hope, well; a girl's gotta hope.

"D'you like flying?" asked Jack.

"It's okay, but I prefer sailing" I replied.

"It would take a lot longer to get to Europe" he joked.

"I know, but I'd be in charge all the way" I replied.

"You're a girl who likes to be in charge" he laughed.

"Show me one that doesn't" I replied and he nodded. I felt comfortable with Jack, he was like an uncle and I settled down in my seat feeling safe, before switching on the in flight movie.

At last we arrived in Paris and after delays at immigration got out of Charles de Gaulle. I was excited as we headed for our hotel in two taxis. After checking in I went straight to my room to freshen up before calling Jack and arranging to meet for something to eat.

"It's well gone eleven o'clock local time and I guess everything is finished for the night, we can only hope for some rolls or something at the bar" he said.

"Okay, I'll meet you down there, I could do with a drink" I replied. It was good to relax after a long journey and although we were all pretty tired, after a couple of drinks and some chicken sandwiches, which the attentive bar man managed to rustle up, we all felt a whole lot better. All the guys were chipper about the trip and looked forward to what Benoir Paints had to show us. Dave and I were the only ones not to have travelled to Europe before and we were looking forward to a quick tour of Paris, although I had decided to do it all on my own.

"You've only got tomorrow, everything kicks off on Thursday" said Jack.

"I'd better get to bed then, I've got some serious sight seeing and shopping to do" I replied.

"You've got Saturday afternoon as well, we don't fly back until eight that evening" smiled Jack.

"Every moment counts then" I replied before wishing them all goodnight and returning to my room to call Mom, Pops and Melodie to let them know that I'd arrived okay.

Next morning after coffee and croissants with Jack and the guys, I set off on my own in a taxi for a whirlwind trip around Paris. Hey, was I impressed or what? The city was beautiful and so old and full of trees in pink or white blossom, I just couldn't get over it. Luckily my driver, Francois, spoke pretty good English and gave me quite a tour. I saw everything from the Eiffel Tower to the Arc de Triomphe and made Francois drive up the Champs-Elysees twice to make sure that I missed nothing. The traffic was manic and the French drove like bats out of hell. I loved Montmartre and persuaded Francois to wait patiently whilst I went into a little shoe shop and bought two pairs of drop dead gorgeous, high heeled, peep toed shoes that fitted perfectly. I thought how envious Karen and Rachel would be, but never mind, that's life and sometimes you get a break. I was an American in Paris for the first time and boy, was I going to enjoy it. When it got to lunch time I asked Francois to drop me at a café and wait, he said he couldn't do that, but he'd come back in an hour or so and pick me up if that was okay. I agreed and when I paid him off I added a hefty tip, I reckoned that way he was sure to return. His eyes widened as he counted the Euro's and he thanked me before assuring me he'd be back at two o'clock, without fail. I believed him and slipped out of the cab and found a seat in a pavement café on the Champs-Elysees.

I enjoyed the coffee and baguettes, full of delicious cheese and Italian ham, then finished lunch with a huge chocolate gateaux. If the girls could see me now! I began to think of Eric as I watched the Parisian men hurrying by and wondered if he would make it over here. I was certain that as he was listening in on all my calls he'd know where I was staying. I could only hope and if he didn't show, then maybe, just maybe, I might meet some guy to fill the gap and make my stay in Paris memorable. I was busting to show off my black lace, rose enhanced underwear!

Francois arrived back on the dot and was all smiles when he spotted me in the café. Soon I was being whisked around the romantic city once more and I must admit I got my money's worth. It was almost five when he dropped me outside the hotel. With many thanks and another large tip I said goodbye to Francois and went to my room for a rest and to call Mom, Pops and Melodie.

I met Jack and the guys in the bar about eight and after a couple of drinks, whilst I gave them the low down on my day, we went into dinner. Jack insisted I sat at the head of the table which was kinda nice, he said that was in Pop's honour as well as mine. We'd only been there a short while when two guys were shown to the next table. One was middle aged and a little overweight whilst the other was a bit younger, slim and quite tall, not as tall as Eric, but nevertheless okay. He had fair, wavy hair, not blonde like Eric, a nice face, blue grey eyes and he was wearing glasses. Now, normally I don't go for guys with glasses but he was different. He reminded me of that English actor, I can't remember his name, he's a Londoner, wears glasses and speaks kinda dramatically, shouts a lot and always points his finger at people. I guessed the guy at the table was English but I couldn't be sure and I caught him looking at me a few times but pretended I didn't see him. Jack insisted that I tried everything on the menu that was new to me, so I let him check with me first and then choose. I ended up with mussels in a sauce to start, which was very good, followed by pheasant breasts in a wine sauce, which was okay and I finished with a sorbet. Jack kept ordering more wine and we managed to keep drinking throughout the meal. The guys really relaxed and were getting pretty damned loud as they drank their way through the bottles of red wine. I noticed the older guy at the next table getting a bit redder in the face every time he looked across at us and I guessed the noise was getting to him. The young one with glasses kept looking at me and eventually I gave him a little smile as I stood up to leave. Whilst Jack and the others went off to the bar I went to my room and called Rachel.

"Hi, Rachel, it's me calling you from Paris, France….."
"Hi, Helen, you okay?" she asked excitedly.
"Yup."
"And tell me all about Paris, did you have a good flight over and what are the French guys like, has Eric shown up and…….."
"Hold it sister, one at a time, eh?" I interrupted as I tried to slow her down.
"Okay, but I'm just busting to know……"
"Sure, I understand."
"So, do tell…."
"Okay, the flight was good but seemed to take for ever, God knows how those air hostesses manage….."
"It's the thought of the captain in the hotel after the flight that keeps them going!" she interrupted and I laughed.
"Probably, and as far as the French guys are concerned, well, I haven't met any yet…."
"What?"
"Well, only one, Francois……"
"What's he like?" she asked.
"He's overweight, almost bald and smelled of cheap cigarettes and garlic….."

"Oh, my God, where did you meet him?"

"In his taxi…."

"Helen….."

"Yeah, I know……"

"Has Eric shown up?"

"Nope" I replied in a resigned tone.

"Seen anybody else?"

"Well, just one guy, looks okay but wears glasses."

"So?"

"I don't fancy guys with glasses" I replied.

"Helen, I promise you, he'll take them off before you get laid" she said and I had to laugh.

"And I think he's English….."

"You only think? Haven't you spoken to him yet?"

"Nope, he just keeps looking at me…."

"Helen, you definitely have gotta see a shrink as soon as you're back home……"

"Probably….."

"What does this guy look like?"

"He's tall, fair haired and he looks like that English actor who wears glasses and shouts….."

"What are you giving me?"

"You know who I mean, he points at everyone……"

"I think you've had too much wine already!"

"Possibly, but I'll think of his name….."

"Sure, now have you been shopping yet?"

"Yup" I replied and told her all about my trip to the shop in Montmartre, the shoes and lunch at the café. She asked so many questions that in the end I told her that as soon as I was back in Atlantic City we'd carry on this conversation in great detail. I knew that she was hanging on every word and living my experience through her imagination. I promised to call again tomorrow as we said our goodbyes.

Deciding to go down to the bar and buy the guys a drink, I tidied myself up, put a touch more lip gloss on and went down in the elevator. I just reached the ground floor when I realised I'd left my purse in my room. Before I could push the button to go back up, the doors opened and the guy with glasses got in. Close too, he was a lot taller than I had guessed, he smiled at me. I thought he looked nice so I asked him "are you going up or down?"

"Up, third floor" he replied.

"So am I, but I've been up once already" I said and realised that I'd said another dumb thing, why do I do it? Perhaps that's what turns guys off me. I decided to try and straighten things out, I didn't want this guy to think I was dumber than average.

"You were in the restaurant tonight" I said.

"I was" he smiled.

"I'm sorry if we got a little loud on our table."

"That's okay" he smiled and I looked into his eyes, they were soft and gentle.

"Not really, I guess we upset people sometimes, especially the British, you are British?" I suddenly panicked, thinking he might be Dutch or something.

"I am indeed" he replied and relief swept over me.

"I guessed you were, and I'm sorry, I could see that the guy with you was getting a little sore with us" I said, hoping he'd think that I was an observant kinda girl as well as a caring one.

"I assure you, it's alright" he replied and this time his English accent came through.

"This is my first time in Paris and you're the first Englishman I've ever met" I said after hastily deciding to tell the truth and not pretend to be too sophisticated.

"Really?"

"Yup."

"I really don't know what to say" he replied and the way he said 'say' it was kinda drawn out and just gorgeous.

"Hey, I love your accent, say something else" I asked.

"Something else" he said and for a moment I didn't catch on then I laughed and he smiled a charming, disarming smile. The lift bell dinged and the doors opened as I decided to go for it and, hoping not to sound too desperate, asked "Hey, as we might not see each other again and you're the first Englishman I've met, I wonder if you could buy me a drink in the bar downstairs and tell me all about old England?"

"Why not indeed" he smiled and I felt good all over.

"Just let me get my purse from my room, I'll meet you back here in a moment and we can ride down in the elevator together" I said and rushed back to my room where I checked my makeup, touched up my lip gloss again and bobbed my hair, before snatching up my purse and hurrying back to the elevator. As I got there the fat guy, his buddy from the next table, stepped out and said something to my guy which I didn't hear.

"Hi" I said, trying to be friendly and the fat guy looked at me and turning to the tall one said "good God, you'll regret this" before high tailing it down the corridor. I felt anxious as I stepped into the elevator and we made our way down.

"He's your boss?" I asked.

"He is."

"Is he unhappy with his life?"

"I'm afraid so."

"Aren't we all" I replied as I thought of Reece and then Eric.

"Only some of us" he replied.

"Are you unhappy too?"

"Unhappily married I'm afraid" he replied and I thought 'here we go again, all the decent guys are married and all the other bums are like Reece or un-available like Eric, and in his case I wonder what un-available means, am I confused or what for Chrissake?'

"I don't even know your name" I said with a smile.

"Peter."

"Hi, Peter, I'm Helen, from the U.S.A" and I held out my hand which he took gently and replied "welcome to Europe, Helen."

"Thank you kindly, sir" I replied whilst I felt my temperature rise a little. This guy was charming and I didn't mind his glasses.

At the bar, Peter ordered two Jack Daniels and we found a comfy table for two in a corner. Jack and the guys were sitting over the other side of the lounge and when they saw me, other than a quizzical look from Jack, they pretended they didn't know me.

"Well, I'm just dying to hear about you and England" I said.

"Really, what do you want to know first?" he asked with a gentle smile.

"Do you live in London?" I asked making sure I kept all my questions around about him.

"No, but my boss, Freddie has an office in Berkeley Square……"

"Oh, how romantic it sounds" I said and he began to tell me all about himself. As he carried on I thought what a nice, homely sort of guy he was and I felt pretty relaxed until he made a crack about me being a secretary or 'something'. Boy, did I yell at that? Did he think I was a hooker for Chrissake? He seemed nervous after that and I needed to calm down a little so I said "I could do with another drink."

"Be my guest" he said before he went to the bar and my thoughts turned to Eric. Oh, why wasn't he here? Peter returned with fresh drinks and suddenly I couldn't have cared less. He rambled on about paints and who he worked for and I didn't pay much attention. I just kept thinking of Eric whilst Peter mumbled on about some Italian piece he was all hooked up with. Typical married man, not yet divorced and already side lining the next one. I couldn't be bothered and just didn't listen to him, besides I'd had too much to drink to care. Suddenly I said "up to bed then" and he replied "it makes sense" and I felt relieved. As we got out of the elevator on our floor I just said "goodnight" and went straight to my room and collapsed on the bed.

I felt awful the next morning and my face looked pale and the black circles around the eyes didn't do me any favours. I showered, hoping I'd feel better but the hot water needles didn't seem to do much for me. I took time with the makeup and managed to hide most of the wreckage under a hefty layer of foundation and blusher. I slipped on the pink blouse and then the dark suit. I looked okay but didn't feel it and at that moment was certainly not looking forward to a day at Benoir Paints. At breakfast, Jack and the boys were kind and sympathetic as they were all nursing some hefty hangovers.

"It was the wine" said Jack repeatedly and the guys nodded as we sat and consumed several cups of sweet, black coffee.

The cab ride to Benoir Paints wasn't the best and I felt as if I was going to throw up any moment soon, but I made it and was glad to get out of the cab into the clear April air. We all stood around breathing deeply before going into the reception and as we were late already I guessed a few minutes more wouldn't hurt. At last we felt that we were all ready to face our hosts and trooped in.

After being given name tags and ticked off a list we went into a crowded room full of guys in suits and I think, other than the girls serving coffee, I was the only woman there. I felt all eyes on me as we homed in on the coffee. Peter and his fat buddy were standing close and I said "hi" as I sailed by. Peter answered but 'fat boy' mumbled something and I knew that he was not fond of me. Anyway, clutching a coffee I decided to take the lead and I introduced Jack and the guys to Peter and his boss. Just then a smooth guy in a grey shiny suit arrived and introduced himself. He was an Italian, I didn't catch his name and didn't bother to peer at his name tag but just smiled and nodded in the right places. I was still drinking my coffee when we were summoned to the training school. I was pretty curious to see how the French were going to spray autos, but I guessed it would probably the same as our guys did it back home. I managed to get up alongside Peter outside the spraybooth and thought that as I'd been a bit feisty last night perhaps I should try and makeup. I apologised and he smiled and said it was okay. I jumped in right away and asked if we could do it again and he replied "possibly", now what kinda answer is that? So I sharpened him up a little and he agreed to give it another shot. His fat buddy was listening and mumbled something about a holiday.

After the guys had finished spraying paint we went back for a lunch of rolls, pastry and wine, which I gave a big miss, staying on orange juice. We were then ushered into a big conference room. I tried to show some interest, but I didn't quite understand the technical chat from the speakers and kept glancing at Peter. I was glad when it was all over and we could go back to the hotel. Jack and the guys didn't seem too impressed by what they had seen but in general, they thought that it might all get better.

When I was back in my room I took another shower, flaked out on my bed and fell asleep. When I woke up and glanced at the time I realised I'd have to hurry along otherwise I'd be late for dinner.

Fully made up and looking better than this morning I slipped into the neat black dress that Reece had bought me, figuring that it would be just right for tonight. I planned to wear my drop dead gorgeous long blue dress at the dinner dance tomorrow along with the lace panties.

After a drink in the bar with Jack and the others, we went into dinner. Peter and his boss were already there and Jack tried to be nice and spoke to fat boy who wasn't too forthcoming, I just smiled at Peter. He did remind me of that actor, but I still couldn't think of his name. The meal was good and I stayed away from the wine as I knew I had to make a speech tomorrow and I did not want to feel God awful, like this morning. Jack and the boys didn't hold back and the wine started to flow like the Potomac and I knew they'd regret it in the morning. At the end of the meal I got up and left them to it and gave Peter the 'come on' look. He followed me and we found a cosy table in the lounge and ordered Jack Daniels before agreeing we shouldn't talk business. I told him about Melodie and Rachel and he seemed interested. When I mentioned Eric he kinda froze and his face looked pale, but I carried on and told him all about my guy, I guess he was jealous.

We talked and drank some more and I wondered if he fancied me, so I asked him if he wanted to get laid and he said "not particularly", I mean, how English is that for Chrissake? And then he blushed and I found that so cute. I really could have had him tonight, but I thought I'd knock him dead with my blue dress at the dinner dance and if Eric didn't show by then, well, I'd give Peter the chance to see the lace underwear. A girl's needs have got to be met, especially in Paris.

We said goodnight and I gave him a quick peck on the cheek, planning to nail him tomorrow night. I called Rachel and we had a long chat, mostly about Eric and Peter and she made me promise to call tomorrow with the up to date news. I promised; then went to bed and slept like a baby.

At breakfast, Jack and the guys seemed quite chipper and I guessed they were getting used to the wine. As we sat drinking coffee Jack told me that he'd had a good evening with Freddie 'fat boy' and they'd talked about cricket, I mean, what's that all about? The bottom line was, would you believe, that Freddie had invited us all to stop over in London for a couple of days as his guests. Well, was that just great or what? I was excited and was sure that Peter would be around to show me London and take me shopping. Wow, I could hardly wait to get back home and tell them all about it!

I was a bit nervous when we got to Benoir Paints and although I'd read Pops speech through a dozen times on the plane and another dozen times back at the hotel, I was still anxious. I felt it was a bit like taking 'Princess' out to sea for the first time on my own.

The day went quite well and I seemed to understand a little more of what was being discussed and when it came to the buffet lunch I was quite relaxed. My speech was scheduled at the end of the open forum in the afternoon and before Jack and Roger LeDuc made their winding up speeches at the end of the day. When the time came I stepped up to the rostrum clutching Pops notes and tried to compose myself. I looked out at the delegates and felt all their eyes on me, believe me, it was a gut wrenching moment.

"Monsieur LeDuc and fellow delegates" I began quietly and then went for it. "Benoir Paints, here at Evry, have been the perfect hosts in the most romantic city in the world, full of sophistication and old world charm" Pops had a way with words and I heard a collective sigh from the audience.

"And I know that I speak on behalf of the other delegates from the United States when I say that the presentation and demonstration of your new, quick system of painting wrecked automobiles has been outstanding and has given us all a lot to think about. I know that we will be taking back to the east coast a lot of information about up to the minute paint technology that could well change the way we repair auto's in the States….." I saw LeDuc nodding at that and felt pleased. "….and it won't stop there, as I'm sure that bodyshops all across America will be anxious to try out the system and to see if they can cut dollar costs on the repair jobs and maximise profits. Finally, I'd like to thank you all for the kindness shown to me. As you see, I'm the only woman at the conference and I really shouldn't be here, but I've stepped in at the last moment to represent my Pops, Joseph Milton, who unfortunately had an accident at work that prevented him from attending. However, there's always a silver lining to everything, and I want you to know that I've bought two pairs of shoes in Montmartre, which is my contribution to the French export drive, a girl can never have too many shoes; I know your wives will agree. Thank you." They all laughed at that and clapped and I felt really something. As I returned to my seat I saw Peter smiling at me and he gave a little wink. Jack then gave a very good speech and he was followed by Monsieur LeDuc, who waffled on for an age before finally thanking us all and reminding us that tonight was party time.

Glad that it was all over I felt relieved when we were back at the hotel. I went straight to my room to begin getting ready for the big night.

After a soak in the tub, where I tried out all the bath gels that were available, I spent time on the makeup. I looked better than yesterday and staying off the wine had certainly improved the bags under my eyes. When at last everything was done, I slipped into my blue dress with the low neckline, which was too low for me to wear my lace bra, and squeezed my tities up a little to try and add the extra umph I needed. I looked at myself in the mirror and had to admit that I didn't look too bad, although my bum is still a bit too big. Finally I slipped into the new shoes that I had bought in Montmartre and clipped on a pair of pendulum ear rings that Pops had bought for me last Thanksgiving. I touched up the lip gloss once more, dabbed a spot of perfume here and there, checked my hair, snatched up my evening purse, wondered about Eric and went down to the bar in search of Jack and the guys.

After a quick drink we went on up to the Rousseau suite and I could hear the band playing as we got close. I was pretty excited and looked forward to a good evening ahead. I saw Peter the moment we entered and he stood up to greet me. I thought he looked very smart in his DJ and bow tie.

"Hi" I said.

"Good evening, Miss Atlantic City delegate" he replied and I knew I'd made a hit.

"Am I okay tonight, Mister Reserved Englishman?" I asked, hoping for the right answer.

"You look stunning" he replied Right answer and I knew if Eric didn't show I could get lucky.

"That's okay, then" I replied. Jack and the others greeted 'fat boy' and then looked for our places. We were on the next table with the Italians and before I joined them I asked Peter if he was going to dance with me later. He said 'yes' and I told him 'nothing heavy tonight' and he nodded. I wanted him relaxed and not all wound up behind his English reserve.

The meal was very good and I enjoyed it whilst trying to limit the amount of wine that the waiters and then Jack kept pouring in my glass. I sat next to the Italian guy, Gillani, who couldn't take his eyes off my cleavage and I nearly asked him if he'd ever seen tities before. He was with a very pretty, young, dark haired woman, who he introduced as Maria somebody or other, his secretary. I nearly said 'in the US the business men normally call them their niece' but I didn't. Hell, it was none of my business. At the end of the dinner the band got going and Jack asked me to dance. It was great and I gave it some go and at the end, poor Jack looked a little pie eyed and sat down whilst I went after Peter.

"Now it's your turn to show me what you can do" I said with a touch of lust. He smiled and said "let's do it." We danced three dances and on the last one, which was a waltz, he held me very close and I liked it. He smiled a lot and I really began to like him and I found his glasses quite attractive. If Eric didn't show then Peter would be a great, short term, Paris only, substitute for the night. I needed the ladies room so I left him to wander out onto the balcony. When I got back, he was at his table and looked as if he'd seen a ghost.

"Shall we dance?" I asked. He nodded and we did. It was another waltz and as he held me close once again, I said that Jack told me that Freddie 'fat boy' had invited us all to stop over in London. He looked concerned at that and when I said I was looking forward to going shopping with him he looked even worse. As the evening went on, Peter seemed to relax a little and we laughed a lot and danced a lot. I was sure that he would be inspecting my panties back in my room later and wondered if he needed his glasses to see close up. People drifted away and it was pretty late when Jack said he'd had enough and wandered off with the rest of the guys. I think Dave was a bit put out that I'd spent so much time with Peter but I didn't care. At last I thought it was time for Peter to go back to my room.

"Ready for bed yet?" I asked with a smile.

"Yes, it's been a bit of a day" he replied.

"Okay, let's go." We left the Rousseau suite and made our way down to the third floor and my room. I opened the door and as I went to step through, Peter said "goodnight then."

"What?"

"Goodnight Helen, thanks for a lovely evening, I enjoyed

it…."

"What?" I almost shouted.

"Thanks…." he replied in a quiet voice.

"Aren't you coming in?"

"No, I don't think that's wise…."

"What's wisdom got to do with it for Chrissake?" I asked as the cloud of disappointment appeared overhead once more.

"Well, I, er, have a fiancé, as you know…."

"You're married, un-happily, remember?" I glared at him.

"I know, don't remind me…."

"Well, I do remind you, and you're getting a divorce so you say, I tell you Mister Reserved Englishman, your 'reserve' is getting right up my ass!" He looked shocked.

"Well, I, er….."

"If you go around disappointing women all the time, you're going nowhere with no-one, get it?"

"I don't know what to say….."

"Either come in and give me a little attention or say 'goodnight' again!" He was stunned.

"Goodnight then" he whimpered and high tailed it.

"See you in London" I called and slammed the door. I sat on the bed and thought 'fuck my old riding boots, me and men just don't mix'. Well, here I was, an American in Paris, alone again. I decided to call Rachel and tell her everything. She sympathized and agreed we'd end up like two old maiden aunts with a sail boat. At last I said goodnight to her and wandered out onto my balcony. I looked at the lights of Paris and felt very alone.

"Helen." Jeezus! I nearly jumped out of my skin at the sound of Eric's voice. I turned to see my gorgeous guy standing by the French window. My heart missed a beat and I rushed towards him with my arms outstretched.

"Am I glad, oh, so glad to see you!" I yelled as I felt his strong arms around me.

"Good."

"How did you get here? Oh, never mind, just kiss me quick..." and he did.

"And again…." And he did. "Now come inside…."

"I've got to talk to you, Helen…."

"Yes, of course, you can talk later, for the rest of the night if

111

you want...."

"Helen...."

"Inside, it's getting cold out here" I said as I dragged him into my room before shutting the windows.

"Now then, sit there" I pointed to a chair near the window and he did as he was told. I took two paces back, steadied myself, unzipped my dress and let it fall to the floor before announcing "it's showtime!" I hoped he'd approve of my black panties, stockings, garters and high heeled shoes. He just smiled.

"Well?"

"Very lovely" he replied.

"Then come and get it cowboy, why don't you!"

"Helen." he began and I sensed another rejection coming on as I put my hands on my hips.

"What?" I demanded.

"It's no good, I can't be involved with you."

"You're one hell of a guy, d'you know that?" I interrupted.

"I know how you feel...."

"Do you?"

"Yes."

"I wonder, I really do wonder, I mean, what's a girl got to do to get laid around here?"

"I've come to guide you and...."

"Great, then guide me into bed!" I smiled in hope.

"Your happiness is important to me...."

"That's nice, so, now you can make me really happy by getting stripped down to bare flesh...." I interrupted again.

"Listen, believe it or not, Peter is the man in your life, he's a kind...."

"Oh, no, no he's not, I tell you what he is, he's a reserved, girl shy, married Englishman who wears glasses and can dance a little, he's no Romeo and he certainly can't take care of my needs!"

"I promise you...."

"Besides, how do you know about him?" I demanded, confused as ever.

"It's a mystery."

"It sure is, are you some kind of mystic matchmaker?"

"Don't ask."

"Why not?"

"It would take too long to explain and you wouldn't understand anyway."

"Here we go again, why is it that guys always think that women wouldn't understand, the trouble is, we all understand everything too damned well!" He sat quiet at that and I knew I knocked him sideways for the moment.

"Will you please just give Peter a chance, I promise you, you'll come to realise that he is the best person for you…."

"I don't want him, I want you" I said as I sat down on the bed and crossed my legs. I hoped he noticed that my tities were firm and didn't bounce much.

"It can never be…"

"Why not? What's wrong with me?"

"Nothing, absolutely nothing…"

"Well then…."

"I'll tell you later why we can't be together, I promise, but for the moment, give Peter a chance, open your heart to him, just a little…."

"No, I won't…."

"By the Gods, Gunther told me the first time was hard but I didn't think it was going to be this bloody hard!"

"I guessed Gunther would show up sometime in all this…." I said angrily.

"It's like trying to steer a longship full of drunk Vikings up a fast flowing, narrow river, full of jagged rocks…."

"What are you talking about?" I demanded.

"Never mind, I must go before I get angry and say too much….."

"Oh, please don't go…."

"I have to, I'll see you again soon." With that he stood up said 'goodbye' and opened the French windows and stepped out onto the balcony. I jumped off the bed and followed him out but he had disappeared. I suddenly felt very afraid and went in search of something to drink from the mini bar. A small bottle of brandy looked promising and I settled for that before falling asleep on top of the bed.

CHAPTER 7

PETER SHOWS HELEN AROUND

Freddie and I arrived at Benoir Paints at ten for the last time. This was the usual meeting to say 'goodbye and thank you for coming and by the way, here's all the sales literature and price lists, we'll be in touch'. The Americans were late and I couldn't understand why, we'd seen them at breakfast at the hotel. I expect they were waiting for Helen. She was just too much and when she invited me into her room last night, well, I was taken aback and glad that I had Sophia in my life. Helen was such a contrast to my beautiful, sophisticated, petite Italian. Although, I had to admit that the American was very attractive and certainly went after what she wanted, but she was too rich for my blood. Freddie was right in his opinion of the Americans, that's why I found it hard to understand why he should suddenly change his tune and invite them back to London. Perhaps he thought that J.B. and George would be impressed.

"Bonjour, bonjour" said Roger in a flamboyant tone as he went to each group of delegates as they arrived. He was followed everywhere by Jacques and two young women dressed smartly in their black, Benoir dresses with motifs. They were there handing out little packs of sales literature whilst fixing everyone with a smile. They reminded me of the air hostess demonstrating the safety procedures on our flight out. I then thought of the return trip and wondered if I could get to see Sophia after we landed at Heathrow.

"Hi" and I was suddenly aware of Helen by my side as Freddie and Jack did the back slapping old pals act, whilst the others looked on.

"Morning" I replied and tried a little smile.

"I'm sorry to disappoint you Freddie, but only Helen and I can take up your offer of a few days in London, all the guys have got to get back State side, you know, business and the bottom dollar and all that" said Jack.

"Oh, shame" replied Freddie and my heart sank. What this meant was that I'd be stuck with Miss Atlantic City whilst Freddie and his best American pal hit the town. I wanted to see Sophia and be alone with her, not bamboozled into fighting off Helen's advances day and night, for however many days Freddie had dreamed up with pal Jack.

"But, we'll keep the flag flying" said Jack.

"I'm sure" replied Freddie.

"Helen's keen to see around London and I guess this is where you come in, Peter" said Jack.

"Yes, indeed, it'll be my pleasure" I replied.

"Spoken like a true gentleman" smiled Jack and I winced inside before glancing at Helen with a fixed smile.

"Shall we get some coffee?" she asked and we all nodded and made our way to the table where more Benoir girls stood ready to serve us.

"I know you're not too happy about being stuck with me in London, but I'll try and keep it painless for you" said Helen as we sipped our coffee, away from the others.

"It'll all be fine, don't worry, I'm looking forward to it" I replied but I didn't convince her.

"Peter, I've been around long enough to know, okay?"

"Helen…."

"I get the message, and as soon as we hit London, all you've got to do is point me in the direction of the shops and leave the rest to me, Jack will see I'm okay in the evenings and if he's out with Freddie boy I'll just go to my room and watch TV or something."

"I can't let you do that" I replied.

"Why not?"

"Well, you're our guest."

"Don't you want to catch up with Miss Italian?"

"Of course but……"

"Well then, go to it cowboy, I'm sure she'll have better luck than me!" Before I could reply Freddie appeared and said "glad to see that you two are getting along" and he winked, I could have hit him.

Roger called us into the conference room where he introduced us to Charles de Fontaine, managing director of Benoir, who rambled on about paint and the links across the Atlantic whilst directing all our thoughts to the future. The only future I wanted was with Sophia, and that, as soon as possible. I felt glad that Helen was stepping back a little and if she would manage on her own in London it meant that I could spend time with Sophia. I smiled at Helen and she smiled back, at last, an understanding.

Other than the usual delays at Charles de Gaulle, the flight into Heathrow was uneventful. Freddie had made arrangements for Helen, Jack and me to stay at a small hotel, around the back of Berkeley Square, that was regularly used by the company. I was quite happy about that as it meant I could stay in London and see Sophia at least until the Americans flew home. It transpired that they now planned to leave on the Wednesday which meant I had to be at Helen's beck and call for three days. I could cope with her as I knew that I'd be able to see Sophia every day. As soon as we arrived at the hotel I phoned Sophia and told her that I'd take her out tomorrow night for a meal. It was a delight to listen to her lovely voice and we made our arrangements before we ended on kisses and sweet nothings. I went to sleep happy and contented whilst reminding myself that I should call Janet in the morning to let her know that I'd be staying in London until Wednesday.

Next morning I had breakfast with Helen and Jack whilst waiting for Freddie to drive up from his flat in Croydon. It seemed that he had already made some arrangements to take Jack away and planned to leave me with Helen for the day.

"It's okay, Peter, you don't have to hang around for me, I'm sure you've got better things to do" said Helen after Jack had spilled the beans.

"I wouldn't dream of it."

"Well, it's up to you" she replied in a disinterested tone.

"You must let me drive you around London and show you the sights at least" I said with a little enthusiasm.

"Okay" she nodded and Jack looked pleased. Freddie arrived soon after and was his usual bumptious self. After enquiring about their rooms and general state of their well being he made his excuses to Helen and left with Jack on a tour of Lords and the Oval. I thought Jack might be bored to death by the end of the day and he certainly had a resigned look on his face.

Sunday is the best day for driving around London and we started the journey in Berkeley Square then onto Piccadilly, down the Haymarket and into Trafalgar Square. Helen was delighted and chatted all the way, asking so many questions that I could hardly keep up. I drove on down Fleet Street to St. Pauls then onto the Tower. That really impressed her and she was amazed that the White Tower was built by the Conqueror almost a thousand years ago. I retraced my route back towards the Embankment and then along to Parliament Square, she thought Big Ben was just the tops, then around Horse Guards and into the Mall. She asked me to drive around Buckingham Palace twice so she could get a second look at it. We finished up at Marble Arch and as the M40 was just up the Edgware Road, I asked if she'd like a run out in the country to Wallingford where I knew a lovely little restaurant by the Thames that served Sunday lunches to die for.

"Oh, yeah, you bet" she smiled and we set off at a cracking pace.

"This place is run by a slightly eccentric widow who has a bulldog" I said.

"You don't say."

"The restaurant is right on the bridge over the river and was originally an inn" I said.

"How old is it?" she asked.

"It was built sometime in the seventeenth century, it's all oak beams and white plaster walls and it seems that Cromwell stayed there when he was besieging Wallingford castle" I said knowing she would be intrigued.

"You've got so much history here, it's unbelievable" she smiled and I felt that as she no longer appeared interested in me, I began to warm to her. She did look very attractive today and she seemed much more relaxed.

We arrived at the restaurant a little late and it was almost full. I smiled at one of the waitresses who managed to squeeze us into a table for two at the back of the dining room. The homemade tomato soup followed by roast beef and Yorkshire pudding was perfect and the homemade apple pie, custard with cream finished the meal to perfection. We chatted all through lunch and she told me a lot more about herself and her life in Atlantic City. I realised that behind that brash exterior was a very nice, considerate woman who had been badly let down by the man whom she had loved and trusted. Melodie was her pride and joy and she was obviously close to her parents, whilst Rachel and Karen also played a big part in her life. Sailing the 'Princess' was her escape from the cares of the world and the drudgery that surrounds work. I had only been sailing a couple of times and had found it exhilarating, so I was interested by her experiences.

"If you ever come over to the States and you're close by Atlantic City, give me a call and we'll fix it to go sailing" she said with a smile.

"I'd like that" I replied.

"Good, now, are you going to take me back to the hotel?" she asked.

"No, I'm going to show you Oxford, it's just up the road and I know you'll enjoy it" I replied.

"Wow, are you a star or what?"

"A star."

"Yup, that's it, you're a star and you look like that film actor, what's his name?"

"Michael Caine" I replied.

"Oh, my God, that's right, has anybody ever told you that you look like him?"

"Only everyone I ever meet, but not a lot of people know that" I replied and she laughed out loud. I paid the bill and patted the bulldog, asleep in front of the open fire, before we left the restaurant and made our way to Oxford.

I stopped on the hill at Botley to show Helen the gleaming spires before descending into the elegant city. I drove around the colleges whilst telling her a little of the history and she was fascinated, again asking so many questions I couldn't answer. When I told her that Shakespeare always stopped in Oxford on his way, to and from London, and was rumoured to have had an ongoing affair with the inn keeper's wife, she was enchanted.

"So much history in this place, you British are so damned lucky, if we had as much as you've got, we'd be a real pain in the butt to the rest of the world" she said and I thought 'forget the history you're a real pain anyway' but smiled and nodded.

It was late afternoon before we set off for London and the traffic on the motorway was quite heavy with everyone returning to the capital. I was concerned that I'd be late for Sophia but I made up time as we got close to Berkeley Square. I stopped outside the hotel and she turned to me and said "it's been a great day and I've really had a good time, so, thanks a lot."

"My pleasure" I replied and then on impulse, I leaned across and kissed her. She didn't respond and when our lips parted she whispered "you didn't have to do that, you know."

"I wanted to."

"Why?"

"Because you've been lovely company today and I just wanted to thank you."

"You could have just said it" she replied.

"I know, but a kiss was nicer, don't you think?"

"Believe me, honey, I don't know what to think anymore."

"Neither do I."

"Well, off you go to Miss Italian…."

"Sophia" I said.

"Whoever."

"I'll see you tomorrow then and I'll take you shopping."

"Okay" she replied as the opened the door and slipped out of the car.

I arrived at Highgate and only had to wait a few minutes before Sophia emerged looking radiant as ever. We kissed for some while in the car before we set off into London. I took her to an Italian restaurant in the Haymarket where we settled down to a meal of soup, cannelloni and ice cream.

"I have some a wonderful news" she said over the ice cream.

"Yes?"

"Some friend of the Parker's wantsa me to do some translation for his a business" she said, her eyes bright with excitement.

"Really."

"Si, and he is going to pay me very wella."

"Good" I replied.

"Mr Parker and his friend, Mr Ray Ashton, have been talking about me and it seemsa that when Mr Ashton knew I could speaka French and Italian, he asked to meeta me."

"Oh" I replied.

"Si, and he came over yesterday and we're all going out

119

for dinner next Saturday…."

"I'm invited?

" I asked.

"Si, I wouldn't go withouta you." I suddenly felt un-easy about this arrangement.

"Okay."

"So, you willa come?"

"Of course, my darling" I smiled.

"Gooda, thatsa gooda." We finished the meal and walked down the Haymarket to Pall Mall where I had parked the car and then drove to Hyde Park where we stopped and kissed and talked for a long while. It was in the early hours when I returned to the hotel and the news of this man Ray Ashton was troubling me, I sensed danger.

Over breakfast Helen said "you really don't have to stay with me, just drop me somewhere near a mall and I'll be okay"

"Listen, I'll take you to Kensington and to Harrods…."

"Then you can drop me" she interrupted.

"I'll stay with you" I insisted.

"You don't have too…."

"Hey, you two, give it a rest will you, you're beginning to sound like an old married couple!" said Jack as he sipped his coffee.

"Sorry" I said.

"Me too" said Helen.

"That's better" smiled Jack before he continued "now Freddie has made arrangements for me to visit Rolls-Royce at Park Royal today and then for us to visit your factory at Stratford tomorrow and in the evening we're all going to dinner and then onto a show."

"That's great, what are we going to see?" asked Helen.

"Oh, I'm not sure, Mama something…."

"Mama Mia, the show with all the Abba songs" I said.

"That's it" replied Jack and Helen smiled whilst I felt unhappy that I would not be able to see Sophia that night.

I decided to take her to Harrod's first of all, hoping that she would spend so much time there that any other shopping would be negligible. I was wrong of course, and having spent all morning buying gifts in that lavish emporium followed by a snack lunch in the cafeteria, Helen was all ready to do justice to the rest of Kensington. My God, is there no power on earth that can stop a woman shopping? So, I held my breath and followed her through all the shops that she decided were a 'must' for any visiting American. Surprisingly, I found the experience pleasant and in some cases almost delightful. She was quite amusing as she tried on umpteen dresses and bought several, with my approval, as well as tops and bottoms for Melodie. At last she had had enough and we drove back to the hotel.

"Well, thanks again for the day, I guess I'll see you tomorrow when we visit your factory" she said as we got out of the car.

"My pleasure, let me help you with these things up to your room."

"Okay."

After I laid her shopping bags on her bed I hesitated for a moment, I don't know why.

"Well, thanks again" she smiled.

"You're welcome." There was a pause.

"You'd better get going otherwise you'll be late for Miss Italian" she said and turned away.

"Yes, right, I'll see you at breakfast then."

"Okay."

I went to my room and phoned Sophia.

"Where would you like to go this evening, my princess?"

"I can'ta see you tonighta" she replied.

"Why not?"

"Mr Ashton has senta some very important letters that he wantsa translated into English...."

"Bloody hell, they can't be that important surely, what if he hadn't met you?"

"I donta know, sweetheart, buta Mr Parker has asked if I will do it justa this once as a biga favour, I can'ta say 'no', I'ma sure you understanda." It was at this moment that I realised that Ashton was going to be a real threat to us, I felt it deep in my bones.

"Okay, my princess, I understand and I have to tell you that I have to work tomorrow night so I can't see you 'til Wednesday."

"Okay."

"We'll go to that lovely restaurant at Harrow, where we went before."

"That'll be nice" she replied. Then with kisses and fond farewells we said goodbye.

I tried to remain calm but felt an anger rising from the very depths of my being. This was irrational, I hadn't even met Ashton, but some sixth sense was warning me of what was to come. This was where I needed some mature help and guidance and I thought of Eric then dismissed him from my mind. All he was likely to do was to advise me once again that Helen was the woman in my life, which proved conclusively that he didn't realise how much Sophia and I loved each other.

Before I went down to dinner I phoned Janet to tell her I wouldn't be going home until Wednesday night. She couldn't have cared less and I was glad when our loveless, one sided conversation was over.

In the dining room I was surprised to see Helen sitting alone at our table.

"No sign of Jack then?" I asked as I sat down.

"Nope."

"Freddie's keeping him out on the town I expect" I smiled.

"I guess so."

"Good for them" I replied as I picked up the menu.

"What's happened to your date?"

"Oh, she has to do some urgent work for a business man" I replied.

"What kinda work?"

"Some translation, some letters...."

"Is that what they call it over here?" She touched a raw nerve with that.

"What d'you mean?" I asked angrily.

"No offence, honey, but working late is always a lame excuse, don't you think?"

"No, I don't....."

"Believe me, you can bet someone's either planning or doing something along the line" she interrupted. I chose to ignore her remark but deep down I felt very uncomfortable. Helen had already ordered and as I didn't fancy much, I just settled for scampi with a salad and trimmings.

"What d'you plan to do this evening?" I asked.

"I guess I'll watch TV" she replied.

"Oh, right."

"And what are you going to do, now that Miss Italian is up to her peaches in translations?"

"I thought I might invite you out for a drink somewhere nice" I replied.

"Sounds good, so tempt me" she replied with a smile.

"How about the Savoy Hotel in the Strand?"

"As soon as we're done here I'll get my coat" she smiled.

We sat in the grandeur of the Savoy lounge drinking brandy and sodas whilst talking, in turns, about London and New York. I wasn't too keen on the 'big apple' but I had only spent a few days there, so I felt that my judgement was probably clouded. Other than Times Square, 42nd Street and Macey's I hadn't seen much of it. Helen was lyrical about the place and said "if you ever come over, just call me and I'll show you around, I know you'll just love it." I felt her genuine warmth and was touched by the way she had invited me, her voice was gentle and soft. We drank a couple more brandies before we returned to the hotel in a taxi.

I escorted her to the door of her room where without hesitation she kissed me full on and said "thanks for a great evening, it's been fun as usual."

"My pleasure, I'm sure...."

"And, no, I'm not inviting you in, you go to your room and worry about Miss Italian and her translations" she said.

"Right."

"And I'll see you in the morning, okay?"

"Okay" and she disappeared into her room leaving me in the corridor, confused as usual. I mean 'what do women want?'

I was unsettled and decided to go for a walk around Berkeley Square to try and think and clear my head. The night was mild and with only a few passers by, it seemed I had this delightful place in the heart of London to myself. I thought about Janet and decided that I'd tell her that I definitely wanted a divorce and then I'd make an appointment to see a solicitor. Having settled my mind on that course of action my thoughts turned to Sophia and that bloody man, Ashton. I was concerned that somehow he would come between me and the woman I loved deeply. On reflection I felt that I was being foolish and irrational, I mean, what harm could really come from a little well paid work on the side? As Sophia obviously loved me too, it was inconceivable that she should be swayed by anybody else. I began to feel better and strode across to the railed garden in the centre of the Square. I wandered in along the path and was about to sit on the park bench nearest the gate when I noticed a man sitting on the next bench. I recognised Eric as he stood and walked towards me.

"Oh, God, not you again" I said.

"Hello, Peter, how are you?"

"Not so sure now you've turned up to harass me" I replied.

"Let's talk" he replied with a smile and waved me to the bench. I sat as commanded and he joined me.

"I don't think we've much to talk about" I said.

"You couldn't be more wrong" he smiled.

"Well if you're going to tell me again that Sophia is not the love of my life, you're wasting your time."

"I'm not."

"Not going to tell me?" I asked.

"No, because she probably is the love of your life…."

"I'm glad you agree at last" I interrupted.

"But, she will bring you the most unhappy heartache…."

"Never…" I said angrily before he continued "that you can possibly imagine and you will always think of her for the rest of your life after she's gone, whilst cursing the day you ever met her."

"She'll never leave me, she loves me too much" I replied with confidence.

"You will find the happiness and contentment you seek with Helen…."

"You must be joking, she'd drive me mad in an instant, no, I couldn't possibly…….."

"Listen, I've spent a lot of time making arrangements behind the scenes to bring you two together…." he said angrily before I interrupted him.

"What the bloody hell are you talking about?"

"Do you have the faintest idea how difficult it's been to get you

124

and Helen to Paris so you could meet?"

"No, I don't and frankly, I don't care."

"Well you should."

"Really?"

"And the timing plan necessary to get two strangers alone in a lift, well...."

"Are you telling me you arranged that?"

"Yes, and apparently even Thor and Odin were impressed."

"You're mad" I replied.

"Possibly, but I am trying to help you...."

"I've heard enough, I'm going" I interrupted and stood up. Eric sighed and said "goodbye, Peter, I'll be around if you need me."

"No chance" I replied before walking off. As I made my way back to the hotel I became more and more depressed with everything and I began to think that I'd never get out of the emotional and financial mess I was in. I went to bed unhappy and confused.

At breakfast, Jack looked a little worse for wear and I gathered that after his visit to Rolls-Royce, Freddie had taken him out for a slap up dinner followed by some serious drinking in a Soho bar that Freddie knew intimately. Jack was not looking forward to the day at the Beauclare Paints factory but he was trying to put on a brave face. It had been arranged that I should drive Jack and Helen to Stratford where Freddie met us mid morning. After coffee and an informal chat in reception we set off on a tour of the factory. They were quite impressed by the process of making paint and when they were shown the ball mills, large rotating drums where pigment and large steel balls mix and tumble, grinding the pigment to fine dust, they were surprised by the simplicity.

"That process will go on night and day for up to three days, it's called a three day grind" said Freddie.

"How romantic, it's every girls dream" said Helen and we all laughed. I looked at her and saw a vivacious, attractive woman who I quite liked but could never love the way I loved Sophia. What Eric had said troubled me and my unhappiness felt like a wet blanket over my shoulders. The tour ended on the filling floor where hundreds of empty paint cans chattered along a delivery system to a point where a measured amount of paint was poured mechanically into the waiting tins.

"And that's how it's all done" said Helen with a smile.

"Now you know" said Freddie.

"I'll tell 'em all about it in Atlantic City" she replied.

"Well, I guess we've seen everything on this trip" said Jack and he seemed relieved that the tour was over.

I drove them back to the hotel so we all could get ready for the night out. Freddie had to stay on to deal with a few problems and arranged to meet us in the Steak House in Trafalgar Square at seven. Helen looked very attractive in a red velvet dress that she had bought in a chic little shop just off Kensington High, and with her neat makeup and the aroma of her perfume she looked tantalisingly lovely as we waited for a taxi.

"How do I look, Mister Reserved?" she whispered as Jack stepped forward to wave at a passing cab.

"Good enough to eat" I replied.

"No chance, Mister, you're strictly on an Italian diet" she said firmly.

"You know how to hurt" I whispered.

"Didn't I ever?"

"Come on you two" called Jack as the taxi pulled over.

The steaks were good, Freddie was on top form and very entertaining and we certainly relaxed as the wine flowed. Helen kept looking at me in a way that disarmed me and I felt my defences slipping. We sat next to each other in the theatre and she held my hand for most of the time. Her perfume was playing tricks with my emotions and I wanted to kiss her passionately there and then. I tried to concentrate on the show, which was really fabulous, but I was so conscious of this amusing and rather lovely woman holding my hand, that I could not. I tried to think that I was there strictly on business, a sort of lay back and think of England attitude, but it wasn't working. I felt something for this woman and the more she pointed me away from herself and towards Sophia made her more attractive to me. God, I was in a mess and it was all Eric's fault.

After the show we all went back to the hotel for drinks and to enable Freddie to say goodbye to the Americans.

Several drinks later, Freddie went over the trip and finished by

126

saying that he planned to go to the States later in the year to visit the Bradley Ponting Consortium, and he would definitely call in and visit Jack and Helen.

"Are you bringing Peter with you?" asked Helen.

"Don't think so, I'm afraid he'll have to stay along with the rest of the sales team and get those sales figures up" replied Freddie.

"Shame, I'd fixed it for him to come sailing" she replied with a smile.

"I'll come over sometime, you can be sure" I said and Freddie gave me a disapproving glance. The company didn't own me completely, at least not yet. At last Freddie said goodbye and shook Jack firmly by the hand and then kissed Helen lightly on the cheek.

"See you next in Atlantic City" said Jack as Freddie left the lounge. I then followed the Americans to their rooms before wishing them goodnight and reminding them that we had to leave by ten in the morning to be sure that I could get them to Heathrow by eleven to check in. As we said goodnight, Helen gave me one of her long, intensive looks before smiling.

"Thanks for a great evening, Mister, I'll see you in the morning" she said as she slipped into her room. I just murmured 'goodnight'.

"You know, you've made quite an impression on her" said Jack.

"You think so?"

"I know so, and I'm going to persuade Freddie to bring you over to the States in the Fall" he smiled.

"That'll be great if you can" I replied. He nodded and wished me 'goodnight' before he went to his room and I went to bed worried about Sophia and confused as usual.

The journey along the M4 motorway was slow but we made it in time to Terminal 3 at Heathrow. The number of cars and taxis unloading passengers outside the Terminal had to be seen to be believed and I struggled to find a gap before eventually giving up and double parking. When their luggage was unloaded on to two trolleys, Jack shook hands.

"It's been a great trip and I've enjoyed it" he said.

"Good."

"And it's been a pleasure to meet you, Peter."

"The pleasure was all mine" I replied.

"And I'll see you in the Fall."

"I hope so." I turned to Helen, who kissed me hard on the lips.

"Goodbye, Mister Reserved."

"Goodbye."

"Now call me soon" she said as she handed me a business card.

"The phone bill will be enormous" I replied with a smile.

"It's okay, you can call 'collect', and Pops will pick up the tab" she smiled.

"I'll probably write" I replied.

"Oh, God, you're like some old antique, you're so English, but I quite like it."

"I'm glad you're pleased with my Englishness" I replied.

"I didn't say I was pleased, I said I quite liked it...."

"I can't handle you...."

"Do you think you're romantically challenged?" she interrupted.

"I'm sure of it...."

"We must be related...."

"Come on, Helen, we don't want to be late checking in" said Jack as Helen kissed me quickly again and said "remember me." They disappeared into the crowd in an instant and I was left slightly dazed by Helen before an irate cabbie called out "come on mate, you can't leave your bloody car parked there!"

Back in the office in Berkeley Square I did some paperwork and then reported to Freddie. He seemed pleased with himself and was in a buoyant mood all afternoon. Time dragged and I was glad when Freddie told me to call it a day. I drove to Hyde Park and waited in the car, thinking about Helen, until it was time to go to Highgate and collect Sophia. She kept me waiting twenty minutes before she appeared looking beautiful as ever in a cream, fitted dress that contrasted with her lustrous black hair and olive complexion. We kissed for sometime in the car before driving off to our little restaurant in Harrow.

"I have missed you so much" she said as we made our way to the restaurant.

"I've missed you too" I replied quickly, anxious to steer the conversation round to find out about Ashton.

"Tell me all abouta Paris" she smiled.

"Yes, I will, my princess, but tell me, did you get all the work done last night?"

"Yes, I dida."

"And what did he say?"

"Who?"

"Ashton."

"He saida everything was okay and he looked forward to dinner on Saturday."

"What's he like?"

"He's an old man, how you say, a stammering old farta" she replied and I laughed.

"Really?"

"Si, first impressions are always righta, you know" she replied and I felt relieved at her discourteous description of this man that I had been unreasonably concerned about.

Dinner was up to the usual high standard and Sophia's coq au vin and my tournedos Rossini were mouth wateringly good. The full, red house wine was just so and we finished with gateaux and cream. We sat outside the house in Highgate, kissing for some while before she went in and with her last words to me about dinner on Saturday night still revolving around my mind, I drove off and back to Wantage.

Janet was in bed and half asleep when I arrived home and other than an unwelcoming grunt from her side of the bed, we did not speak. I decided not to tell her that I wanted a divorce until after the weekend.

On Saturday I arrived at the house in Highgate just after seven and pulled up behind a dark blue Jaguar parked right outside the front gate, which I guessed was Ashton's. Sophia opened the door to me and I was shown into the lounge and introduced to the Parkers, he tall, elegant and called George, she, also tall with straight shoulder length blonde hair and called Fiona. Then I first set eyes on Ashton and disliked him on sight. He was a short scrag of a man, about sixty years old, with greasy grey hair and shifting gimlet eyes behind gold rimmed glasses. He was wearing a badly fitting black suit with a white shirt that had gone grey and a poorly tied, red patterned tie.

"Pleased to meet you" he stammered as we shook hands.

"How do you do" I replied.

"And this is my wife, Jean" he said half turning in the direction of an un-interesting lump of a woman with short grey hair, dressed in a dark grey suit, seated on the settee.

"How do you do" I said and held out my hand.

"Hello" she replied in a disinterested tone. I received the message loud and clear, she was here in ill disguised sufferance.

"Well, what will you have to drink, Peter?" asked George Parker, sensing the cold atmosphere.

"A scotch and soda, if I may" I replied.

"Ah, a scotch man, I always have a gin and tonic before dinner" said Ashton as he sat beside his wife.

"Really" I replied in an disinterested tone.

"Oh, yes" replied the old man. I turned to Sophia, looking radiant in a green dress, and smiled.

"How are you tonight my darling?" I said in a loud half whisper so everyone could hear.

"I'm a fine, Peter" she smiled as George arrived back with my scotch.

"So, cheers everyone" said George and we all raised our glasses after mumbling 'cheers'.

"So, where are you taking them to eat tonight?" asked Fiona and I was surprised that the Parkers were not coming with us.

"A little place I know round the back of Regents Street" replied Ashton.

"Oh, very nice" said George.

"Yes, the food's good and I can always park the Daimler there" grinned Ashton. I was most concerned that Sophia and I were going to have to spend the evening with this old goat and his unhappy wife.

"What's it called?" asked George.

"The French Partridge, it's all nouvelle cuisine and I'm sure Sophia will enjoy it" said Ashton as he looked hard at Sophia. I didn't appreciate his comments or his leering glance at Sophia and I began to feel my hackles rise.

"So, what do you do for a living, Peter?" asked George in a friendly tone.

"I'm a paint representative" I replied.

"Oh, you're a salesman, a necessary evil, so my sales director tells me at board meetings" said Ashton with a sneer.

"My boss doesn't think so" I replied.

"And what sort of paint do you sell, white emulsion to Woolworths?" Ashton said with a grin.

"No, automotive repair paint" I replied.

"Oh, really" smirked Ashton.

"Yes, for instance, if you had an accident in your Jag...."

"It's a Daimler!" interrupted Ashton quickly.

"No it's not, it's a Jaguar with Daimler badges, it's called badge engineering in the industry."

"You think so do you?"

"I know so, it's where manufacturers build the same car and put other badges on it so gullible and pretentious people think they are getting something that they're not, and then part up with a lot more money for the privilege." Well, he looked furious, I felt pleased with myself and it set the trend for the evening. That was one in the eye for the patronising, stammering old goat.

"Another drink, Ray?" enquired George sensing the mutual hostility.

"I think I should, it will calm my nerves" replied Ashton through clenched teeth. Fiona tried, with gentle conversation, to lift and lighten the mood by asking Jean about holidays.

"I doubt if Ray will be able to get away this year, he's got so much on" replied Jean.

"Yes, I'm dealing with the Italians and the Turks, big business" said Ashton loudly.

Now it was my turn to have another go at the old man.

"What sort of business are you in, Ray, I may call you Ray?" I smirked.

"My directors call me R.J., I prefer that" he replied.

"R.J. as in the American style" I grinned and he looked uncomfortable and didn't answer.

"Peter has been in Paris last week on business with Americans" said Sophia proudly and that news shook Ashton and his gimlet eyes widened. Obviously, in his book, paint salesmen didn't go to Paris on business. At that moment George arrived with his drink.

"Here, better drink up, you don't want to be late for dinner" said George.

"Indeed not" replied the old man before he took a swig of his gin and tonic. I sat and watched him whilst George warbled on about their last holiday in Tuscany, and when he made references to Sophia, Ashton looked at her and I watched him mentally undress her. Jean watched the performance with tired and resigned eyes, she must have seen his behaviour a hundred times before and I guessed more would come out over dinner. At last we were ready to go to Regents Street and visit the French Partridge. As we approached his car Ashton did a silly little dance before opening the rear door for Sophia. It's the thing that old men do to try and impress a young woman. Jean squeezed her portly frame into the front seat and I sat in the back with my lovely Italian whom I kissed and said loudly "you look lovely tonight, my darling."

All the way to the restaurant we had to listen to Ashton as he informed us of his business deals and his smart moves to avoid tax and liabilities.

"Everything's in Jean's name, it allows me to operate without being held back by red tape" he chortled.

"Really" I replied.

"Yes, you wouldn't know what it's like for an entrepreneur like me to be stifled by red tape" he said.

"It's there to stop people abusing the system. When my father had his business, he managed to play by the rules and still make money" I replied and that shut him up.

The nouvelle cuisine served up by the restaurant was as shallow and un-interesting as our host. Very small portions on large plates with various sauces 'drizzled' over the top were the order of the day. Ashton undressed Sophia a hundred times during the meal and his non stop, self centred observations bored me rigid. I only perked up once when I heard him say that he was looking for a bi-lingual PA to visit Turkey with him. I sensed the danger and watched Jean's eyes half close in anger. The old man was after Sophia and I had to do my best to stop him. Like a wife who knows her husband is being unfaithful, a man can tell when another man is after his woman, it must be an instinctive smell or something. I was relieved when it was time to leave and the journey back to Highgate was in silence. I never wanted to see this old man and his wife again, ever, and I had to warn Sophia and keep her close to me. We said goodnight and I took Sophia to my car and we kissed whilst waiting for Ashton to drive off.

"That awful man is after you, my princess."

"No, you're imagining it, darling."

"I just know he is, and he's going to ask you to go to Turkey with him."

"I've never been to Turkey" she replied and my heart sank.

"You mustn't go with him" I said.

"Why nota?"

"Because he just wants you for his next mistress…."

"Darling, you're being silly" she interrupted.

"Oh, God, I promise you I'm not!" She didn't reply and we just kissed for a while. At last we said goodnight and I set off for home in a sad and confused state once again.

CHAPTER 8

HELEN RETURNS HOME

Jack and the guys had been discussing Freddie's invitation to stay in London for a few days but as they had been to Europe before they decided to stay on schedule and get back to the States. It meant Jack and I were going to be the only ones to take up the invitation and I think he stayed back, just to keep an eye on me. I'm sure he felt responsible for me and he owed it to Pops to see that I was okay.

We were late arriving at Benoir's place at Evry and anxious to get a coffee before all the final hullabaloo started. Peter and Freddie were already there and I said "Hi" as we arrived whilst Jack told Freddie that it was just going to be him and me in London. You should have seen Peter's face when he heard that, he looked as if he'd lost a dollar and found a dime. I decided to let him off the hook, as I guessed he had plans to catch up with Miss Perfect Italian, and told him it was okay to point me at the shops and leave me. He said he was looking forward to showing me around, but he was just being polite and I realised then that the poor guy could never tell a lie, his face was an open book. I thought that he was out of place working in sales, I guessed he'd be happier running a little shop in New England, selling home made cookies and cakes, he was that sort of guy.

We were all shown into the conference room where the final speeches and wind up took place and I gave Peter an encouraging smile or two. I was sure he had had enough of me over the last few days and I thought it fair to leave him to the tender mercies of Miss Italian. I felt a touch of something about her, not jealous, exactly, but just a little irritation. Perhaps it was because I'd been unable to reel in Peter or Eric in Paris, of all places. Rachel and Karen were just going to die when I gave them the whole story.

I was excited to be in London and Freddie boy had made reservations for us in a small hotel, near his office in Berkeley Square, until the Wednesday. The place was alive with black cabs and red buses all rushing about and I couldn't wait to get out and look around. Freddie boy arranged to take Jack off for the day on the Sunday and Peter was left to show me London in the spring.

After breakfast, Freddie boy arrived and whisked Jack away on some trip he'd planned and I gave Peter the option of leaving me, so he could go and attend to his Italian piece, but he insisted he drive me around for the day and I guess I was pleased at that. You have to see London to believe it and I was mightily impressed as we drove round the old city. I couldn't believe that the Tower was a thousand years old, and when I think of all the history, well, it made me almost speechless, which is a rare condition in a girl from Atlantic City. Buckingham Palace is like a fairy castle and I made Peter drive around twice so that I could get a good look at it. We finished up at Marble Arch where they used to hang all the felons in days gone by, and when Peter suggested we went to some place in the country for traditional Sunday lunch, I jumped at that.

We drove out to a spot on the Thames called Wallingford. He took me to this little restaurant on the bridge over the river where we had a roast beef and home made apple pie, which was to die for. He told me over lunch the name of the actor who he looked like, it was Michael Caine and I was glad I got that settled in my mind at last. The lady who owned the place was quite a character and had a huge English bull dog that dozed in front of an open fire. The dog was so ugly he was cute. I felt that I was right in the heart of England and when Peter told me that the place had been an inn where Cromwell stayed, well, I was just amazed. After the meal I took plenty of snaps of the place to show all the folks when I got back. He then surprised me by taking me to Oxford, where after a trip around the old place, I felt as if I'd had enough history for one day and I couldn't possibly store up any more memories.

Arriving outside the hotel, Peter kissed me and I was surprised. He said he'd enjoyed the day and it was his way of saying thank you. Well, he could have just said it, but I was glad he gave me a kiss. It was just nice, I mean, he's nice but too reserved, but it grows on a girl. He's so wrapped up with his new love that he's no time for anybody like me, anyway, I comfort myself with the thought that I belong to Eric. That crazy, good looking hunk of an un-obtainable guy, or so he thinks, and I wondered when he was going to show up next. Peter rushed off to be with Miss Italian and I went to my room to call all the folks. Mom and Pops were fine and Melodie was, as usual, wondering what I was going to buy her in London. I said that I'd find something nice for her and if she promised to be good, I might buy one or two little extras. She promised and we said goodbye. I then called Rachel.

"Hi, babe."

"Hi, you globe trotting business woman" said Rachel with a laugh.

"Right as usual" I replied.

"So tell me all the news."

"It's just great, and everything is good, I'm good and...."

"What about the guys?" she interrupted.

"They're fine" I replied.

"Both of them?"

"Yup."

"You're a lucky girl, Helen Milton, do you know that?"

"I do."

"So, spill the beans, honey and let's get to it!" I told her all about Eric and then Peter. Rachel just kept asking questions and I guessed that when I got back home it would take me months to go through everything again. I knew that this trip meant as much to her as it did me and I felt glad that I'd had the opportunity to get to Paris and London, although I wish it had not been due to Pop's accident. Still, he was getting better quickly and I knew he'd soon be back at the business.

It was quite late when I'd finished the call and went down for dinner. Jack was still out with Freddie boy and I settled for a light, prawn salad with all the trimmings. I planned to go to bed and get a good night as tomorrow I intended to hit the shops at full speed with my plastic at the ready.

Peter took me to Harrods first of all and was I impressed or what? I reckon it's better than Macey's and Bloomingdale's put together, and that's saying something. We started in ladies fashion where I bought a couple of dresses and a skirt for Melodie and then slowly worked our way through the store. Peter was his usual calm and charming self and I asked for his opinion on everything I bought. He seemed to be quite enjoying it, which is a bit unusual in a guy, they normally hate shopping, I know Reece does and I wondered about Eric. After I had spent a good few dollars more than I intended Peter took me to the snack bar for lunch where the soup, sandwiches and cakes were the very best. Harrods certainly know how to do it. When we'd finished up in there I was ready to bust the rest of Kensington and we worked steadily through the shops that were a must for any American tourist. Peter was relaxed and a bit detached, but he smiled a lot and he seemed to be a very tolerant kinda guy. I liked him for that, it makes a girl feel secure somehow, especially when she's seriously involved with retail therapy.

When it was eventually all over we returned to the hotel and unloaded the bags in my room. Peter seemed reluctant to leave and I had to chase him off to see Miss Italian. Eventually he went and I spent some time unpacking and going over everything I'd bought, wow, what a day!

There was no sign of Jack by seven and so I went down to dinner on my own as I guessed Freddie boy had lured him into some fleshpot somewhere. I was just starting my meal when Peter appeared. He looked disappointed as he sat down and I realised that Miss Italian had stood him up. He told me she was working late; I said it was a lame excuse which made him a little touchy. He then asked me out for a drink and I was more than happy to see more of London as I didn't fancy staying in my room watching TV.

The Savoy Hotel in the Strand is so English it hurts you nicely. We sat in the lounge, drinking brandy and soda, whilst waiters hurried about in their quaint outfits. It was straight out of a vaudeville show and I was only sorry that my folks weren't there to see it all. Peter and I just talked and talked about London and New York and I promised him to show him around the 'big apple' if he could get over. After we'd had too much to drink we went back to the hotel in a cab and outside my room I decided to give the guy a big sloppy kiss to thank him. I then told him that he wasn't coming in for the night and reminded him that Miss Italian was probably still translating, he looked hurt at that.

I went to bed and started to think about Eric. I couldn't get him out of my mind and I wondered if he was close by. I guessed I'd never figure the guy out and I felt a bit depressed and confused before I fell asleep.

At breakfast Jack looked awful and I guessed he wasn't looking forward to the trip around the paint factory, but he rallied, kept the flag flying and we eventually set off in Peter's auto. We met Freddie boy at reception and after coffee he rushed us around the place. I must admit I found it all very interesting but somehow kinda funny, I guess it's the same as a glue factory, there's something slapstick about it. When it was all over Jack looked relieved and Peter drove us back to the hotel to get ready for a night out. I took my time and had a good soak in the tub before spending longer than usual on the makeup. Only God knows what we'd do without it. I decide to wear a neat, red velvet dress that I had bought in a boutique earlier because I knew Peter liked it, and I was going to tease him a little as it was our last night in London. After a good touch of perfume, I was ready to knock'em all dead.

We met Freddie boy in a steak house in Trafalgar Square and had a great meal before setting off to the theatre. The show was fabulous and I enjoyed it immensely whilst sitting next to Peter and holding his hand. He appeared a little formal and didn't seem to relax and I guessed he was worried about Miss Italian and her businessman.

After the show we all went back to the hotel where, over drinks, Freddie boy made a long goodbye speech. I was glad when he'd gone and went to my room for a good sleep knowing that tomorrow we were headed back across the pond to Atlantic City; then Eric came into my thoughts, so I was restless for a while.

Next morning, as we said goodbye to Peter outside the Heathrow Terminal, I gave him a big kiss, along with my card, and told him to call me. He said he'd write! Can you believe this guy? I wondered about him, but I hoped he'd stay in touch. I wanted to know how he got on with Miss Italian, well, a girl has to know about these things.

Jack and I dozed for an hour or two on the flight before we had lunch, which wasn't too bad, and after a Jack Daniels each ,we started talking about the trip. Jack said he was not that impressed with Benoir Paints and their quick paint system. He thought that technical problems would arise and if we painted wrecked autos that later showed up faults, the customers would be calling their lawyers before they called us. Nothing new there then. We fell silent for a while and I gazed out of the window at the beautiful cloud formations below before Jack startled me by saying "that Peter's a nice guy."

"Yes" I replied.

"He's so polite...."

"He's married, Jack" I interrupted quickly so as to head off the conversation.

"Okay, but I'm sure he's got a soft spot for you...."

"Jack, trust me on this one will you? He's married and he's already got some Italian all lined up to be the next Mrs Coltman, okay?"

"I was just making an observation that's all...."

"So leave it will you?"

"Hey, you're a might touchy about it" he replied.

"Sorry, I've got a lot going on at the moment and I guess I'm tired and a little confused."

"That's okay, I understand." And he did, that's what I liked about Jack. He changed the subject and we talked about my shopping in Paris and London. After a couple more Jack Daniels I relaxed some more and thought about Eric before eventually falling asleep watching the clouds glide silently past underneath.

We landed on time and Jack said goodbye at the cab rank outside the terminal before we went our separate ways. I was glad to be back and wanted to get to bed. Thankfully Mom, Pops and Melodie understood and I hurried my little girl home after spending a short time with them, promising to catch up tomorrow.

I settled down over the next few days and spent time with Mom and Pops after work. There was a hell of a lot to catch up on and I was surprised that Pops had not rushed back to the office, it seemed he was taking it easy on Moms advice. I was glad about that.

At the weekend I decided to go sailing with Melodie and invited Rachel to come along. She was pretty excited and I looked forward to her company. With still lots to talk over it was going to be a real girlie session out on the rolling Atlantic. I hoped that Eric had been listening in on our phone call so that he would know where I'd be on the Saturday and show up. Late Friday night Reece called as I was about to go to bed.

"Hi, babe."

"Hi, Reece."

"How are you?"

"Fine thanks."

"How was your trip to Paris?"

"It was good" I replied in a dead tone.

"Only 'good'?"

"Yup."

"What a disappointment" he said cheerfully.

"What do you want, Reece?" I asked in a tired voice.

"I'd like to take Melodie to a show tomorrow, is that okay?"

"What kinda show?" I asked suspiciously because Reece wasn't normally busting a gut to spend time with his daughter.

"It's a Spring Fair and County Show out at Burlington" he replied. I knew the place and it wasn't so far away so I guessed it was okay.

"I'll ask her if she wants to go" I said before calling up to Melodie. She said that a day out with Reece would be pretty cool, so it was arranged that he would collect her at about nine and drop her back to Mom and Pops in the evening and I would pick her up from there.

Next morning, when I collected Rachel from her apartment she was all ready to go and bright eyed with anticipation.

"I've got cheese and ham rolls, pizza slices, cream cakes, cookies, chocolate and loads of coffee to keep us going" she said as soon as I arrived.

"Great, a few pounds more won't do me any harm, how about you?" I asked and she laughed and replied "no, but does my bum look big in this wheelchair?"

We chatted all the way to the marina at Cape May and I was almost exhausted with answering all her questions about my trip to Europe. We parked up and got the food aboard the 'Princess' before struggling as usual to get her and the wheelchair on board. I wished that Eric had been there to help but there was no sign of him and I tried to hide my disappointment from Rachel.

Eventually, after getting her settled and wrapped up warm, we cast off and chugged out toward the harbour entrance. The morning was fresh and clear with the spring sunshine quite strong with the sea beyond looking gentle and calm. A light offshore wind was gusting as I cut the motor and raised the mainsail. The wind caught the 'Princess' and we started making way to the sound of the gentle slap of the waves against the bow.

"Isn't this just too good?" asked Rachel.

"Sure is, honey."

"Do you ever wish that you could sail on for ever?" she said.

"Often."

"Have you ever thought of sailing right across the Atlantic to Europe, or even around the world maybe?"

"I've thought about it, but realised a while ago that I wasn't that adventurous" I replied.

"I'd come with you if you ever did" she smiled at me.

"Sure, I know that, but I guess all I want is to settle down somehow, I'm not as ambitious as you" I replied and she laughed.

"Helen, I've only got you and dreams of what might be and settling down with some guy and having a bunch of kids will never happen for me, I'm a realist and I promise you, sitting in a damned wheelchair brings it all on." I felt so sorry for her and the way she said it touched me deeply. Why do awful things happen to such good people for Chrissake?

"Well, you never know what's around the corner as Mrs Dawson would say."

"Who?"

"Mrs Dawson, my next door neighbour" I replied.

"Oh, yeah, I remember her, the eyes and ears of the street" she laughed.

"That's the one" I said as I brought the 'Princess' around a few degrees to catch more of the breeze. Once we were out about a mile or so, I swung the 'Princess' on to a southerly course, keeping a safe distance from the coast line. I planned to sail for about three hours and then turn one eighty and return to the harbour. Rachel was enjoying it as much as I was and we started on the rolls and coffee, just to get us set up for the voyage. We talked about Mrs Dawson and wondered what it was like to be old, then we reminisced about our first dates at high school and finally we got onto Eric and Peter.

"I just can't believe that you didn't nail one of them down in Paris, I mean, Helen...."

"I know, I know, I'm a failure...." I interrupted.

"Can you imagine Karen letting them get out of her room alive?"

"Nope."

"You're damned right, she'd have had them both spread eagled on the bed naked and riding away on top like a jack rabbit."

"For sure...."

"And she'd have chosen one of them and got the date of the wedding all tied down."

"I know...."

"So, while you try and think what went wrong, let's have some chocs to keep us going!" I laughed and passed her the bag she'd brought with all the food. I worried inwardly about my failure to entice Eric whilst putting Peter at the back of my mind. After all, he had met someone who was obviously going to make him happy, and that fact made him un-available to me. Not like Eric, he said he was un-available, but hell, what was the guy playing at?

We sailed on whilst eating too much chocolate and when it was all gone we had a rest before starting on the pizza slices. The sea remained gentle and the 'Princess' glided smoothly through the rolling waves. The green, Maryland coastline lay about two miles off to our starboard side whilst the sun shone down from an almost cloudless sky. I felt relaxed and comfortable as I listened to Rachel telling me how I should try and line up my elusive guy into some kind of on going relationship. We laughed at some of her ideas before finishing lunch with the cookies and coffee.

"Time to turn around, Helen, we've run out of food" she said.

"Rachel, you should be as big as a Texan steer" I replied and she laughed as I began to slowly turn the 'Princess' on to a homeward bound course. The wind had shifted a little and we made slower headway on the return leg, but it didn't matter as we were both enjoying the experience and time was not important. Eventually we entered the harbour and I moored the 'Princess' in her berth. I looked around and along the jetty in case Eric was there, but I was disappointed. With a lot of silly giggling and struggling we managed to get Rachel off the boat and into her wheelchair. As I gathered up my sports bag and a few other bits, Rachel sped away along the jetty, calling out "I'll race you to the end!" I didn't bother but just smiled and thought 'she's crazy'. I looked back at the 'Princess' for a final check over before turning just as Rachel crashed off the end of the jetty and screamed. I saw the wheelchair drop off onto the hard standing and Rachel flying forward, rolling once and laying still. I ran as fast as I could whilst calling her name. Two guys, who were working on a boat nearby ran to help and we all arrived together.

"Rachel, Rachel, are you alright?" I cried out as I bent down over my friend. Her face was gashed and bleeding and her lip was swelling up.

"I think so, but my wrist hurts like crazy, just get me up, I'll be okay in a minute" she replied.

"D'you want us to call 911?" asked one of the guys.

"No, thanks, just get me back in my chair, I'll be okay, honestly" she replied. He righted her wheel chair and the other guy lifted her from the hard standing and put her gently into her chair. She looked pale and all shook up with blood running down her face from the gash on her cheek. I grabbed a tissue from my bag and wiped her face.

"I bet I look a helluva mess" she said.

"You're okay, babe" I replied.

"It's my wrist that hurts" she said.

"Better get to hospital with that and have it checked out" said the first guy.

"We will, and thanks for all your help" I said.

"No problem, ladies, you take care now" he replied with a smile. I drove my Chevy as fast as I could back to Atlantic City and straight to the A and E department at the hospital. I stopped outside the entrance and as I started to get Rachel out of the passenger seat some jerk, and there's always one, said "you can't stop here lady."

"Just help me get this injured person into the hospital, will you?" His attitude changed and we soon had Rachel in her chair and through the doors into reception. I went through the formalities with the receptionist and we were asked to wait. Rachel was in pain and looked pale and shaken.

"What an end to a lovely day" she said with tears in her eyes.

"Never mind, babe, you'll be okay and then we'll do it all again, only next time you'll wait for me to wheel you along the jetty." She smiled at that just as a nurse arrived and said "the doctor will be along in a moment, I'll put you in a cubicle so he can examine you." The nurse pushed Rachel into the corridor and I followed on. We were then left in a cubicle for a short while before the handsome young doctor, who had examined Pops, arrived and Rachel's eyes lit up.

"Hi, I'm Doctor Williams, so tell me what has happened to you then" he smiled and I saw Rachel melt a little.

"I fell off a jetty down at Cape May and hurt my wrist" she said holding out her left hand towards the Doctor.

"Did you fall very far?" he asked as he gently took her hand.

"No, not really."

"Okay, let me examine it, now tell me when it hurts as I move your hand" he smiled.

"Okay" she whispered. He very cautiously moved her hand in various directions and she winced just a couple of times.

"Okay, now have you suffered any other injuries?" he asked.

"Only my face" she replied.

"That's okay, we'll get that cleaned up while you're waiting for an x-ray" he smiled again.

"Is it serious, Doctor?" Rachel asked.

"No, I don't think so, but I'd like an x-ray just to make sure" he replied.

"Yes, of course."

"I'll send a nurse in to attend to your face whilst I contact the x-ray department and then I'll be back to check you over, okay?"

"Yes, that's fine." He smiled and was gone in a moment.

"Oh, my God, he's gorgeous" whispered Rachel.

"Isn't he just" I replied.

"I hope the nurses can concentrate on their work with him around" she said.

"I wonder what else he wants to 'check over' on you" I said.

"Everything, I hope, I hope" she smiled and I laughed. A nurse arrived and started to attend to her face.

"Doctor Williams is very nice isn't he, nurse?" asked Rachel.

"He sure is" replied the nurse as she continued to wipe the gash in Rachel's cheek.

"He must be very popular with the patients" persisted Rachel.

"He sure is" replied the nurse in a dead tone.

"Is it difficult to work with him?" asked Rachel.

"No, not at all, the difficult bit is talking about him to all the women patients who ask" she snapped and Rachel shut up and blushed slightly. Well, she asked for that one. Nurse finished the job with a plaster and left the cubicle.

"I wonder if he'll send me home tonight" said Rachel.

"Don't count on it" I replied as the handsome one returned.

"Okay, x-ray will see you in about twenty minutes or so" he smiled.

"Okay" whispered Rachel.

"That gives me time to check you over before nurse takes you down" he smiled.

"Shall I wait outside?" I asked.

"If you wouldn't mind" he replied.

"I'll let Rachel's folks know what's happened" I said.

"Thanks, that would be helpful."

"Will I be going home tonight?"

"I don't think so, I'd like to keep you in overnight for observation, if that's okay" he replied.

"Oh, yes" Rachel smiled and I left the cubicle with a grin on my face and thought 'Mrs Dawson is right, you never know what's around the corner.'

I called Rachel's folks who were anxious when I told them what had happened, and her Pops said they would hurry on down straight away. I was glad that I had arranged for Reece to drop Melodie back at Mom and Pops, I gave them a call to let them know what had happened to Rachel and that I'd be along later to collect Melodie.

I waited in reception and had a couple of coffees before Rachel's parents arrived. They were pretty anxious and I tried to re-assure them that their baby was not hurt bad, but just a little shaken up. Doctor Williams eventually arrived and told us that Rachel had broken a bone in her wrist but it was not serious and she was now in plaster and comfortable in a side ward. He invited us to follow him along to see his patient. She was sitting up in bed as pretty as a picture and she managed to calm her protective parents with smiles and assurances that she was just fine now and in the very capable hands of Doctor Williams. She announced that the Doctor was keeping her in overnight for observation as she'd been a little shook up.

I could see that Rachel was loving it all and when the handsome one said he'd call by later in the evening to see how she was I was sure to God that her wrist got a whole lot better there and then. He smiled and wished us all good evening before he left the ward.

"Is there anything you want, Rachel?" asked her Mom.

"Only him" she smiled and her Mom laughed and replied "he's a pretty handsome, guy, I must admit." We stayed for about another hour and retold every moment of the accident to her relieved parents. I promised to come back in the morning to collect her and I could see she was getting anxious that we should leave.

"I want to be alone when he drops by to check on me" she said firmly.

"There's nothing too much wrong with you, honey" said her Dad with a smile as we left the patient to enjoy her over night stay in hospital with Doctor Williams in attendance.

It was almost ten o'clock when I arrived back at Mom and Pops feeling tired.

"Where's Melodie?" I asked as I slumped into a chair.

"She's not back yet" replied Mom a little anxiously.

"What?"

"Reece hasn't brought her back" said Pops in a firm and disapproving tone.

"Not yet, Joe" said Mom hastily.

"Oh, my God, I hope that they're okay" I said.

"I'm sure they are" said Mom.

"I hope Reece isn't playing up with her" I said anxiously.

"So do I" replied Pops. It was something I always dreaded, Reece holding on to Melodie to somehow blackmail me into getting involved with him once again. He had let me down so many times before that I really felt that I couldn't go another round with him. He'd messed up my life and I was now at a stage where I couldn't forgive him. Mom made some coffee whilst I told them all about the adventures of the day and they were relieved that Rachel was okay. We talked on for a while and although Mom tried her best to calm me down I was getting more anxious by the minute. I suddenly felt a strong compulsion to go outside and I made an excuse to go out to my Chevy, I guess I needed some air and a moment to think.

It was quite cold as I wandered down to the sidewalk and gazed along the road in both directions. I don't know why, I suppose in the hope that Reece's Compact would suddenly appear, but it didn't and I just glanced along the row of neat houses across the street with their porch lights and drawn blinds. I turned to go back in and saw Eric standing by my Chevy in the driveway. My heart missed a beat and I called his name as I rushed towards him. He held out his arms to me and smiled. I felt his strong, warm embrace and we stood for a minute before I spoke.

"Eric, thank God you're here."

"Yes, I'm here."

"I'm so worried about Melodie."

"She's quite safe, I assure you and she'll be back tomorrow......."

"How the hell do you know?" I interrupted angrily, thinking that he was messing with my mind.

"Calm down, will you?"

"No, and what are you doing here anyway?"

"I've come to re-assure you that your daughter is safe and you'll see her in the morning after you've collected Rachel from hospital." Well, I was speechless, how come he knew so much about what had been going on? I mean was he some kind of mind reader or what? Boy, was I confused.

"Now go inside to your parents and wait for a call from Reece" he said with a smile.

"Are you coming in to meet my folks?"

"No, not this time, Helen."

"Why not?"

"It's for the best at the moment" he smiled before kissing me so gently.

"Oh, do that again will you?" I whispered and he did.

"Now, go in and wait and I'll see you soon."

I didn't know what to think but I turned away and walked up to the house, stopping to wave to him but he had gone. I looked up and down the empty street and felt very uneasy. Perhaps I was beginning to imagine Eric. It was almost eleven when the phone rang.

"Hi, babe."

"Reece, where are you?"

"Still out in Burlington" he replied.

"And?" I asked waiting for an explanation.

"We've had a great day at the show and I met some folks I know from Baltimore and we've had dinner with them and...."

"Reece, are you bringing Melodie home ?" I interrupted.

"Er, no, babe, I've booked us into a motel and...."

"Reece! Bring Melodie home now!"

"Babe, I've had a bit to drink and it's better that we stay here for the night, trust me on this one will you?"

"Put Melodie on"

"Okay, here she is."

"Hi, Mom" said my daughter.

"Hi, honey, are you okay?"

"Yup, I'm good."

"Okay, have you had a nice day?"

"It's been great, the show was something else and we met loads of people that Reece knows and I've been invited to stay with Daniel and his folks...."

"Who's Daniel?"

"He's a really nice kid and his Pops said that he'd take us out to see his boat...."

"Okay, honey, you can tell me all about it when you get home tomorrow" I interrupted feeling relieved.

"Okay, Mom, Reece says we'll be back about lunch time."

"Okay, honey, sleep tight, love you."

"Love you, Mom."

"Put Reece on, honey."

"Hi, babe...."

"Just make sure your back here by lunchtime, okay?"

"We'll be there, trust me."

"I stopped trusting you a long time ago, Reece" I said before I put the phone down. Mom was smiling and Pops raised his eyebrows.

"There, she's okay then" said Mom.

"Yup, so, I'm going home and I'll call round about lunch time after I've got Rachel home" I said.

"Okay, dear, I'll have something ready for us all to eat then."

"Thanks, Mom" I smiled and gave her and Pops a quick kiss before I drove home.

At the hospital reception the next morning, Rachel was waiting in her wheelchair, she was all smiles.

"Hey, have I got news for you" she said as soon as she saw me.

"Surprise me, no, let me guess, Doctor Williams came by late last night and you got laid, and he's only just gone home to sleep!"

"Almost" she grinned.

"Rachel...."

"I know, lets get out of here and I'll tell all!" Well, I couldn't wait and as soon as we were in the car I demanded to know every little detail. Doctor Williams must have found her quite sweet and to his taste because according to Rachel did he open up to her or what? Apparently he's single, not gay, no woman in his life at present, lives in an apartment over on Brooklyn Avenue West and has a sailing boat that he keeps moored up in Chesapeake Bay.

"Oh, my God, have you struck lucky" I said as we pulled up outside Rachel's apartment block.

"Let's get in and get the coffee on, there's lots more to tell" she said, her eyes bright with excitement.

"Okay, but I can't stay long, Reece is dropping Melodie off at Mom's soon."

"Right, so you make the coffee while I just talk!" Well, she never stopped and it seems that the good Doctor sat with her for a long while as he was at the end of his shift and happy to stay with his fast recovering patient. He said that the speed of her recovery was almost a medical miracle and I thought 'you can say that again'. There was one drawback apparently, every time he took her pulse her blood pressure went up but it went back to normal when he left the side ward and the nurse took the reading. That somehow, didn't exactly come as a shock to me. Rachel had the 'hots' for this handsome guy and it seemed he was attracted to her. I can understand that because she has a very beautiful face and a great, crazy personality to go with it. When she told him that we'd been sailing before the accident he asked her if she'd like to go with him for a sail around Chesapeake Bay after she's fully recovered. She said she hesitated for about a second before saying 'okay'. The thought flashed through her mind that she didn't want to appear too eager so a one second delay seemed in order before she agreed and told him that she felt much better already! What is she like? The Doctor said he will give her a call to fix a date after she's been discharged from his care. Was she excited? You better believe it! It been a long while since I've seen my lovely friend so happy and I was sorry that I had to leave her.

"Don't worry, Helen, Mom and Pops are coming round this afternoon and that just gives me time to call Karen and tell her all!" I laughed, kissed her and told her that I'd catch up later.

Melodie was already at home when I arrived and I was both pleased and relieved to see her. I heard all about the county fair in Burlington and all about Daniel and his folks. It seemed that my daughter had had a very good time with her father. After lunch Pops and Melodie wandered off to watch a baseball game on TV whilst I stayed in the dining room with Mom. I felt that something was bothering her. I reckon that I can always sense when she's a little tense and wants to off load to me. We sat at the table whilst the dishwasher churned away in the kitchen.

"Pops is a whole lot better" I said.

"He certainly is."

"When does the Doctor say he can get back to work?"

"In a week or so, he wants to see him again before he gives him the okay" she smiled.

"Right." There was a long pause whilst Mom studied her finger nails and I thought 'here it comes'.

"Helen...."

"Yes, Mom."

"Pops isn't getting any younger you know, and, well, this accident has shaken him up a bit...."

"I'm sure it has" I interrupted.

"Whilst he's been at home he's had time to think about things...."

"What kinda things?"

"Well, the business for a start" and at that moment she looked at me and I somehow guessed what was coming next.

"And?"

"Pops has given it a lot of thought and he wants to retire."

"Okay...."

"And he wants to leave you to run the business...."

"Oh, no, Mom, never, I couldn't do it, I just couldn't...."

"Helen, if you don't do it, then Pops will sell it, lock, stock and barrel."

"Mom, believe me, I couldn't cope with it now."

"Helen..." she just said my name when Pops walked in and asked "where's my coffee and my grand daughter wants to know if we've got any cookies?"

CHAPTER 9

PETER TRAVELS TO MILAN

It was a week since I said goodbye to Helen and Jack at Heathrow and I'd tried to settle back into work but I kept thinking of Helen whilst I worried about Sophia. On top of that I dreaded telling Janet that I was going to get a divorce. Work seemed to be running in second place to all my personal problems. I decided that without fail, I'd tell Janet this coming weekend that it really was all over. I waited until Sunday lunch time and after we had finished our meal and were still sitting at the dining table I said "Janet, I've given it a lot of thought and I've decided that the best thing for us now, is to get a divorce."

"Well you finally got round to it then, talk about the blinding bloody obvious...."

"Really?" I interrupted.

"Yes, really, you silly fool."

"I, er...."

"Look Peter, I realised a long while ago that it wasn't going to work and all you've done is made the situation worse by dragging it out."

"I didn't mean to...."

"I don't love you or even care about you now, to me our whole marriage has been a bloody mistake from the word go."

"I never knew that you felt like that about me" I replied feeling a bit sorry for myself as well as relieved that there obviously was not going to be a bad tempered fight over the divorce.

"Well I do, so, as far as I'm concerned you can see a solicitor and get things moving as soon as you like."

"Right...."

"And I want the house sold, half of what's left after we've cleared the mortgage, plus all the furniture and a decent amount of money each month to live on."

"You have given it some thought haven't you?"

"I have."

"Where will you live?"

"None of your business" she replied firmly.

"Right."

"Now that's out of the way, let's get the washing up done." I thought 'women are so practical when compared to men and it's no wonder they win all the time'.

After the washing up was finished and Janet had settled down in front of the television with a box of chocolates I left the house and drove up to the White Horse hill to think things through. I parked and wandered along to the mound where I had sat with Eric and gazed over the rolling countryside spread out before me. It seemed that the fickle finger of fate had, for once, eased my path to freedom and my lovely Sophia. Hopefully I could arrange a 'quickie' divorce and marry Sophia within a few months and take her somewhere new, well away from Ashton.

"Hello, Peter." I heard the voice behind me and my heart sank. I did not want to turn around and I didn't have to, because he then sat down beside me.

"Hello, Eric."

"It's a lovely view from up here" he said.

"It is" I agreed whilst wondering what was coming next.

"Do you like wide open spaces?"

"Yes, sometimes."

"America has plenty of space."

"I know, I've been there" I replied.

"You should go again."

"Why?"

"It would be good for you."

"I should take Sophia with me for a holiday…."

"No, Peter, you should go alone."

"Why?"

"Because it's the best thing for you to do."

"I'd rather go to Milan to meet Sophia's parents." Eric sighed at that and replied after a long pause "if you must."

"I must" I replied. At that he stood up and looking down at me said "You're making things very difficult for me as well as yourself."

"Oh, dear, well hard luck, Eric, that's life at the moment" I replied.

"It certainly is." With that he wandered off back up towards the top of the hill and I watched him as he disappeared from my sight over the brow. I thought 'what a pain he is and why is he so concerned about me for God's sake?.'

I sat for some while planning what I should do next before returning home to my wife.

Janet left early for work the next morning, so I phoned Jessups and Partners, the solicitors in Oxford who handled our house purchase, and made an appointment to see their Mr. Oakwood. Apparently he was the matrimonial affairs expert and I was assured by his secretary that he was very professional and always managed to sort out any difficulties with consummate ease. I was glad to hear it and felt relieved. I then phoned Freddie at his office in Berkeley Square.

"Morning, Freddie."

"Is it?"

"Yes, of course...."

"I'll let you know about that after you've told me what's gone wrong now" he said.

"Freddie...."

"I'm waiting."

"Nothings gone wrong, I just want to book a short holiday...."

"You're always on holiday, your sales figures prove that!"

"You know how to hurt...."

"It's Monday morning and it's the thing I do best on Monday's."

"Seriously, I need a few days off...."

"What for?"

"I just need to get away...."

"You've just been away with me to Paris...."

"That was work" I interrupted.

"You were working?"

"Yes."

"You could have fooled me" he replied.

"Freddie, please" and he obviously heard the desperation in my voice.

"Okay, if it's really necessary...."

"It is, I promise you."

"I'll make a note and let personnel know."

154

"Thanks."

"When are you going?"

"From next Monday."

"How long for?"

"Better make it a week."

"A week! You said a few days….."

"I know, but a week would be better."

"Might be for you but it's not so good for the sales figures."

"I know, I know, but I promise that I'll put in a big effort next month and my figures will surprise you…."

"I look forward to the surprise."

"Good."

"Let me know if you have any problems before the end of the week."

"Thanks, Freddie, I will."

"And where are you going for your break?"

"Milan."

I phoned Sophia "my darling."

"Peter, it's so gooda to hear you, where are you?"

"At home at the moment but I'm coming to take you out for dinner tonight….."

"Oh, I can't come out, I said I woulda do some more work for Ray tonight……"

"Ray? You mean Ashton don't you?" I asked as my hackles rose.

"Yes, but….."

"Well tell him your going out to dinner with your fiancé who has a big surprise for you."

"A surprise? What is it?"

"A surprise, I'll pick you up at seven, okay?"

"Okay."

"A thousand kisses until then" I said and put the phone down. That bloody man was getting closer to Sophia and I knew that all he wanted was to start an affair with her. God, how I hated the decrepit, bumptious old creep

I made several calls round Reading, popping in as a courtesy call to Marparts and then on to Westons Body Repairs in the Oxford Road to try and bring a smile to Charlie Walters face. He was the paint shop foreman and had unfortunately suffered more than his fair share of mis-matched colours from our paint mixing scheme. Luckily, Charlie was of the old school and always managed to tint 'off shade' colours by eye and get a match that was acceptable to the customer. If only there were more like him. After a coffee and a genial chat I left Charlie and went out to see Bob Cummins at Reading Coachworks in Tilehurst. Bob was not a happy man and gave me a hard time over colour problems and soft paint after the low bake process.

"The finish is still bloody soft and marks easily" he complained.

"Are you getting up to panel temperature in your oven?" I asked.

"Yes, I called your lab and complained, so they sent Jimmy, your technical chap, down from Stratford last week to set up a test probe to check; he said the oven is working perfectly." I had no answer to that and could only surmise that either Bob's painters were spraying too much paint on the cars or there was something wrong with our paint formulation. As I stood in his office listening to all his woes I thought that there must be an easier way of earning a living than this. When Bob had finally wound down, I made my excuses and left. It was late afternoon when I drove to Caversham and parked near the bridge over the river. I went for a walk along the river bank and began to think of Helen and our lunch together at Wallingford. It had been a very enjoyable day with no hassle and I appreciated that oasis of peace in what seemed to be a turbulent time. My mind turned over in myriad ways and I was unsure whether I was becoming more or less confused. I let it all rest and made my way back to the car and set off for Highgate.

Sophia made me wait for twenty minutes before she appeared at the front door looking radiant in a yellow, high neck dress. I waited by the car and kissed her as soon as she was with me.

"Darling, you look lovely."

"Thanker you, now where are you taking me and whatsa my biga surprise?"

"I'll tell you on the way" I replied as she slipped into the car. I pulled away and before we had driven to the end of the road she asked "well?"

"We're going to our favourite restaurant in Harrow tonight and then..." I paused.

"Yes?"

"We're going to Milan next week!"

"Oh, Peter, darling, thatsa wonderful!"

"Yes, it's time I met your parents."

"Oh, I'm a so happy, so happy!"

"Good."

"I'll phone them when I get home tonighta."

"Okay, now then, can we stay with them?"

"Yes, of course, of course, they will be so happy to meet you, I've told them all about you."

"Good" and I was pleased that I only had to find the money for the flight plus any meals we might have out in Milan. The meal was excellent at the restaurant and when we had finished and were lingering over coffee I decided not to spoil the evening by mentioning my concerns regarding the old crone, Ashton. I was not even going to speak his name on such a pleasant occasion when my lovely Sophia was so happy and radiant. We drove back to Highgate in a relaxed mood, listening to late night music on the radio. We kissed for some while before we parted and I watched my fiancé until she gave me a final wave from the front door and went inside.

The week dragged by and I was late back from work every night, except on Wednesday when I kept the appointment with the solicitor, Mr Oakwood of Jessups, and started the divorce proceedings. We agreed that the grounds would be mutual irretrievable breakdown. Other than phoning Sophia each day, I didn't see her until the Saturday morning when we were booked to fly out from Heathrow. Janet wasn't interested in the fact that I'd be away for a week and I was relieved about that. Sophia had made all the arrangements with her parents, who were going to meet us at the Milan airport, and it seemed we were all set for a very enjoyable visit to Italy.

Jacqueline and Mario Portovecchio were waiting for us when we eventually cleared the baggage hall. Jacqueline was a beautiful, mature version of Sophia and Mario was a tall, distinguished looking man with a mop of black hair tinged with grey. Their faces were wreathed in broad smiles when they caught sight of Sophia and Jacqueline waved frantically. After hugs and kisses the conversation started and it seemed that they were all talking at once in their musical, lilting language. At last they stopped for a moment for Sophia to introduce me and as I spoke not one word of Italian, all I could do was to smile and nod gently. Mario shook my hand and Jacqueline planted a light kiss on either cheek. It seemed that they approved for the moment. Soon we were on our way through the traffic in Mario's BMW seven series and I guessed that he had a good, well paid position in business.

They all talked incessantly until we arrived outside a smart block of flats in the Via Agostini.

"We're home, darling" smiled Sophia.

"Oh, good."

"I'm sorry we all talker so much, but we're Italian and they are pleased to see me."

"I understand."

"Papa says I musta teach you Italian straight away" she laughed.

"Right."

"Now, Papa has arranged to take us out for dinner tonight."

"That's nice."

"It will be, now help Papa with our cases" Sophia said as she slipped from the car.

The Portovecchio's flat was spacious and luxurious with décor that was sophisticated and beautifully understated. Sophia led me to her bedroom, that was to be ours whilst we stayed in Milan and I was impressed.

"Is thisa okay?" she asked with a winsome smile.

"Very nice indeed, my Princess" I replied as I looked at the double bed and the fitted wardrobes all along two walls of the spacious room.

"Mama and Papa approve of you and when I tolda them that we were going to get married, they were very happy and everything is okay."

"That's wonderful" I replied as I took her in my arms and kissed her passionately.

"Tonight will be a gooda night, Papa wants to celebrate."

"That's fine by me."

"There is justa one thing, darling...."

"Yes?"

"My parents are Catholic anda I can't tell them that you're married, so, you musta never let them know, because Papa would stop us."

"Okay, I promise I won't ever tell them, but surely they would want you to be happy?"

"Of course, but if Papa knew you were married he'd stop my allowance and never leave his money to me."

"That's important to you is it?"

"Yes, of course, darling, we can't a live for a day without money anda you can never have too much" she replied with conviction. For a moment I suddenly worried about Ashton and wondered if his plan to seduce my fiancé revolved around finance, I shuddered at the thought of her in his scraggy arms. Money can be an excellent aphrodisiac with some women. I dismissed the unhappy thoughts and kissed Sophia once again.

Mario took us to an excellent restaurant, situated just off the famous Milan Piazza, where the Portovecchio's often dined. The menu was extensive and I struggled for a while before Sophia came to my rescue. I started with fabulous Parma ham and followed that with the most delicious cannelloni that I have ever had. We drank Chianti throughout the meal and finished with ice cream of many flavours. All through the meal, Sophia had to keep translating the conversation, backwards and forwards, as Papa asked me so many questions about relatives, work and prospects. He finished with a 'bombshell' when he asked when we were getting married. That stumped me and I looked at Sophia for inspiration, but there was none, so I blurted out 'in September.' She translated and they all smiled and I smiled back in hope rather than certainty. From then on I surmised that Sophia and her mother would be making all the arrangements for an autumn wedding in Milan. On the plus side I thought that having a future mother-in-law a couple of thousand miles away and who couldn't speak English was a positive situation.

The rest of the week was pure bliss as I was introduced to

various members of the family and visits to them were punctuated with shopping sprees with Jacqueline. My lovely future mother-in-law bought several pairs of expensive shoes for Sophia and me and I was taken aback by her generosity.

It seemed that the Portovecchio's were quite a wealthy family. Mario's father had started a metal fabrication business after the war and had managed to secure several government contracts which proved to be very lucrative. The business had flourished and when Mario took over the management of the operation he had been able to expand it further into Europe. There was financial success on a grand scale and the Portovecchio's enjoyed their wealth and their lives together. Mario hinted more than once that I should learn Italian very quickly as there were well paid management opportunities in his ever expanding business for a future son-in-law. Naturally, it was expected that Sophia and I would live in Milan immediately after the wedding and Mario said that a suitable flat would be found in time. I was overwhelmed by all this and was glad when we at last waved goodbye to Sophia's parents and boarded the plane for the return flight. I needed time to think.

"Mama and Papa are very fond of you, darling."

"I realise that and I must say they are very kind and generous to a fault." She smiled at that and held my hand before gazing out of the window as the aircraft was pushed back from the terminal.

The flight was uneventful and other than the delay in the baggage hall at Heathrow Arrivals, everything went smoothly. I dropped Sophia home and drove back to Wantage in the Sunday evening traffic, thinking about the trip to Milan and all its implications. Supposing I couldn't get divorced in time? What if the Portovecchio's found out I was already married? What would they do to me? Did Mario have connections with the Mafia?

A thousand questions rose up in my mind and I didn't have answers for any of them. Then I thought of Helen and our few days together and somehow my restlessness seemed calmed by the memories. I remembered my first sight of her in the hotel and the meeting in the lift, how attractive she looked in her blue dress when we danced together, the red dress when we went to the theatre, and then... I had to stop, this woman was invading my senses. I tried to concentrate on the driving, but Helen kept coming back into my thoughts so I decided I would ring her, just as a friend, to chat about her trip over to Europe.

I was glad to be back at work and other than calling Freddie in Berkeley Square, just to check in and to assure him I was all ready to go and hit those sales targets, I dedicated myself to business in the hope of reaching budget and getting a monthly bonus. I knew that money was a priority from now on as there was so much to pay for. I hadn't even started looking for an engagement ring for Sophia and I was worried about the ever mounting debt on my three credit cards. God, those bits of plastic are the devils own work because no matter how hard I tried to pay them off the debt stubbornly remained the same each month. It must be me.

I travelled down to Swindon, the farthest place to the west of my area, and had a good day visiting the various paintshops. I picked up quite a few orders and the success of the sales gave me confidence and I pushed ahead for the next two days in Reading, which proved to be similarly rewarding.

I phoned Sophia on the Thursday morning to make arrangements for the weekend, when I had planned to take her shopping for a ring.

"I'm a so sorry, darling, but Ray has asked me to go to Turkey with him tonight......."

"What?" I screamed down the phone.

"Darling, it's a very important meeting he has to go to........"

"I don't care! I don't want you to go and that's that!"

"Don'ta you trust me?"

"Yes, but I don't trust him!"

"Darling, I'ma not interested in this old man......."

"I should hope not....."

"But he's paid me very well for the work I've done and he says he needs me to be at this meeting........."

"No!" I interrupted.

"I'll only be gone for a couple of days, I'll be home on Sunday......."

"Sophia, I don't want you to go......."

"But, darling, I've never been to Turkey and........"

"I don't care..."

"It's for such a short time anda you know I love you, so, please let me go" she pleaded and, like a fool, I slowly relented.

"Well, where are you going exactly?" I asked half heartedly.

"It's a place called Izmir, it's near Istanbul."

"And when do you fly back?"

"On Sunday, Ray will dropa me home in the afternoon, so we coulda go out in the evening, okay?" she sounded happy and I knew I had to let her go.

"Okay, I'll be there at seven and we'll go for a meal and you can tell me all about your trip."

"Oh, darling, thanker you for being so gooda, I do love you so much."

"And I love you too……."

"I'll phone you when we arrive, okay."

"Okay, and take care."

"I will, darling, goodbye."

"Goodbye" I whispered and my heart sank as I put the phone down. The old bastard had managed to get her away for a few days and I knew he'd work hard on her for his own nefarious ends.

The rest of the day dragged and so did Friday until Sophia called me at home late in the evening. Luckily, Janet had gone out with her friends for a 'girls only' night at the pub.

"Hello, darling" she said brightly.

"Oh, darling, it's good to hear you, are you okay?"

"Si, I'ma fine, the flight was delayed and so thatsa why I'ma calling you late."

"Never mind, so tell me, how's your hotel?"

"It'sa very nice and my rooma over looks the sea."

"That's nice."

"And the food is good, we had a nice meal with some business people."

"Good."

"But, I'm a sorry, darling, I won't be home on Sunday……"

"What?" I shouted as my hackles rose once again.

"Ray says that we have to stay until Wednesday……."

"Why for God's sake?" I shouted as I knew what was going on and the game the old lecher was playing.

"We have to go to an important meeting with the mayor of Izmir…."

"Why?"

"Because he has to approve of the work that Ray's business is going to do if he gets the contract."

"I don't like it one bit, Sophia, I tell you that that old man is going after you and you'll end up as his next mistress!"

"Darling, you're so wrong, I'm a not interested in him, it's you I love."

"Well, wait and see, but I'm sure he'll try as hard as he can to get you and believe me that old creep will ruin our lives."

"Darling, listen to me, I love you, now I have to go because we're going to have drinks with some more people, I'll phone you tomorrow, I promise."

"Okay, I love you."

"Love you too, goodbye." I put the phone down and the sheer despair and disappointment made me feel quite ill.

The weekend dragged and was made worse because Sophia did not call as promised. On the Monday morning I phoned the Parkers to see if they knew anything. Mrs Parker answered the call.

"Well, to be honest, Peter, I don't know when they are coming back, it's all a bit inconvenient as far as we're concerned."

"I'm sure."

"I mean, without an au pair these days you're just stuck with the children all the time."

"Yes, indeed."

"I called Jean last night and she said that she didn't expect Ray back for at least ten days, which was news to us, I mean we were told they'd be back Sunday." My heart sank further at that as I realised that the old fart would keep Sophia with him for as long as it took to seduce her. I felt sick to the very pit of my stomach and I knew I could do nothing about it but wait.

"Yes, Sophia told me she'd be back on Sunday" I said, not letting Mrs Parker know that it had been put back to Wednesday at the earliest. I hoped that Ashton would fall further in the Parker's esteem.

"We'll just have to wait until they turn up, I suppose" she said wearily.

"Yes, well, thank you Mrs Parker, I'll be in touch if I hear anything."

I went through the motions of work for the rest of the day and Tuesday was more or less the same. Wednesday came and went and it was on Thursday evening, when I had just about given up all hope that Sophia would call, that Janet answered the phone and after asking who was calling, just put the receiver down and said, stony faced, "it's for you."

"Darling, I'ma so sorry that I've not called you, but we've been so busy and Ray has had to take me to so many meetings, well...."

"So you're okay then?"

"Si, we had a little break this afternoon and we stayed by the pool for a rest...."

"By the pool?"

"Si, I went for a swim, it was so gooda."

"Really?"

"Si, Ray had to buy me a little swimming costume, because I didn't bring one."

"Indeed, well you were originally only going for a few days."

"Si, and darling, I'ma sorry but we won't be coming back until late Sunday night, so it'sa best if you give me a call Monday evening."

"Okay, I'll phone about seven."

"Okay, darling, I'll talka to you then."

"Bye now" I said and put the phone down. Janet didn't ask who it was but just kept her eyes firmly glued to the television whilst I went to the kitchen to pour a stiff whisky. I felt dreadful. The rest of the week was a blur of work as I decided to bury myself in sales calls and concentrate my mind to keep out the anger, disappointment and utter frustration that I felt over the situation. How this cunning old man had managed to manipulate Sophia for his own ends was indeed a mystery. Was she that gullible, that naïve? Only time would tell and at the moment it hung heavy with me.

At last Monday arrived and other than Janet giving me the name and address of her solicitors, Maxwell and Jones in Wantage, the time had passed without incident. I phoned Sophia at seven on the dot and she answered with her lilting voice.

"Oh, darling, you're back at last" I said joyfully.

"Of course I am, Peter, did you think that I'da run away?"

"No, of course not, darling, but I'm glad you're home."

"Si, and I had a very gooda time, it was very interesting."

"That's good, you can tell me all about it over dinner tomorrow, okay?"

"Si, my darling."

"I'll pick you up at seven and we'll go somewhere new."

"Okay."

"I love you, Sophia, and I always will."

"I love you too, darling."

"See you tomorrow."

"Bye."

I felt so much better all of a sudden and thought that perhaps my fears were groundless. Perhaps it was all innocent and the old man was genuine. I went off to Reading the next day to begin my round of sales calls with a light heart, knowing that I'd be seeing Sophia later.

Working steadily through the morning I moved on to Windsor in the afternoon, picking up several good orders for primer and thinners from the car refinishers situated underneath the railway arches. It was late afternoon when I set off for Freddie's office in Berkeley Square, where I planned to update him on my sales figures.

When I arrived Paula told me that he'd been called to a meeting at the works in Stratford and would not be back today. As I had time to spare before driving up to Highgate, and was feeling light hearted, I decided to give Helen a call. It was almost five o'clock in London so it would be about midday in Atlantic City. I sat at Freddie's desk and dialled the number on Helens card. It rang for only a moment before a sweet female voice answered.

"Hi, this is Milton's auto repairs..."

"Hello, may I speak to Helen Milton, please?"

"Who's calling please?"

"I'm Peter Coltman, she knows me."

"I'll just see if she's available, Mr Coltman, please hold."

"Thank you." I waited for a few moments before the line clicked and the sweet voice said "putting you through, now."

"Hi, Peter, how are you?"

"Fine, thanks, Helen, and you?"

"I'm good and even better that you've called on my birthday…"

"Your birthday?"

"Yup."

"Well many happy returns from this side of the Atlantic."

"Thanks, it's a shame you're not here to help me celebrate…."

"I wish I was, are you hitting the town tonight?"

"You better believe it!"

"Great, so where are you going, and more importantly, who with?" she laughed at that and I thought how good it was to hear her.

"I'm out with my two best friends, Rachel and Karen…"

"No boyfriends?"

"Nope, we're dead short of eligible guys in Atlantic City…"

"Really?"

"Yup, they're all either married, gay or nerds, I swear to God there's nobody left for us full blooded American babes."

"I don't believe you!" she laughed at that.

"Well come on over and see for yourself, hey, and while you at it, bring some handsome English guys to make up the numbers."

"I might just do that."

"It would be great if you did" she replied in a wistful tone.

"Well if the invitation is still open…"

"You can bet your sweet bibby on that" she interrupted.

"I'll certainly look into it" I said.

"You gonna bring Miss Italian? And by the way, how is she?"

"She's fine, thank you, I'm taking her out to dinner tonight."

"Lucky girl."

"Thanks….."

"So, are you gonna come over soon, or what?"

"I'd like to."

"Well, do it then, I promise I'll take you sailing, get dolled up in that red dress I bought in Kensington and I'll take you to dinner at Rolfe's, I know you'll love it." She was plucking at heart strings and I felt attracted to this 'up front' American woman. She painted a good picture and for some reason without thinking, I replied "I'll talk to Freddie and see if I can wangle it."

"Wangle? What's 'wangle'?"

"Arrange it" I replied and laughed.

"Okay, so you'll be coming alone then?"

"Yes, it will be a business trip."

"Like Paris, but without the French?"

"Yes."

"Okay, Mister Reserved, make it soon, and call me, d'you hear?"

"Loud and clear."

"Good."

"And Helen."

"Yup?"

"Happy birthday and I send you a big sloppy kiss."

"Why thank you, kind sir, you certainly know the way to a girl's heart!" I laughed at that.

"Bye, Helen."

"Bye, Peter, and call me!"

"I will." I put the receiver down and sat for a while meditating on the trans-Atlantic friendship and felt very good about it.

Sophia kept me waiting for half an hour before she emerged, radiant in a red dress and with her hair swept up into a French roll. When she sat beside me in the car, we kissed and kissed again until we were both breathless. As we drove over towards Richmond she told me all about the trip. It seemed that all had gone well and the old man never said or did anything untoward. I was relieved and the evening was off to a good start.

The meal at the Steak House, just by the river bridge, was excellent and we both enjoyed Tournedous Rossini accompanied by a mature bottle of Mouton Cadet. Crepes suzette finished the experience, leaving us well fed and very relaxed. After coffee and brandy we left the restaurant all smiles and wandered along the side of the river. Sophia started talking about her Turkish adventure whilst I tried to steer the conversation on to the subject of our marriage and the new life in Milan. It seemed all in vain as she kept going back to what Ray had done, and what he had said to whom, and what he planned to do next. I was not happy and had to tell her to shut up about the old man because I was not interested. I feared the old goat had had quite an influence on Sophia. We drove home in silence and I was angry at myself for spoiling the perfect evening as much as I was furious that Ashton had invaded our privacy. We kissed goodnight and she relaxed in my arms. I felt all was well until she said "darling, Ray has asked me to go to Paris next week for a meeting with some of the people we met in Izmir." I was stunned and just whispered "oh, dear God."

"You don't mind, do you?"

"No, darling, if it makes you happy" I replied, full of apprehension.

"Gooda, I do love you so."

"And I love you."

"Phone me tomorrow?"

"Of course." We kissed some more before she left the car, giving me a little wave as she went into the house.

I was just about to drive off when a tall figure I recognised came striding along out of the darkness and bent down by the car. I wound the window down and Eric said "it's time we had a long talk, Peter."

CHAPTER 10

HELEN TAKES OVER THE BUSINESS

I looked at Pops across the dining room table and for the first time realised that his age was beginning to show. Perhaps it was the accident or I just hadn't noticed it before, but now it was plain for me to see.

"Pops, I'm glad that you've decided to retire, but really, I can't run the business."

"Why not, honey?"

"I haven't got the experience and...."

"You never know what you can do until you try" he interrupted.

"Sure, and that's easy to say, but...."

"There are no 'buts', I know you can do it, you've got Mitch running the workshop and Naomi helping you with the paperwork."

"I know..."

"And the rest of the guys, Frank, Ted and the others, all think the world of you and I know you'll get all the help you need."

"Pops, I'm not sure I want to do it...."

"Look, honey, I'll be around to back you up all the time, and, hey, I'm not going to just drop you in it, I'll plan a slow, careful, handover so you're not left wondering about anything."

"I know that you'd do the right thing, Pops, but....."

"I promise you, honey, the business is simple, so trust me on this one, you know the drivers around here wreck their autos faster than we can fix them, they bring 'em to us and we repair 'em with new panels and fresh paint, then give 'em back, all shiny and new."

"I know, Pops...."

"And the insurance pays up with a nice cheque, what could be easier?"

"Pops, I've got to think about this...."

"What's there to think about? It's not as if you're going to get married soon or anything." That hurt and knocked me back a little.

"You don't know that" I replied firmly.

"Okay, where's this guy 'Eric' your Mom and I have heard so much about?"

"He's not ready to see you yet."

"Well, as far as I can make out, no one has seen him yet, so are you sure you're not imagining him?" That really struck home and I guessed that my face showed my embarrassment.

"Well, honey?" Pops persisted.

"I'll have to think about it all, so give me a moment, will you?"

"Okay, think it over and let me know, but I'm telling you now, if you don't take it on, then I'm selling the whole damn kit and caboodle." There's nothing like a bit of pressure to ensure you make a quick, and possibly, wrong decision.

Next day, in the office, I decided to tell Naomi that Pops was thinking about retiring and she asked so many questions that I wished I hadn't told her.

"Who'll run the business then?"

"Well, I will."

"That'll be great, so will I get your job?"

"We'll have to see how it pans out, but I guess so...."

"Hey, will I get a raise?"

"I expect so...."

"Does Mitch know?"

"Not yet, so don't say anything, leave that to Pops."

"Okay, it'll be our secret" she smiled and was all excited.

"Yup, and let's keep it that way."

At lunch time I went to the deli for rolls and a chocolate bar, well, it helps me think and I've lost a bit of weight off my hips, so why not? I sat in the park and looked at the fat birds, who were eyeing me up and down, whilst I wondered if Eric would show. I thought about running the business and all the problems and responsibilities that came with it and was unsure whether I could cope with it all. I didn't need any more complications in my life. I just wanted to have Eric with me, to love and care about me, surely not too much to ask.

My mind wandered back to Peter and the good time I'd had in Paris and London with him. Jack was right, he is a nice guy and just the type for a girl to settle down with and raise some kids. I felt a little jealous of Miss Italian, boy, had she got him on a plate!

Rachel came into my thoughts, and I kept seeing the look on her face when the Doctor examined her. She fell in love with that guy at first sight, and I hoped he'd take her out and treat her well, if nothing else. It seemed everybody I knew and liked was getting lined up with someone, except me.

I had just taken a large mouthful of cheese salad roll when Eric appeared and sat down next to me.

"Hello, Helen."

"Why do you do turn up and do this to me every time I've got a mouthful of food?" I flustered angrily as bits of cheese spattered in his direction. He laughed out loud.

"You're very lovely when you're angry" he replied and I just melted, couldn't speak but chewed quickly.

"So...." I managed to say through the food.

"I've come to see how you are and talk for a while" he smiled.

"Suits me" I replied, swallowing as fast as I could with a beating heart.

"I know things are troubling you at the moment, like sailing in a rough sea, it's unpleasant, but soon the waves will become less and eventually the sea around you will calm down. Life is like that, full of storms and fast currents that take us from our course, but its how we deal with those that prepares us for what might come next and makes us appreciate the calm and happy times in between."

"Oh, good, now kiss me will you?" I asked, not listening to much.

"I shouldn't, but I will as soon as you wipe your mouth" he smiled and I knew I had salad dressing all over as usual. I found a tissue and wiped fast.

"There, okay now?"

"Perfect." He took me in his arms and gave me a smooth and, oh so tasty kiss.

"That's better" I sighed.

"Yes, now where were we?"

"All at sea" I replied and he laughed.

"Yes, well, I want you to think very carefully about what I'm going to tell you."

"I'm listening."

"You must trust me and put yourself completely in my hands"

"No problem...."

"I know it's hard for you to understand, but I'm only interested in what's good for you...."

"Oh, you're good for me alright" I interrupted.

"Helen...."

"I promise, not another word, I'll just eat if that's okay."

"That's good, now first of all, don't hesitate to take over your father's business...."

"How d'you know about that for Chrissake?"

"Will you be quiet and listen?" I nodded before zipping my mouth up and Eric shook his head at that.

"What I'm going to tell you, I shouldn't and you won't believe....."

"I believe anything you say...."

"Helen!"

"Oops."

"As I was saying you won't believe, but trust me please, now, I'm an angel...."

"You sure are, honey pie...."

"Helen!"

"Oh, stop getting so shirty and kiss me some more...."

"You're not taking this seriously...."

"I am, I promise I am" I smiled at this gorgeous man with his tan and twinkling blue eyes.

"As I said, I'm an angel sent to try, and that's the operative word, try to guide you through difficult times...."

"Okay, honey, you believe that if you will, but I know your secret...."

"My secret?" he looked puzzled.

"Yup."

"What secret?"

"You're really a line man working for the phone company who's a bit of a hippie and is probably married with a couple of kids someplace...."

"I am certainly not, I'm Eric Blood Axe from Storvigga."

"Is that near Baltimore?" I interrupted with a giggle.

"No, Helen, it's near Trondheim...."

"Don't know it honey."

"Listen to me woman" he said firmly and I just loved the way he said that with his clipped accent and in such a masterful way. I could be his sex slave and no mistake.

"I'm listening, honey."

"It's best if you forget about me for the moment...."

"Never...."

"And tell your father that you'll run his business...."

"Don't start that again...."

"You will get help from a person you least expect...."

"I'm not into that....."

"Helen, it's for the best, I promise you...."

"No dice" I replied firmly.

"Very well, but you're making a mistake."

"You may think so."

"I must leave you now, but consider my guidance carefully before you say 'no' to your father and disappoint him." That took me back for a moment.

"I have done my best to guide you and now it's up to you, so, goodbye." He suddenly stood up and strode away towards the trees, leaving me open mouthed for a moment before I whispered "goodbye, angel."

I tossed the rest of my roll to the fat birds and returned to the office with my chocolate. This guy was really messing me up and I compared him unfavourably to Peter with his calm, predictable, reserve, especially when shopping.

The next few days dragged and although Pops didn't mention taking over the business again, I knew it was at the top of his agenda and he wanted my decision as soon as possible. I called Rachel to chat about things and get a feel for what she thought but she was so starry eyed about the Doctor that I couldn't get any sense out of her. I hoped he would call her soon and put us both out of our misery.

I decided to go sailing on my own and hoped that some quiet time alone on the sea would give me a moment to think things through as I was still undecided and just needed some time to myself. I called Pops at home and told him that as everything was up to date in the office and Mitch had the workshop well under control, I planned to take the afternoon off and go and think about things on board the 'Princess'. Pops sounded please at that and I guess he figured he'd soon get a decision out of me, one way or another.

It was a bright, sunny spring afternoon, once again and I quite enjoyed the drive down to Cape May. I felt as if I was bunking off from school, kinda naughty but nice and I guess life is made up of little moments like that, the trick is to learn how to enjoy them. I was soon aboard my baby and heading for the harbour entrance with the comforting sound of the auxiliary motor throbbing away in the background of my thoughts. A brisk off shore wind was blowing as I cut the motor and raised the mainsail to catch the breeze. In moments the 'Princess' was heading out at some speed into the rolling, grey green, Atlantic. The sound of the waves slapping on the bow and the rise and fall of the boat as she plunged into the ocean throwing up great showers of spray that hissed and sparkled in the sunshine almost drowned out the cry of the sea birds overhead. I felt exhilarated, free and happy.

I tried to clear my mind of all the emotional baggage that I was carrying and just concentrate on sailing and my sense of freedom. I was on my little boat, alone and hassle free, it did not matter what I looked like, or how old I was, or what I thought about the men in my life. The 'Princess' didn't care and neither did the sea, they were just there for me and me alone and I loved the feeling. The 'Princess' increased her speed as the wind gathered strength and soon the waves pounding on the bow were breaking over the boat and drenching me at the helm. God, this was rugged and I suddenly thought of Eric and wished he was with me to share the moment. I tried to stop thinking about him but couldn't and then Reece wandered into my mind followed by Peter. Oh, my God, how was it that I'd fallen in love with a line man who was unavailable; had a baby with a two timing, absolute loser and spent a relaxed and enjoyable time with a guy who was married and about to get married again to somebody else? Pops was right, I should take over the business because, as he said, it wasn't as if I was about to get married soon or anything else, whatever that meant. It was now obvious to me that I would die a lonely old woman with a lovely kid and a boat.

I made my mind up there and then, I would say 'yes' to Pops as I had nothing to lose and just at that moment a huge wave broke over the bow and absolutely drenched me to the skin in cold sea water. I had had my moments to think and the cold water had concentrated my mind wonderfully so I thought I would sail on for an hour or so in a content frame of mind, enjoying the challenge of the sea, before heading back.

Once home I called Mom and told her I'd be round later to collect Melodie, have a bite to eat and stop to have a 'quality time' chat with Pops. She sounded pleased at that and after I put the phone down I poured a Jack Daniels and toasted myself as the new business woman in Atlantic City. I had a hot soak in the tub and emerged feeling great before having another scotch to celebrate. I drove round to Mom and Pops feeling pretty pleased with myself.

"Well, honey, have you had a moment to think about it all?" asked Pops as we finished the meal. I could tell that he was impatient to know so I didn't hold out.

"Yes, Pops, I have...."

"And?" he interrupted and I saw the eagerness in his face and I glanced at Mom, who was willing me to say 'yes'.

"I'll do it...."

"Oh, my baby, that's great, absolutely great!" he said with his face beaming with pleasure.

"But I'll need help...."

"Of course, honey, I'll see you get all the help you need to be a great success, I promise you." Then Mom, with tears in her eyes, came and kissed me on my cheek. I guess she was relieved that Pops could step back now and take it easy before over-work gave him a heart attack. It happens to so many folks and I guess it's a fine balance of timing, knowing when to stop before the body packs up and leaves you stone dead. It was late when I eventually left and took Melodie home, leaving Mom and Pops in a very happy and relaxed frame of mind.

I felt pretty chipper in the office the next day and after Pops had come along in the morning and told Mitch and the guys that he was 'stepping back a little' as he put it, I moved into his office. Everybody was just great and they all said they'd help me all they could. I was pleased with that and it made me realise how much respect they all had for Pops and what he'd achieved as a good businessman and boss. It was late in the afternoon when Jack called and said Pops had told him the news, he said he was delighted and wished me well in the future. I seemed to have a bunch of nice folks around me but no man in my life. Still, I guess there's always hope.

My birthday was in a few days time and Pops had booked a table at Rolfe's for us all, including Rachel and Karen. I called the girls to make sure they could make it and they told me that they wouldn't miss it for the world. Rachel was still in plaster and waiting to hear from Doctor Gorgeous, whilst Karen was preparing a 'tender man trap' for a new partner in her law firm. Ralph was twice divorced, naturally, and that fact gave him a kinda world maturity that she thought was appropriate for a girl like her. Apparently he was quite tall, reasonably good looking, and most important of all, very wealthy. As Karen said 'after the ceremony, the love thing only lasts a year at the most, but the money goes on for ever.' She's all squared up with the realities of life, that one.

It was almost lunch time on my birthday and so far I'd had a very good day. I was just about to wander along to the deli when the phone rang and I heard Naomi answer it. My phone then rang and when I picked it up she said "there's a Peter Coltman on the line, shall I put him through?"

"Yes, please..." my heart skipped a beat in time with the line click.

"Hi, Peter, how are you?" I asked with enthusiasm.

"Fine, thanks, Helen, and you?" he sounded as pleased as I was.

"I'm good and even better that you've called me on my birthday..." I said, thinking that would surprise him and it did. After wishing me a happy day he asked about my plans and I told him all before inviting him over once again. He said he'd try and 'wangle' it and I laughed before checking if he'd be coming alone.

"Yes, it will be a business trip" he replied and I smiled knowing that if Freddie boy was picking up the tab, Miss Italian was out of the picture and boy, did I feel good about that.

"Like Paris, but without the French?" I asked whilst thanking God for that.

"Yes."

"Okay, Mister Reserved, make it soon, and call me, d'you

hear?"

"Loud and clear."

"Good."

"And Helen."

"Yup."

"Happy birthday and I send you a big sloppy kiss" Oh yes, the 'man trap' was closing rapidly on him and there was no escape.

"Why thank you, kind sir, you certainly know the way to a girl's heart" I replied whilst thinking that he needed a bit of guidance to the other parts that required attention.

We said goodbye and I knew that he'd come to Atlantic City and spend some quality time with me and, as sure as God made little apples, I was gonna make certain he saw me stripped for serious activity. I figured if Eric wasn't going to meet my needs, much as I loved him, I would have to let Peter have some action, I mean, I was getting a little frantic these days, what with the pressure of business and all.

Karen was a little late when she arrived at my house and as Melodie and I were all ready to go we didn't even stop for a coffee. Apparently the drive over from Baltimore was worse than usual because of some road works just out side Atlantic City that snarled up the Freeway in both directions. We hardly talked in the car as I hurried round to Rachel's apartment. She was already to go and busting to say something as soon as we arrived.

"You'll never believe this..." she said, her eyes sparkling with delight and I knew what was coming.

"Go on" I said.

"He called me this afternoon when his shift finished...."

"Who called, baby?" asked Karen.

"Doctor Gorgeous" I said.

"Yes, oh, my God, yes!" exclaimed Rachel.

"Who?" persisted Karen.

"Doctor Guy Williams...." replied Rachel in dreamy ecstasy.

"And?" I asked.

"He wants to take me sailing on Chesapeake Bay as soon as my plaster comes off...."

"When's that, baby?" asked Karen.

"Tonight if I could manage it" she replied and we all laughed.

"Seriously though" I said.

"Next Monday, at out patients, he's gonna check if my wrist is okay" said Rachel.

"And will it be?" asked Karen.

"You betcha" I said and we all laughed again. I was very happy to see Rachel so alive and excited, I only hoped that the good Doctor would not disappoint her.

Mom and Pops were already at Rolfe's when we all arrived. We sat in the reception area whilst a waiter brought us drinks and menus.

"Well, here's to you, birthday girl" said Pops as he raised his glass and everyone else followed on whilst Melodie gave me a big smile and a wink.

"Thanks" I murmured.

"My little girl is now a business woman, and I'm proud of her" announced Pops. Why do parents say things like 'little girl' that embarrasses you in front of friends? They all do it for some reason, God knows why.

"Business woman?" queried Karen.

"Yup, I'm retiring and my little girl is taking over" said Pops with a big smile.

"Wow, you never told us" said Karen.

"I haven't had a chance " I replied.

"True, we've been too busy talking about Doctor Gorgeous" said Karen.

"Who?" asked Mom.

"Doctor Williams, he looked after Pops when he had his accident" I replied.

"That good looking one" said Mom.

"Yup" I nodded.

"I gotta see this guy" murmured Karen.

"What about him?" asked Mom.

"He's taking me out on a date" announced Rachel as if she was broadcasting coast to coast on CNN Television.

"Really?" queried Mom.

"Yup"

"Well, good for you, Rachel, I wish Helen could find someone decent to get hooked up with, but I guess now she's got the business to run, it's pretty unlikely...." said Pops.

"Thanks, Pops" I interrupted whilst thinking 'I do love you but for Chrissake stop embarrassing me'.

"You're wrong, Joe, I can promise you that now Helen is in business, she'll attract a more mature guy, who's usually rich and good looking, although he may be dragging some ex-wives and alimony along with him" said Karen with conviction and I was so pleased with her support.

"You think so?" asked Pops.

"I know so, because I've just been dated by the new senior partner in my law firm..."

"Really?" asked Mom with a smile as she must have been thinking there was hope for me yet.

"And he wouldn't even look at a girl who wasn't at least senior management" said Karen.

"So there you go" I said with a smile and Pops looked hard at me.

"What about that strange guy you see occasionally?" asked Pops.

"D'you mean Eric or Peter" I replied enjoying the moment.

"There's more than one?" asked Mom.

"Yup, Peter called from his office in London today...."

"What?" asked Pops with a stunned look."

"And I had lunch with Eric a couple of days ago" I hammered that in and really was beginning to enjoy my birthday night out.

"What did I tell you?" asked Karen with a big smile.

"Are you ready to order yet?" asked the waiter at that precise moment.

The meal was well up to standard and when we had all finished our T-bone steaks or duck breasts with black cherry and vodka sauce, with all the salads, trimmings and then some, along with several bottles of a sweet rose wine from California, we settled for pecan pie with ice creams and coffee. At the very end, Pops had arranged for a birthday cake and the waiter brought it to our table and presented with a flourish whilst everyone sang 'happy birthday'. I looked around at everybody at the table and saw happiness and pleasure in their faces as I smiled and blew out the candles with one blow and they all clapped.

The wine had loosened us up, especially Karen, who had had

more than her fair share, and she started telling stories about her Aunt Mame, who lived in Boston. We all laughed as Karen revealed the truth from behind the façade of correctness in Boston society. Aunt Mame had three husbands and outlived them all, collecting a hefty inheritance and life insurance pay out after each had 'passed on' as she described it. We all were amused by the stories and she finished up by telling us that husband number three, Albert Hunsecker, a man much older than Mame, expired on his wedding night just after he had consummated the marriage in the bridal suite of the Adelphi Hotel, in Colorado Springs. Aunt Mame told Karen that 'Albert came and went!' We all laughed at that and whilst Mom looked a little straight faced, Pops roared out loud.

After saying goodnight to Mom and Pops we drove back to Rachel's apartment where we settled down with coffee and brandy. Melodie fell asleep on the couch whilst we girls got down to serious talk about everything in general and men in particular.

"So, tell us about Ralph then" said Rachel.

"Where shall I begin...." Karen said.

"You choose" I interrupted.

"Okay, he came to the office about a month ago from a law firm in San Francisco...."

"West coast to east coast, quite a move" I said.

"Yup, apparently he had been pretty successful over there and made a pile that any girl would be proud to help spend" said Karen.

"I like him already" said Rachel with a smile.

"What made him decide to leave?" I asked.

"It seems that Jerry Buxton, one of our partners, who's due to retire, heard about Ralph and recommended him as a partner to the others, a kinda replacement for himself, and they okayed it, the rumour is, that he was made an offer he couldn't refuse."

"You don't say"

"Yup, but personally, I think Ralph wanted to put the whole continent between him and his ex's."

"Really?" I asked.

"Troublesome are they?" enquired Rachel.

"Not too bad, Ralph tells me he's got alimony down to a manageable amount, after all, he's a smart lawyer..."

"Sure."

"And both ex's have got homes out of it...." said Karen.

"And kids?" asked Rachel.

"Two, one from each marital disaster, a boy and a girl..."

"Are you planning to be Mrs Ralph number three?" I asked.

"I think it's about time that I brought some regularity into my life, and marriage can do that you know, regular bedtimes with a regular guy after a regular night out...."

"And regular expensive shopping in the mall" interrupted Rachel.

"That goes without saying, honey, it comes with the territory" replied Karen.

"I can't imagine you married" I said.

"Neither can I" said Karen.

"What are the chances with Ralph?" asked Rachel.

"Well, it's looking good, so far, but I had to frighten off Angie Ward after she first set eyes on him, she's head of corporate finance, a wayward divorcee with big boobs and an 'oh so tight' ass" replied Karen in a firm tone.

"No other competition then?" I asked.

"Nope, not that I'm aware off, and boy, is my ear close to the ground" replied Karen.

"So, it's an easy run home now then?" asked Rachel.

"Not yet honey, he's pretty well hooked, but he's a little nervous of commitment, just at the moment" replied Karen.

"Tell me about it" I said.

"Yeah, so update us on Eric and the London guy, Peter" said Karen.

"Well, it's like this..."

"Both shy?" asked Karen with a grin.

"Yup, Eric is gorgeous, and he's the one I could settle for" I said.

"Then go for him, honey" said Karen.

"I'm trying, I really am..."

"But the problem is that nobody's seen him yet, so he's really shy or Helen's just imagining him" interrupted Rachel. She touched a raw nerve with that and I suddenly felt embarrassed. Then I thought, as Naomi had seen him with me on the park bench and Mrs Dawson had caught him skulking around my home, Eric was not a figment of my imagination, he was real and a good kisser on top of that. I was just about to tell the girls when Karen asked "so how do you meet?"

"He just shows up, kinda unexpectedly" I replied.

"I'd think I'd have to move him down my list, he sounds like a guy you can't control, and honey, that's just not a viable situation these days" said Karen.

"So, what about Peter?" asked Rachel.

"He's so cute, very English and too reserved really, but he'd make a dependable husband" I said thinking of his easy charm.

"Sounds good" said Karen.

"He's married, but getting a divorce, but then, he's already got the next wife all lined up, so, he's sort of between wives at the moment" I said lamely.

"He sounds all 'buts', that's the time to hit him hard, get him over here, take him to Rolfe's, show him the town and then get him spread eagled someplace romantic and unhook the sex beast in him" said Karen with a smile.

"That's what you'd do isn't it?" asked Rachel.

"You bet honey, you bet, now how about another brandy?" replied Karen as she held up her empty glass. Rachel smiled and poured more of the golden liquid into Karen's glass before topping me up.

"And what about Reece these days?" asked Karen.

"Don't mention him" I replied.

"That creep is one of the few guys that I know that has had a personality bypass for certain" said Karen and we all laughed.

"Yup, he's nothing but a pain in the butt" I replied as I shook my head.

"See him much?" asked Karen.

"Nope, but he did take Melodie to the fair at Burlington recently" I replied.

"Good of him to show some interest in his kid" said Karen in an offhand tone.

"Yup."

"Helen doesn't seem to have much luck with the men she picks" said Rachel.

"Believe me, Rachel, I've had no luck with the men I've picked until now" said Karen, Rachel and I smiled at that.

The conversation drifted on and we heard all about Doctor Gorgeous and the planned boating trip on Chesapeake Bay before we decided to call it a night. Karen stayed the night at Rachel's and I drove home slowly with my sleepy daughter after a great birthday.

The next few days were busy at work and Pops came in for a day and went through some of the ordering system for parts from GM and Ford. I was happy when he was about and I spent time with him and Mitch in the workshop seeing how we repaired the wrecked autos using alignment jigs. I had never taken much notice before but now that I was officially in charge of the business, everything changed. It was very interesting and I was impressed by the care and attention that went into every repair.

The boys in the paint shop were magicians and it was great to see how they primed up repaired parts and finished them out in colour to perfection. I didn't think that Benoir Paints 'quick system' would have a place in my business as the guys in the paint shop were doing a great job and, as the saying goes, 'if it ain't broke don't fix it'. There is a lot of craftsmanship in making a good auto repair and I was impressed by what I'd seen and my confidence grew as each day passed.

At the end of the week I relaxed in a hot tub with a Jack Daniels and was just about to have another soap all over when the phone rang. Melodie answered it and I couldn't make out who was calling. She then came into the bathroom and said "Mom, it's Reece…."

"Oh, my God…." I said.

"He wants to talk to you, he says it's important."

"Okay, honey, tell him I'm in the tub and I'll be out in a moment." Melodie rushed off whilst I cursed and got out of my warm bath and wrapped a towel around myself.

"Reece, what do you want?"

"Hi, babe, sorry to get you out of the tub, but I've got to talk to you."

"Well you're talking" I said firmly.

"Yeah, now can we meet up soon?"

"What for?"

"I want to talk business opportunities with you."

"What?"

"Business opportunities…."

"I heard you the first time, now then what's this all about, Reece?"

"Now you've taken over Pop's business, I thought that…."

"How do you know about that?" I demanded angrily.

"Naomi told me when I called your office today…."

"Oh my God!" I interrupted feeling angry at the stupid kid letting Reece, of all people, know about it.

"So, I thought if we could meet up, I could lay out my plans…."

"Lay out plans? You must be kidding, Reece."

"I'm not, babe, I know I could be a real asset to the business, I mean I'd be happy to take a reduced share but in time I'm sure I could work up to be an equal partner…."

"Over my dead body, Reece, over my dead body!" I slammed the phone down and went back to the bathroom with tears in my eyes.

CHAPTER 11

PETER'S MOTHER

After Janet had gone to work I called Adams, the estate agents in Wantage, and spoke to a Mr Carter, who promised to come out and value the property before putting it on the market. He said the housing market was buoyant at the moment and he expected a quick sale as our house was ideal for 'first time' buyers. I was pleased to hear that and arrangements were made for him to come the next morning. I felt satisfied that I had started the ball rolling with the divorce and now the house sale. I planned to live with my mother in Reading before the major change in my life when I moved to Italy and married Sophia.

Everything was gently sliding into place for a very happy and successful future for me with my lovely Italian fiancé. I would be bloody glad to leave the sales pressure and complaints of work behind me but would miss Freddie and the other boys in the sales team. The only fly in the ointment was Ashton and I was concerned that he was taking Sophia to Paris 'on business'. I didn't trust the old fart for one moment, but I decided to keep my thoughts and fears to myself so that I did not upset Sophia. Least said, soonest mended. I had kept my plans for the future a secret but now decided that I would have to tell my mother and then take Sophia to see her. I expected a lot of opposition, especially when I announced that I was going to marry her and live in Milan. Mother did not approve of foreigners in general and I knew that it would be an uphill struggle to convince her that Sophia was the one for me.

I set off for Reading, did a few sales calls and bought a 'teach yourself Italian' book in Smith's, before I popped into see my mother to tell her that Janet and I were going to get a divorce.

"I'm not surprised, not surprised at all, you were never suited and I told you that before you got married" said mother before she sipped her tea.

"I knew you didn't approve of her...."

"Wasn't a question of approval, I just knew that you were not suited, that's all" she interrupted.

"Well, it's all over now, bar the shouting, and I'm putting the house up for sale straight away…."

"That's a bit premature isn't it?"

"Don't think so, Mum…."

"You're not divorced yet."

"I know, but my solicitor said the divorce would all go through quite quickly as we both wanted to separate" I replied.

"Where are you going to live?"

"I thought with you, if that's alright…."

"With me?" she asked in a shocked tone.

"With you…" She remained silent for a few moments.

"Well only for a short time, just until you find a place of your own" she said firmly.

"Yes, it would be for just a few weeks…."

"Oh, that's alright then" she smiled with relief.

"And, I've met someone else…."

"That was quick" she interrupted.

"Yes, she's a lovely person and I'd like you to meet her…."

"Oh, really?" she queried.

"Yes."

"What's her name?"

"Sophia."

"She sounds foreign to me."

"She's Italian, Mum…."

"I thought so, where on earth did you find her?"

"Actually, I gave her a lift…."

"What?"

"She and her friend were hitch hiking……"

"You picked her up on the side of the road, for God's sake?" she asked angrily.

"Well, yes, sort of…."

"Sort of? You either did or you didn't!" she exclaimed as she put her cup down on the occasional table.

"Yes, actually, I did…."

"And what type of woman gets picked up by the side of the road, I wonder?"

"Well, she's from a very good family…."

"Sounds it."

"Look, please meet her, I know if you do, you'll like her…."

"That remains to be seen."

"Please."

"Oh, very well then, bring her for tea next Sunday" replied Mother in a resigned tone.

Mr Carter arrived mid morning the next day and armed with his clipboard he toured the house. He went around tapping walls and stroking paintwork, as if he really knew what he was doing, before announcing a 'realistic price' for a quick sale. It was a little lower than I expected but if it sold for the price he quoted then we'd make a profit of thirty thousand over what we paid for it when we bought it new. After clearing the mortgage it would leave about forty thousand to be shared between Janet and me. I thought that would be a nice little amount to start a new life with Sophia in Milan, with presumably everything being paid for by her parents. I would have to clear my overdraft and the credit cards, but that still should leave me plenty to relax and enjoy life for a while.

I thanked Mr Carter and confirmed that Adams could be the sole agent and a quick sale would be appreciated. When he had left, with smiles and promises of an instant sale, I phoned Mr Oakwood at Jessups and asked if I could be divorced and free by September. He told me that was unlikely but he would do his best and confirmed that he was in contact with Janet's solicitors, Maxwell and Jones. There was nothing I could do now but wait and I reasoned if we couldn't get married in September it would have to be later in the year.

The next few days came and went and I managed to notch up quite a few sales whilst dealing with the usual run of colour complaints. I phoned Sophia every night and told her that we were going out for the day on Sunday ending up at Mother's for tea. She seemed pleased but reminded me she was going to Paris on Monday with Ashton and didn't want to be too late getting home. I tried not to get angry but I boiled up inside, the bloody man was affecting our lives too much.

On Friday evening, Freddie called me at home.

"Are you busy with anything special on Monday afternoon?" he asked.

"No, boss, I was just going to do some local calls in Oxford, nothing planned."

"That's good, I want you to come to Berkeley Square for a meeting with George and me, at three."

"Okay, what's it about?" I asked anxiously, thinking that it might be bad news.

"Nothing to worry about, Peter, George wants you for a special project and I think you'll find it interesting….."

"Come on, Freddie, give me a clue" I interrupted.

"No, you'll have to wait until Monday, dear boy, and don't be late!"

"I'll be there."

"See you then." And he was gone leaving me intrigued.

I arrived at Highgate mid-morning on Sunday and waited only a few minutes for Sophia to appear. She looked as lovely as ever in a light blue trouser suit over a white lace blouse and her hair and makeup were just so.

"I thoughta I'd better look good for your mother" she said after I had complimented her on her appearance. I kissed her and smiled.

"You always look good" I said.

"Thanker you, now where are you taking me firsta?"

"To a lovely little restaurant I know on the river at Wallingford" I replied and she smiled.

"Thatsa very nice."

"It is and I know you'll like it" I replied. We set off towards the motorway and no sooner had we joined the weekend traffic heading out of London, when Sophia started.

"I don'ta want to be late back, darling….."

"Why not?" I interrupted.

"Because, I have so much to do before I go to Paris tomorrow with Ray."

"You told me that you're only going for a few days" I said touchily.

"Si, but I've gota things to do."

"Like what?"

"Wash my hair, have a bath and pack all my thingsa" she replied.

"All that for a couple of days?"

"Si, you have to be a woman to understand" she replied but I was getting more than annoyed.

"Okay, what time do you want to be back?"

"About six o'clocka."

"I tell you, Sophia, I'm not happy about all this."

"All whata?"

"You and this old man Ashton."

"You're silly, I'ma not interested in him, but I'ma learning a lot, he's a very clever businessman and…."

"I'm sure his wife is very proud of him…."

"You're jealous…."

"I don't trust him…."

"Oh, Peter…."

"I only care about us and I know that he's after you, I've seen the way he looks at you."

"Of course he looks at me, I'ma working for him and he's paying me for what I do…."

"Sophia, you just don't understand, I promise you, a man knows when another man is after his woman, it's a primeval instinct!"

"Darling, you're wrong, believe me."

"Okay, I'll believe you but be warned…."

"Si, I'ma warned."

"And I don't want to talk about him anymore today, okay?"

"Si, okay."

We had a relaxed lunch at the little restaurant on Wallingford bridge and Sophia was intrigued by the eccentric lady who owned the place and her bulldog. After roast beef and Yorkshire pudding, followed by apple and blackberry pie with ice cream, we needed a walk along the bank of the river. We talked about the future and Sophia told me more about her family and they were indeed, very wealthy. Her parents were pleased that we were getting married and they were already talking about lots of grandchildren. It all sounded to good to be true and I was sure that if I could keep Ashton away from Sophia, then the future looked very bright.

We left Wallingford at three and drove to Mother's in Reading. I was a little anxious when I introduced Sophia, but Mother was very polite and reserved. If she didn't approve of Sophia she certainly didn't show it. Mother was all smiles and gentle conversation as she poured tea from her silver teapot whilst offering slices of her home made fruit cake. She asked a lot of questions and did not seem unduly perturbed at me moving to Italy, which surprised me. When the mantelpiece clock struck five I decided we had to leave so that I could make Highgate by six. Mother understood and kissed us both whilst telling Sophia that she hoped she would come again soon.

As we returned to London, we both were in a buoyant mood and I felt more relaxed about the trip to Paris. Sophia said they were coming back Wednesday afternoon and I could call for her at seven and take her out for dinner at our favourite restaurant in Harrow. We kissed for some while and said our 'goodbyes' before she slipped away and into the house.

On Monday morning, I called up a few customers who were having problems with colour matches or flaking primer and tried to settle their complaints with assurances that the lab boys from Stratford would come down and sort things out. Hopefully, I had done some good work before I left for Reading to find out what Mother thought of Sophia. I planned to arrive about lunchtime when I was sure of tea and sandwiches before I set off to Berkeley Square for the meeting at three.

"So, what did you think of her?" I asked as I bit into a chicken sandwich.

"She's a very pretty girl" Mother replied as she sipped her tea.

"Isn't she just" I smiled and added "but what did you think?"

"Well...." Mother paused and I heard the alarm bells ringing loud and clear.

"Yes?"

"I hope you'll be very happy with her, but I doubt it."

"What?"

"She's not the one for you." Mother said and I thought she sounded like Eric.

"How do you know?" I asked angrily.

"A woman's intuition" she replied.

"But I love her and she loves me" I blurted out.

"Possibly, but I think she'll deceive you...."

"Never!"

"Never say 'never', dear...."

"You don't know what you're talking about, Mother, you really don't" and as I said that I thought of Ashton and my heart sank into my boots.

"We'll see" replied Mother in a calm tone before asking "more tea, dear?"

I arrived at Berkeley Square just before three and smiled at Paula as I knocked on Freddie's office door and marched in.

"Ah, there you are, dear boy, come and sit down, George is upstairs with J.B. at the moment, but he'll be down shortly." I smiled and sat down opposite Freddie and asked "come on, boss, what's this all about?"

"Just be patient and wait for George, dear boy" he replied with a smile and I knew it had to be something good when Freddie called me 'dear boy'.

"Okay" I grinned.

"So, how are sales?"

"Good, I've done quite well over the last week or so....."

"Making up for your holiday in Milan then?" he smiled.

"Indeed."

"So how was it in Italy?"

"Wonderful, everything was wonderful" I replied as the door opened and George Paton rushed in with his round face wreathed in its usual smile. He looked dapper in a light grey suit with a bright red tie and matching handkerchief flowing out of the breast pocket. I stood as he hurried past me and then 'shooed' Freddie from his executive seat. He sat down in it and bumped up and down and then said with a grin "this is comfy, I might pinch this off you, Freddie!" My boss laughed and I knew that George was on top form as Freddie pulled up a chair next to George and smiled.

"Now then, Peter, Freddie may have told you that I've a special project in mind for you" said George.

"Yes, sir, he did mention it" I replied.

"Who said communication was dead in this company?" he said with a smile and Freddie and I laughed.

"Not me" replied Freddie.

"Seriously now, as you may know, Peter, we've been

negotiating with the Bradley Ponting Consortium in the States...."

"Yes" I nodded.

"And J.B. and I have been backwards and forwards to Chicago for no end of meetings about a proposed technology and sales merger...."

"Right."

"Well, at last it seems fairly certain that it will all go ahead" said George with a smile.

"It could be a very good deal for us" said Freddie.

"Freddie, it will be a very good deal because we will make it so" said George.

"Yes, George" replied Freddie.

"So, this is what I want you to do, Peter" said George as he concentrated on me.

"Yes, sir."

"I want you to come off sales for the moment and be our link man in Chicago...."

"Really?" I asked.

"Yes, you have good product knowledge and I want feed back on how their finishes compare with ours, from the sales and marketing point of view...."

"It's a great opportunity" grinned Freddie.

"Yes, and working alongside you on the technical and formulation side, will be Jeff Harrison from the lab at Stratford" said George with a smile.

"You know Jeff, don't you?" asked Freddie.

"Of course" I nodded as the thoughts of leaving Beauclare Paints to start a new life in Milan became confused in my mind.

"Okay, now I want you to go out to Chicago the first week in June, your contact is a man called Hector Flanagan, Freddie has been dealing with him, and you'll be out there, first of all, for about ten days" said George.

"Yes, sir" I replied as my brain raced.

"Freddie will fill you in on all the details, okay?"

"Right" I smiled anxiously as George glanced at his wristwatch.

"Must go, another meeting, it's all meetings these days, so good luck, Peter and I'll see you when you get back" said George as he stood up and left the office like a small tornado.

"Well, what do you think of that?" asked Freddie as he sank back into his executive chair.

"Unbelievable" I replied.

"It's a great chance for you" he said.

"Yes" I nodded.

"And it'll give you a break from sales."

"Yes."

"And that's good, because you're a 'below average' salesman" said Freddie.

"Oh, thanks" I replied.

"Well you are and that's a fact."

"Okay, don't rub it in." Freddie ignored that and called through to Paula for two cups of tea before studying papers on his desk.

"Now George wants you to go out on Monday the third of June and you'll be met at Chicago International and taken to your hotel. You'll have you first meeting with Hector at Bradley's on the Tuesday, and Jeff will already be there." said Freddie.

"Right."

"Now it did occur to me that you might like to stop off on your way out at Atlantic City, to see Jack and Helen…."

"That would be good" I smiled.

"Okay, I'll see if we can book a flight there arriving on the Friday before, so you can spend the weekend with them before going onto Chicago."

"Thanks, Freddie."

"You'll have to pay for your own expenses and any hotel bills for that weekend, because officially you're not due in Chicago until the Monday and the finance department upstairs would never agree to any other expenses" said Freddie.

"That's alright, boss."

"If you let Helen know in plenty of time, you might get to stay with her, it would save you money and you might get your leg over into the bargain" he grinned.

"You're so romantic" I replied.

"I know" he smiled as Paula arrived with the tea. We remained silent as we sipped the tea and my thoughts were cascading down from the surprise of my new job to how it would affect just about everything. I then thought about money.

"Do I get any extra salary for this new project?" I asked.

"Well, not really, because it's a sort of sideways promotion, you see...."

"No, I don't see, Freddie, I am going to be away from home and travelling a lot in my own time" I interrupted.

"Okay, I'll see if George will agree to another five hundred a year...."

"That's not much!"

"It's better than a kick in the bollocks!" he replied loudly.

"True, but it's still not much" I replied and he grinned.

"Okay, I'll see what I can do, but no promises mind."

"Right, now, as we're busy saving money, I'll take your advice and phone Helen...."

"Okay, but keep it dead short" he said. I nodded, picked up his phone and pressed nine for an outside line before dialling Helen's number. The sweet little voice answered and when I told her who was calling she put me straight through.

"Hi, Peter, how are you?"

"Fine thanks, Helen, and you?"

"I'm good, so, it's nice to hear from you."

"Yes, I've got some news" I said.

"What is it?"

"I'm coming out to Atlantic City on the thirty first of May, and I wondered if we could meet?"

"Are you kidding me?"

"No, I'm not."

"Oh, my God, of course we can meet up" she said excitedly.

"Great."

"What time does your flight get in and how long are you staying?"

"I don't know the flight time yet, but I'm only in Atlantic City for a couple of days because I have to be in Chicago on the third of June...."

"Okay, let me know the time of the flight and I'll meet you...."

"That's very kind of you."

"Hey, what are friends for?"

"To be there for you."

"Right answer."

"And I'd be very grateful if you could book a small hotel room for a couple of nights...."

"Don't you worry about that, I'll take care of everything."

"Thanks, now I'll have to go now as I'm calling from Freddie's office and he's worried about the phone bill" she laughed at that.

"Okay, give him my best wishes, and I'll talk to you soon."

"Bye, Helen." I replaced the receiver and said "there, all fixed up." Freddie grinned and asked "what will your wife and fiancé say about all of this?"

"I don't know Freddie, but I'll find out in due course."

It was Wednesday morning and I was just about to set off for the day with planned calls in the Newbury area when the phone rang.

"Hello, darling, it'sa me, calling you from Paris" said Sophia in her lilting voice.

"My darling, how are you?"

"I'ma fine, justa fine."

"Good" I replied while sensing I was about to hear something unpleasant.

"Looka, darling, there's been a change of plan….."

"Oh, yes" I said, knowing what was coming.

"We have to fly out to Turkey straighta away for an important meeting with the mayor in Izmir."

"Really" I replied in a dead pan tone.

"Si, I'ma sorry, darling, but Ray says it'sa very important."

"Does he now."

"Si, I'ma so sorry."

"When will you be back?"

"I don't a know yet, in a few days, probably."

"A very long meeting then."

"We have to go to the site of a new factory as well, its'a all very complicated."

"I'm sure it is where Ashton is concerned."

"Darling, don'ta be cross…."

"Well, I am, Sophia, you said you'd be back tonight and now all the nonsense with that old man starts all over again, I tell you, Sophia, he's after you and he's going to wreck our lives!"

"No, no, darling, he wont, I promise you, now I must go, Ray is waiting for me, I'll call you from Turkey, bye."

She was gone and I was so angry again, because the old bastard had pulled the same trick once more and I'd let him get away with

195

it. I somehow knew then that he would destroy us and I felt very sad and deeply upset. I had found, by chance, a lovely woman whom I adored and wanted to marry, and I knew deep down that another man would take her away.

The following days dragged and I tried to concentrate on work but found it very difficult. Two young couples came to look over the house one evening, but they didn't seem that interested in the place and left quickly without asking many questions. Then Sophia called on the Friday night and told me that she wouldn't be back until the following Wednesday. It seemed there were 'complications' and 'unexpected developments' keeping Ashton in Izmir. I didn't believe a word of it and was sure that the end of our relationship was close at hand. I looked at Janet on the settee, munching chocolate and I despised her and Ashton, both of whom had come into my life and made it very unhappy.

The weekend seemed unending and the monotony was only broken by a couple who came to view the house at lunchtime on the Sunday. They seemed nice, reasonable people and I told them that there was no upward chain as Janet and I were going our separate ways. They appeared quite interested and as they were first time buyers it could be a fairly straight forward sale. When they went I felt hopeful that they would buy the place; they said they had one other property to look at, but they would let me know on Monday.

I drove up to the downs and wandered along in the afternoon sunshine hoping I wouldn't see Eric. Janet had gone to her mother's for the day and it felt good to be on my own. My mind churned through all the latest developments in my life and I felt as if I was sailing along in a very thick fog, not being able to see my way ahead. No matter how I tried, I could not see any upside or silver lining to my present situation, although the trip to America in a couple of weeks time would certainly take my mind off things here. I did not see Eric, thank God, and I went home feeling better after a long walk in the fresh, open air.

Things started well on Monday when Mr Carter phoned and told me that the couple who had viewed the house yesterday had made an offer. I was delighted and accepted it without hesitation before calling Janet at work and telling her. She was surly and non committal, which was what I expected, still, the dye was cast and there was no going back. The day went downhill from then on with as many complaints over colour matches as there were over poor deliveries in the Reading area. It seemed that every paint shop I called at had a problem and by the end of the day I felt relieved that it was all over and I looked forward to the American trip as relief from the pressure of it all. Tuesday was marginally better but Wednesday took a dive when Sophia called first thing and Janet answered it, before handing the phone over to me with a stony face.

"Your woman friend for you" she scowled.

"Hello, Peter here."

"Hello, darling, I'ma calling you from the hotel, I'ma afraid I'ma not coming back until Friday, okay?"

"Not really, but I'll wait and see you then, if you actually arrive...."

"Si, I will, I promise" she interrupted.

"Okay, call me when you're back."

"Si, I promise."

"I'll see you sometime" I said.

"Si, and if I'ma too late on Friday, you can take me out for dinner on Saturday."

"Yes, okay."

"Bye, darling."

"Bye." As I put the phone down I mentally gave up and was convinced that this was the beginning of the end of Sophia and me, I felt utterly wretched.

The rest of the week was a kaleidoscope of complaints and small orders whilst I rushed around the area trying to improve my monthly figures. Friday came at last and Sophia did not call as promised, which somehow, did not surprise me. It was Saturday lunch time when she phoned and told me she was back at Highgate.

"Come and see me tonight, Peter."

"Okay, about seven as usual?"

"Si, I'll be ready" she replied and the tone of her voice told me that all was not well. I arrived at Highgate just after seven and

Sophia came out almost immediately. She kissed me when she sat beside me in the car, but the kiss was light and reserved.

"Where are youa taking me?"

"The steak house in Richmond, okay?"

"Si, thatsa okay."

"Now, tell me all about your adventures in Paris and Izmir" I said as I drove off. By the time we arrived at Richmond I had heard enough about Ashton and how wonderful he was to last me two lifetimes. I tried to steer the conversation away from this paragon of perfection but Sophia would not let him go. Even when I told her about my new job in the States she seemed uninterested and went back into her mantra of 'what Ray said' and 'what Ray did' and 'what he did next'. The meal was very good as usual but I did not feel that hungry and I sensed something was coming that would upset me. She waited until we arrived back outside her house before she told me.

"Peter, I thinka that you are a very nice person, a very gooda person, but, I can't marry you...."

"Why not?" I asked in a whisper.

"Because, its'a big world out there and being with Ray has made me realise whata I coulda be missing if I get married too soona...."

"Oh, really...."

"Ray thinksa that too many people get married when they are too young, he says that'sa why there are so many divorces...."

"Well, bollocks to what Ashton thinks, I love you and want to marry you and you loved me and wanted to marry me before you met him!"

"Peter, its'a no good, I've made up my minda, Ray has asked me to work for him and travel the worlda, opening up new business....."

"Oh, yes?"

"Si, he needs me and he says that if I help him he can build a business as big as my Poppa's...."

"And what does his wife think about all this?"

"I don'ta know."

"Have you slept with him?" I asked and looked into her eyes which began to water and she whispered "si." I didn't go mad straight away but asked "when you betrayed me did you think, as you looked at his old, scraggy face, 'this is the most wonderful man in the world', or did you think 'I'm now going to betray Peter, the person who loves me more than life itself and when he finds out, it will destroy him?' She burst out crying and before I could stop her, she leapt from the car and ran to the front door and disappeared inside. I slammed both hands onto the steering wheel again and again as the tears coursed down my cheeks, shouting "the old bastard has won!... he has won!... he has won and he has destroyed us!... God, I could kill him!"

The next few days were dream like and it was on the Wednesday that I decided to take some action. I phoned Highgate and spoke to Mrs Parker, who, without much reticence, gave me Ashton's home number. I hoped that his wife would be in and I was in luck.

"Hello, Mrs Ashton?"

"Yes...."

"It's Peter Coltman here, Sophia's fiancé, we met at the Parker's a while ago...."

"Yes, I remember."

"I'm sorry to tell you that I've got some bad news for you."

"Oh?"

"Yes, your husband is having an affair with Sophia, my fiancé."

"I'm not surprised, dear, she joins a long list...."

"What?"

"I think it's an illness with him...."

"And you tolerate it?"

"It's a case of having to, I gave up with him a long time ago and I have my own life and interests now."

"I can't believe it."

"Well, that's how it is" she replied in a matter of fact tone.

"Can't you stop him?"

"No, besides why should I? If these women are stupid enough to fall for his 'big business' talk as he flashes money about that he hasn't got, well, more fool them."

"You stagger me."

"I'm sorry for you, dear, and my advice is to give up now because if you don't, you'll make yourself very unhappy."

"Why do you say that?"

"Because, I know him, he's a cunning little bastard that'll undermine you and anyone else who gets in his way, I know how he operates and believe me, he's a past master at deception." I wanted to die when I heard that.

"My, God" I whispered.

"It won't last that long with your fiancé, he'll finish with her when either he goes bankrupt again or finds another young thing to chase into bed."

"I just can't believe what your saying to me."

"Some of them think he'll marry them but what he doesn't tell them is that everything is in my name, the house, business, car, the lot, so when he goes under, the creditors can't get anything, he owns nothing, it's all mine and I'm keeping it, so, there's no hope for your fiancé, I'm afraid she's lost."

"Good God, what an evil, manipulative bastard your husband is."

"Exactly, dear, and I'm sorry that it's come to this for you, you're not the first life he's ruined and you certainly won't be the last."

"I am lost for words."

"It's Sophia I feel sorry for, but never mind, that's life, I'm afraid."

"It seems so."

"Goodbye, dear." She hung up abruptly, but I suppose there was nothing else to say. I called the Parker's to speak to Sophia but was told that she had gone out with Ashton and was not expected back tonight.

I could not bring myself to phone Sophia again and I felt desolate and dead to the core of my being. I kept asking myself 'how could this happen to me?' but there was no answer and my mind was a blank. I took the next afternoon off and went up to White Horse Hill, parked the car and wandered along to the mound where I had sat with Eric when we first met. I thought of him and began to seriously wonder who he really was. I sat and gazed over the rolling fields below and tried to think clearly when I heard something behind me and I turned to see Eric striding down from the hill top towards me with a big smile on his face. I turned away and waited for him to sit beside me.

"Hello, Peter."

"You're late, too bloody late!"

"What for?"

"For me, that's what for! You say you're a guardian angel, well why is it that you're always too late to guard against something bloody awful happening to me?"

"I know, I do have some problems in that area, but I am trying to improve, believe me."

"Not good enough, Eric, I reckon you're an under achiever and you'd better give up being an angel and go back to being a Viking."

"Funny you should mention that because that's what Gunther said to me."

"I should take his advice if I were you."

"I can't do that I'm afraid, I have to go on with my missions."

"In that case, you're going to let a lot of people down" I replied.

"I'm determined to improve" he said with a smile.

"Well, if you are my guardian angel, you can show me how good you are by getting Sophia out of the clutches of that old bastard, Ashton, and back to me" I said whilst looking hard at him. He turned away from me and gazed out to the horizon remaining quiet for several moments.

"I can't do that for you, Peter, I'm sorry."

"Why not?"

"Because your life is going in another direction without her."

"But I don't want that...."

"I know you don't want that at the moment, but I promise you, it's for the best."

"I don't think it's for the best...."

"Well it is, I assure you."

"Why can't you do something about Ashton?" I demanded.

"I'm sorry to say that he's one of the 'life wreckers' in this lifetime and cannot be stopped...."

"Life wrecker? You can say that again!" I exclaimed and added "who the devil are these people?"

"These are people who, by their selfish actions, wreck other peoples lives, and in many cases, totally destroy them, they are murderers, moral thieves, adulterers, rapists, violent men who beat their wives and children, abusers of all kinds...."

"And what are you doing about it?" I interrupted.

"I can do nothing, except try and guide you away from such people."

"So you let them get away with it?"

"No, I promise you that there is a balance in all things and these people suffer to exactly the same degree as the suffering they inflict...."

"Oh, yeah?"

"I assure you, it's too complicated to explain how at this moment, but whatever Ashton has done to you and Sophia he will be made to suffer the same desperate unhappiness that you feel."

"I'll believe it when I see it."

"You'll never see it."

"Pity."

"Now, you're going to America this week...."

"How do you know that?" I interrupted.

"I know because, as I keep telling you, I'm your guardian angel and know everything, and you only have to think of me and I will be with you" he smiled and I was genuinely frightened.

"Oh, God" I murmured.

"No, only an angel" he smiled.

"I don't know whether to believe you or not."

"It doesn't matter, Peter, because I will always be here."

"So, what now?"

"You will go to America and meet Helen again and if you just relax and let things take their course, I promise you that you will find unexpected happiness there."

"I look forward to it" I replied unenthusiastically.

"Good, you'll have a safe journey" he smiled.

"Because you know, I suppose?"

"Yes, I do, and it's such fun just 'knowing'" he smiled and then stood up.

"Goodbye, Peter, I'll see you next in America" and with that he strode off, back up the hill, leaving me totally confused and as frightened as ever. The Tahitians have a saying 'either you eat life or life eats you' and I felt as if I was being eaten.

For the rest of the week I kept busy and tried not to think of

Sophia but hoped deep down that she would call me; the call never came. At the weekend the couple who planned to buy the house phoned and asked if they could look around once more. That was arranged for the Sunday and when they came Janet showed them everything they wanted to see and answered all their questions in a pleasant and friendly manner. It reminded me of how she used to talk to me when we first met and I wondered 'what makes people change? Other people, I guess.

I called Freddie on the Wednesday and he told me that my sales area was going to be split up between Doug Henshaw, who covered the Bistol area and Tony Barnes who was responsible for the Home Counties. I was happy about that because both of them were good salesmen and I knew my patch would be in safe hands until I returned to sales.

Freddie said that Paula had managed to book a flight on Friday, departing at two o'clock from Terminal 3 at Heathrow, scheduled to arrive at two fifteen, local time, in Atlantic City. He wished me luck and told me to come into Berkeley Square on Friday morning to collect my ticket and leave my car in the staff car park to keep costs down. I was pleased at the arrangements and called Helen to let her know. She sounded excited and promised that she would be there to meet me and I didn't have to worry about a thing because everything was taken care of.

Thursday came and went and I only made a few calls in the morning before returning home at lunch time and getting packed. That night I thought of phoning Sophia but decided against it, Ashton's wife was right, there was no way that I could beat such a devious bastard without going down a long, sad, road of frustration and eventual despair. Sophia had made her decision and I had decided to walk away from the woman with whom I had fallen deeply in love. As they say, better to have loved and lost than never to have loved at all.

Janet appeared mildly interested that I was going to America for a couple of weeks and asked what she should tell my 'lady friend' if she called. When I told her that it was very unlikely that she would ever phone again, Janet seemed surprised. I gave her the telephone number of the hotel in Chicago and told her that I would not be there until Monday, so if anything urgent cropped up, it would have to wait until then.

I set off the next morning for London, feeling relieved that I was going away for a couple of weeks so I might have a chance to think things through. When I arrived at Berkeley Square, Freddie had gone off to a meeting at Stratford so Paula wished me good luck as she handed me my tickets and travellers cheques in exchange for my car keys. A taxi took me to Heathrow and arrived at Terminal 3 Departures in plenty of time to get checked in.

Eventually I boarded the 747 that was going to fly me to the States and settling down into an aisle seat, I read the safety notice whilst other passengers sorted themselves out around me. I felt a tingle of excitement as the aircraft was pushed back and then, under its own power taxied to the end of the runway. We all waited in silence until the captain received clearance from the tower, the throttles were opened up and the mighty aircraft began to roll down the runway, gathering speed all the time and then after a final bump, it was airborne and I was on my way to Atlantic City.

After a mediocre meal and several cups of coffee I settled down to watch an in flight movie. I chose the musical 'Chicago' as I felt that was very apt and I liked to watch the dancers. Those girls have got great bodies and they certainly know how to show them off. At the end of the film I dozed for a while before falling asleep and I was brought back to reality by the stewardess asking if I would like a drink before we landed. I was surprised when she told me that we'd be arriving in about an hours time, so I ordered coffee and began to liven up. The captain eased the 747 down smoothly onto the runway, some twenty minutes ahead of schedule, whilst I sighed a little sigh of relief and began to feel excited about seeing Helen again.

After a long delay at immigration I at last made my way through into the Arrivals area where I saw Helen almost immediately. She rushed towards me and flung her arms around my neck and plonked a great big sloppy kiss on my lips without saying a word. Not usual for an 'all American babe'.

"Hi, Peter, how are you?" she asked when she eventually let me go.

"All the better for seeing you" I replied.

"Oh, you're so sweet" she smiled and suddenly I felt more relaxed and happier than I had been for some time. It was as if I had been walking down a grey, damp, foggy street and then turned the corner into a sunlit square.

"I'm glad to be here" I said.

"And so am I, honey, and boy, have I got things planned for you...."

"Really?" I interrupted.

"Oh, yes" she smiled and as the Americans say 'I felt good'.

CHAPTER 12

HELEN HAS A SURPRISE

The day after I had spoken to Reece I called Pops and told him all about the call.

"Don't worry about that no good sonofabitch, honey, I can sort him out and then chase him away, no problem" said Pops firmly.

"Thanks, Pops."

"That's okay."

"I'm so glad you're around when I need you" I said thankfully.

"That's what I'm here for, honey, now don't you give it another thought, and if he calls again, tell him that you're talking things over with me and we'll be in touch."

"If I say that he'll get the idea that he's got a chance to horn in."

"Sure, but don't worry about it, because we'll set up a meeting at the office and I'll have Matt Franklin, my attorney there, and he'll flatten Reece Jackman outa sight when he shows up!"

"Oh, Pops, thanks a lot, I've worried about this all night."

"Hey, don't you ever go losing any sleep over that no brainer!"

"Okay, Pops, I promise I won't."

"That's my girl." We said goodbye and I settled back on the couch feeling relaxed and so grateful to Pops.

I called Rachel to see how she was managing the crisis of having to wait another week before Doctor Gorgeous would allow the plaster on her wrist to come off. He had told her at the hospital on the Monday that he wanted to be certain that her wrist was healed and he was fully satisfied that everything was okay.

"I'm the one who needs fully satisfying!" she complained.

"I know, honey, but just be patient, you've only got a couple of days before you see him and I bet your bottom dollar that he'll have that plaster off and you'll be sailing on Chesapeake Bay before you know it" I replied.

"Yup, I've waited this long for a date so I guess a day or so will make no difference" she replied glumly.

"There you go."

"And I've been thinking, even if he takes me out just once, that'll be fine by me" she said.

"You're kidding?"

"Nope, I mean it, the fact that he's even said he'll take me sailing, a girl in a wheelchair, is something special and I'm not getting my hopes up any higher on this one." I thought that she was as brave as she was realistic and a tear ran down my cheek.

"Honey….."

"Helen, a guy like him, good looking, professional with a great future can have any girl he wants and I'd be stupid if I really thought he'd settle for me."

"You don't know….."

"I know and you know so let's not kid ourselves" she interrupted.

"Okay, I guess you're right" I replied.

"You know I am, now, have you seen Eric?"

"Nope, it seems he's disappeared again."

"He's a strange guy, so, has Peter called?"

"Nope."

"Another strange one."

"I'm surrounded by them" I laughed and added "but Reece called."

"Oh, my God, what does he want?"

"A partnership in Pops business" I replied.

"You've gotta get rid of that guy, he's a menace…."

"I know, Pops says he'll take care of it."

"Good."

"Now then call me Monday at the office and let me know if Doctor Gorgeous has made you a free woman…."

"You betcha, babe!" she said, I laughed and we said goodbye. The rest of the weekend was busy around the house and then over to Mom and Pops for Sunday lunch. Melodie and I had an easy relaxed day and Pops never spoke about the business, which suited me fine.

It was Monday lunch time and I just got to wondering how Rachel was getting on at the hospital when the phone rang and Naomi patched her through.

"Hi, and guess what?"

"Your wrist is okay and he's married" I replied.

"One out of two's not bad" she replied with a laugh.

"So he's married then?" I teased.

"Not yet, but I'll be working on it when he takes me sailing on Chesapeake Bay next Saturday!" she shrieked down the line.

"Oh, babe, I'm so happy for you…."

"He's going to pick me up about ten, so can you come over before that and check me out and say 'hi' to him?"

"Sure, I'll be there about nine."

"Oh, God, is this really happening to me?"

"It is, Rachel, it really is" I replied.

"Don't be late will you?"

"No, I promise….."

"I don't think I'll go to bed Friday night, I mean, I'll never sleep, so I guess I'll stay up and get ready for him…."

"Okay" I laughed.

"I must call Mom and Pops and then Karen and then…."

"Watch the call charges" I interrupted and she laughed.

"Okay, now call me if anything dramatic happens, like Eric appears or Peter calls….."

"Okay, I will."

"But if nothing happens just call me tomorrow and let me know if I'm dreaming!"

"I'll do that, I promise" I replied and she laughed a sweet, happy laugh.

I was very busy for the rest of the week at work and other than a late night call to Rachel, nothing else happened. None of the men in my life showed and I gave up thinking about them. The driver's around Atlantic City were wrecking their cars faster than Dan, our recovery driver, could haul them in on his rig. We had so many damaged vehicles about the place that we could hardly move and Mitch said if it carried on at this rate we'd have to turn work away until we could get some of them fixed and back to their owners. The business was certainly going places and I thought that I would soon need help running the outfit.

I arrived at Rachel's apartment just before nine on the Saturday and she was so excited that she looked a little pale.

"Hey, calm down, honey, you don't want to make yourself ill" I said as I poured some coffee.

"That's okay, I've got my own personal Doctor with me" she smiled and I laughed.

"Well, I must say, you look great…."

"Thanks." And she did. She'd put on a pair of white trousers with a blue and white striped T shirt and was wearing a neat little blue jacket over the top. Her hair and makeup were good and I said so.

"I don't know why I bothered because once we're on the boat I'll be all blown to hell as usual and looking like a drowned beaver" she said.

"No you won't and besides, he'll see you like this before you go and first date impressions count…."

"You're so good for me" she smiled as I handed her a coffee.

"Have you got plenty of food to eat?" I asked.

"Yup, there's a hamper over there ready to burst" she replied as she nodded towards the kitchen bar.

"Good, then I guess you're all fit to go."

"Yup, but, Helen, I'm so nervous" she whispered.

"Don't be, honey, remember, he must like you a lot to ask you out on a date, I mean Doctors don't usually do that."

"You're right, I guess."

"You know I am" I smiled. Doctor Guy Williams arrived at a quarter before ten and I let him in. When he strode into the apartment I watched Rachel melt.

"Hi" he said.

"Hi" she whispered in reply and then added "this is my very best friend, Helen."

"Hi, there, how are you?" he asked as he held out his hand and shook mine. His smile was just gorgeous and his soft brown eyes just melted a girl's resistance to nil.

"Okay" I croaked.

"You were with Rachel when she was first admitted to Accident, weren't you?"

"I sure was."

"And I've seen you before…"

"Yes, you took care of my Pops after his fall at work."

"Yes I remember, how is he now?"

"He's good, yup, thanks."

"That's fine, now then Rachel, we're off to Chesapeake Bay for a days sailing, so I hope you're good and ready."

"I certainly am…."

"Not a 'definite maybe' then?" he laughed.

"No, Doctor" she blushed.

"Hey, I'm off duty so it's Guy, okay?"

"Okay" she smiled.

"Good, let's go then" he said as he gently took her wheelchair and pushed it towards the door.

"Will you bring the food out, Helen?"

"Yup."

"You're bringing food?" asked Guy.

"Sure" Rachel said.

"Okay, but there's no need, I plan to anchor up in a secluded cove I know and cook you a meal you'll always remember…." and I thought 'oh, my God, he can cook too!'

"Okay, hold the hamper" Rachel said with a laugh as Guy wheeled her out to his estate car, a smart new Pontiac. I stood by the passenger door after Guy had gently lifted Rachel into the plush seat and had gone to the tailgate to fold her chair and stow it away.

"Can you believe this?" she whispered to me with a smile.

"No, I can't, but I believe fairy tales do come true, sometimes" I replied.

"I guess this is one of those times, eh?"

"You'd better believe it, honey" I replied.

"I'll call you later when I've got back and woken up from this dream."

"You do that" I replied as Guy slid behind the wheel and said "that's it, off we go, see you again sometime, Helen."

"Bye" I waved and the Pontiac swept off up the road whilst I stood on the sidewalk and cried tears of happiness for my dear, lovely friend on her first date since the riding accident that had paralysed her.

After I had pulled myself together, I decided to go into work. I thought as we had so much on, and Mitch and the boys were working like crazy, it was only right that I should be there for them. Mitch was pleased to see me in the office and when it got close to lunch time he came in and asked if he could get me anything from the deli. I thought that was nice and I had him get me a cheese salad roll with mayonnaise and I smiled as I thought that the fat birds in the park were on a loser today. The rest of the afternoon flashed by and just after five I went off to Mom and Pops to collect Melodie, leaving Mitch to lock up after all the boys had gone. I arrived back home with my little girl at about seven and was just settling down to watch TV when the phone rang.

"That'll be Rachel" I said excitedly to Melodie as I pushed my TV dinner to one side.

"Hi" I said first.

"Hi, babe" replied Reece and my heart sank.

"Oh, it's you, Reece."

"Right first time, babe."

"Well?"

"I've been thinking about what I said to you about the business...."

"Oh, yeah" I interrupted.

"I guess that I caught you at a bad moment...."

"All my moments are bad for you, Reece" I replied, and he ignored that.

"I think I was a touch hasty and didn't make it clear to you what I have in mind" he said.

"Well, hold it right there, I've been talking things over with Pops and he said it would be a good idea if we had a meet at the office to discuss it all" I said, knowing he'd jump at that.

"Oh, babe, that's great!"

"Pops said to tell you that he'll be in touch with you soon to fix up a convenient time, okay?"

"Yes, indeedy, babe, yes indeedy...."

"So, goodbye Reece."

"Bye babe, I'll be seeing you." As I put the phone down I thought 'just one more time and then not until hell freezes over'. I had just got back to my TV dinner when the phone rang once more and I hoped it wasn't Reece calling again as I was ready to bust his balls this time.

"Hi" I said.

"Is that Helen Milton, friend of Rachel Grover? You may

remember Rachel, she's the one who goes sailing on a gorgeous Doctor's luxury yacht in Chesapeake Bay...."

"Hi, honey, hi, tell all!" I replied excitedly.

"Are you sitting down?"

"Give me a moment...."

"Have you got a Jack Daniels close by?"

"Nope, but that can be arranged."

"Arrange it then...."

"So this is going to be a long call?"

"The longest."

"Wow, hold everything" I said as I put the phone down and rushed to pour a full glass of the golden relaxer.

"All ears, honey, so go for it" I said as I slumped down with my drink.

"We got to the mooring on the bay and I couldn't believe how beautiful his yacht is...."

"Really?"

"Yup, Guy said she was a forty eight footer and she's called 'Lady be Good' with everything on board anyone could wish for...."

"Wow...."

"He owns half with his brother, Richard...."

"You mean there's another one like him at home?"

"He's not at home, the Navy has got him, he's a flyer...."

"Oh, my God!"

"Wait, it gets worse...."

"It can't...."

"He flies F16 jet fighters and is often mistaken for Tom Cruise...."

"Don't tell Karen."

"No way!"

"Stop for a second, while I drink to steady up...."

"Guy says Richard has got a Jaguar sports coupe and they've had to make a special scraper for him to scrape women off the side of it so he can get in to drive!"

"I believe him...."

"And here comes the back breaker.... he's not married!"

"Oh, my God!"

"Precisely."

"What ever you do, don't tell Karen" I said as I took another mouthful of Jack Daniels.

"Never…."

"Go on."

"So, we got aboard and after a tour of the cabins, which took a while as Guy had to carry me everywhere…."

"Poor you."

"I know, and then we just sailed away in the sunshine." She paused and I waited.

"And?" I asked eventually.

"I thought I'd died and gone to heaven…."

"What happened next?" I asked.

"After about an hour we sailed into this little cove and anchored up, it was so beautiful and quiet, and he asked if I was ready for lunch."

"Were you?"

"By then I was ready for anything, honey" she laughed.

"So?"

"He carried me into the cabin, put me in a cosy chair and poured me a glass of white wine which I drank whilst watching him cook the most amazing meal…."

"I don't believe this" I interrupted.

"It was a Thai rice dish with fresh shrimps and a mixture of all kinds of green veggies with a rich, sweet sauce over…."

"Oh, my God…."

"He learned how to cook when he was in medical school and sharing a room with a young Doctor from Thailand…"

"I think you are in heaven…."

"And it was delicious, unbelievably so…."

"I bet."

"Guy said it was good for me, full of all the right kind of things a girl needs."

"Yup, it sounds like it!"

"Then we had ice cream and more wine and then we went sailing again…."

"Will this never end?"

"This time, he insisted I steer the boat and he made me hold onto the wheel whilst he stood behind me and put his arms around my waist to hold me tight…."

"So you wouldn't fall over…."

"Yes."

"You poor thing!"

"I know, but I was ready to sacrifice myself…."

"Sometimes a girl has to…." I replied and we both laughed.

"We sailed for about another hour before stopping in another small cove for more ice cream then coffee and cookies…."

"Hey, honey, with all that food did you ask him if your bum looked big in his boat?" I said and she laughed.

"Then we talked for a long while about everything and I just found him to be so lovely and kind, so caring and so…."

"Yes?"

"Disappointing…."

"What?"

"Disappointing…."

"Why?"

"He never kissed me, touched me, stroked me, nothing…."

"Well, he's a gentleman, you've got to…."

"Never mind all that 'gentleman' stuff, honey, I want to be well and truly groped and then laid by this wonderful guy…."

"You will be in time, I'm sure."

"Please God if you're listening……"

"And then what?"

"We sailed back with me steering and he had to keep taking over as I was just wandering all over the place…."

"No concentration, huh?"

"Got it in one, honey! With his arms around me I was a hopeless mess."

"Tell me more…."

"We moored up and then he said he wanted to take me home before I got too tired…."

"He's so sweet."

"And driving back, I thought 'if he dates me again, it'll be wonderful, but if he says 'I'll call you' which means it's over, I'll invite him in to knock me up, kiss him goodbye, and be very grateful that I've had a wonderful day with a wonderful guy……."

"Oh, honey…..."

"I've always got the memories…."

"Rachel…." I said softly.

"But he didn't! When we got back he asked me out to dinner next Friday, he knows a romantic little Italian restaurant someplace outa town that does the most delicious cannelloni...."

"Oh, my God, what did you say?"

"I told him I'd have to check my diary and then call you and a few other friends to see if they'd got anything planned for me and if I was free, I'd let him know next Wednesday or Thursday...."

"Rachel!"

"That's me."

"You're crazy....."

"Just kidding, when he asked me I just said 'I love cannelloni, what time are you picking me up?'"

"That's better...."

"He said 'about eight and I'll call you tomorrow to see if you're okay and then again on Tuesday evening, about nine when I finish my shift'...."

"Oh, Rachel, baby, I'm so happy for you, I really am...."

"I know you are, honey, but please don't say any more because you'll make me cry...."

"Okay."

"I'll call you tomorrow after he's called me...."

"Okay, honey."

"Bye, Helen."

"Bye, Rachel" and I put the phone down and burst out crying.

"What's the matter, Mom?" asked Melodie with an anxious look on her face.

"Nothing, honey, I'm just so happy for Rachel...."

"Why?"

"She's got a wonderful man who's paying her some attention."

"And you're crying?" she asked, shaking her head, and I nodded before taking a large gulp of Jack Daniels.

Rachel called the next evening and we talked for an age about the man in her life and at the end of it I felt so happy for her and hoped that maybe, just maybe, I'd find someone like him who would care for me. I thought that it would be Eric but I'd now given up a little on him, as I was sure I was right, he was a line man, married with a coupla kids someplace. I promised Rachel I'd to go to her apartment on Friday to check her out before Guy

215

arrived to take her to the romantic Italian restaurant and I felt as excited as she was.

It was mid-morning on Monday and I had just stopped for a coffee break when my phone rang and Naomi said "It's Peter calling you from London…."

"Patch him through" I said excitedly, and she did.

"Hi, Peter, how are you?"

"Fine thanks, Helen, and you?" He sounded as if he cared.

"I'm good, so, it's nice to hear from you" and I meant it.

"Yes, I've got some news" he sounded pleased.

"What is it?" I asked, hopefully guessing.

"I'm coming out to Atlantic City on the thirty first of May, and I wondered if we could meet?" I was so pleased that I had guessed right and I asked if he was kidding me.

"No, I'm not."

"Oh, my God, of course we can meet up" I replied trying to keep some of the excitement out of my voice. I asked what time his flight was and how long he was staying and he said he'd let me know flight times later but he was only staying for a couple of days on his way to Chicago. I was a little disappointed at that and then he asked me to book him a room in a cheap hotel but I was ahead of him there, I planned to have him stay with me, which was for free and you can't get any cheaper than that. He was calling from Freddie boy's office so I sent my best wishes to him before we said goodbye. I went into Naomi's office and said "he's coming over at the end of the month."

"That's great, so I'll finally get to meet a guy that you like."

"Yup, you will" I replied.

"That'll be one up on that other one you talk about…."

"Eric?"

"That's the one, he's a guy I'd like to see" she said.

"You saw him in the park with me" I said.

"Nope, I didn't" she replied and the back of my neck tingled.

"Sure you did, you told me that you saw us together and you said how tall he was…."

"Well, if I did, I don't remember…."

"Naomi…." I said firmly whilst my neck tingled some more.

"I honestly don't remember seeing him, perhaps you imagined

it all." I was just about to have another go at her when the phone rang again and this time it was Pops. I took the call in my office and told him that Reece had called on Saturday night and Pops said that he'd fix a date with Matt Franklin and get back to Reece directly. He told me not to worry about a thing and I said I wouldn't and then I gave him the news that Guy had taken Rachel sailing. He was pleased at that and hoped I'd meet someone nice soon, I told him that Peter was coming over from London at the end of the month, he was really happy and said he looked forward to meeting him.

The rest of the week passed quickly at work as we seemed to get busier and busier. Mitch and the boys were fixing vehicles faster than I could get all the new parts in to finish them and so there were holdups getting some of them back to their owners. I realised that I'd have to get more help with the business and I decided to have a serious talk with Pops about it. Other than Rachel calling late on Tuesday, after Guy had called her, nothing much happened until the Friday evening came with a rush. I left work very late and hurried to Rachel's apartment to find her ready to go out and kill. She was all dressed up in a low cut, red satin number, with perfect make up and looking like a million dollars.

"You look great" I said.

"Thanks, but do you really think so?"

"Yup, of course, and don't start getting any damned fool ideas that you don't" I replied and she smiled.

"I haven't gotten over last Saturday yet" she smiled.

"Sure, I understand, and now you're off out on a second date."

"I know, I can't believe it."

"What did Karen and your folks say about your day out sailing?"

"Oh, Mom and Dad were just so happy for me and Karen, when she got over the shock, spent time out telling me how to nail Guy to the floor...."

"She would" I laughed as the door bell rang.

"That's him" whispered Rachel and I smiled before letting Guy into the apartment. He looked really cool in a dark blue jacket with a white shirt, neat red tie and grey pants.

"Hi, Helen and hi, honey" he smiled at Rachel.

"Hi, do I look okay to go out?" she asked in an anxious tone.

"You look gorgeous, doesn't she Helen?" he smiled and we both went a little weak.

"She does" I managed to say.

"Okay, off we go and I hope you're hungry and don't have to be back too soon" he said.

"Oh, no, I can stay out all night if necessary" she replied and I thought 'don't push it, baby'. Guy smiled and said "I'll bring you home sometime to get some sleep." He took her wheelchair and headed for the door as she whispered "pity." I followed on and closed up the apartment. Rachel said she'd call and I told her not to bother tonight as she was bound to be late. I waved as the Pontiac swept away up the road.

Late Saturday night the phone rang when I was in the tub, relaxing after spending a long day at work as we tried to cope with the never ending stream of wrecked autos being recovered from a multiple on the Freeway. Some drivers are just plain stupid, it was a bright dry day and because they drive up too close together, when one has to pull up quick, the others pile into the back of one another. Mitch just threw up his hands as Dan, driving the recovery rig, just kept on coming in with more damaged vehicles. Melodie answered the call and then came into the bathroom.

"It's Karen...."

"Okay, tell her I'm in the tub and I'll be out in a moment" I replied.

"I told her that all ready" she said as she left. I was out and draped in a towel in seconds, snatching up the phone by my bed before sinking down onto it.

"Hi, Karen."

"Hi, so are you clean all over?" she asked.

"You'd better believe it" I laughed.

"Okay, if you can try and stay that way, I'll invite you to my engagement party...."

"What?"

"And get your hearing fixed before you come...."

"Oh, Karen, that's great, congratulations...."

"Thanks, honey...."

"So, you nailed him then?"

"Yup, but not without a struggle, I had to take him out no end of times to really expensive restaurants, then away for a weekend at a golf club in Connecticut to get him laid! Then I had to chase him around his office every night after work for a whole week, until he finally realised that I was fully committed to his bank balance and gave in and said 'yes'!" I laughed out loud.

"You kept all this secret" I said.

"Yup, it was must, honey, and I'll tell you later, but never mind, you know now and the party's at Ralph's apartment next Saturday night."

"I'll be there and hey, can I bring a man?"

"Sure, if you can find one" she replied.

"No problem, I'm shipping one in from London on Friday" I replied.

"Hey, is Peter coming over?"

"Yup."

"That's great, I look forward to meeting him."

"Have you invited Rachel?"

"I'm just gonna call her now."

"Good, and she'll want to bring Doctor Gorgeous."

"Sure, and I'm looking forward to meeting him and I might get him to check me over at the end of the evening...."

"Karen, you're spoken for!"

"Not until I say 'I do'...." and she laughed.

"Is that date fixed yet?"

"Yup, the ceremony is going to be at the Hilton Hotel, Baltimore on Saturday the nineteenth of July, you'll all get an invitation."

"Great."

"Okay, now I'll e-mail you Ralph's address with a little map and if you could bring Rachel and her Doctor on Saturday that would be great."

"I'll do that, honey, and congratulations once again, I never thought you'd ever get married...."

"Neither did I and neither did Ralph until I told him" she laughed and we said goodbye. I went downstairs and poured a large Jack Daniels and thought 'what a week this was turning out to be'.

Rachel called Sunday and told me all about a great night at the restaurant with Guy last Friday. She had just called him with the invitation to Karen's party and he said he'd be there. Rachel was just getting so excited with everything I worried in case she had a heart attack or something. I told her that Peter was coming over and would be with us at the party, she was so pleased that I really wondered if I shouldn't have kept it as a surprise.

The week was frantic at the business and we all worked like crazy to get as many vehicles repaired and back to their impatient owners as quickly as possible. If only you could run a business without the customers it would be just great. Pops came in on the Thursday and Friday to help out and told me that he arranged a meet with Matt Franklin and Reece the following Wednesday afternoon. I was relieved about that and felt okay and excited as I set off to the airport on the Friday afternoon to meet Peter, leaving Pops in charge of everything. I had arranged with Mom for Melodie to stay over for the weekend so I could be alone with Mister Reserved and she had smiled at that.

The London flight arrived early but it was a while before Peter got through immigration and collected his baggage. At last, I saw him and rushed up and gave him a big, all American, welcome kiss.

We said 'hi' and he told me that he was glad to be here and he did looked pleased.

"So, have you got me booked into an hotel tonight?" he asked once we were in my Chevy.

"Sure have, and it's the cheapest in town" I replied.

"Oh" he sounded a little alarmed.

"Don't worry, you'll love the place, it's warm and cosy and the room service is the tops" I smirked.

"Oh, good, that sounds very nice indeed" he replied.

"It's more than very nice indeed" I teased as we drove out of the short stay car park.

"Really?"

"Yup, and it's not to far away from me."

"Oh, good" he replied and I thought 'right answer'.

"I'm taking you to where you're staying first of all" I said.

"Thanks, I need a shower or something after the flight, I always feel so grubby, don't you?"

"Yup, I always feel 'grubby'" I replied and tried not to laugh. We chatted about our time together in Paris and London and I felt at ease with this reserved Englishman because he was so charming and certainly very different from the guys I had known in Atlantic City. We arrived at my place and I swung the car onto the driveway and killed the motor.

"This isn't a hotel, is it?"

"Nope, but it's where you're staying until you go off to Chicago on Monday" I replied as I got out of the car just in time to see Mrs Dawson heading on down from her porch at speed.

"Hi, Helen, how are you? Haven't seen you lately and I wondered if everything was okay?" she said as she arrived at the picket fence.

"Hi, Mrs Dawson, yup, everything is just fine, thanks" I replied as she craned her neck around me to look at Peter.

"Aren't you going to introduce me to your gentleman friend?" she asked with a knowing smile.

"Sure" and I turned towards him "Peter, come and say 'hi' to Mrs Dawson." Peter joined us at the fence and said, in his perfect English accent "how do you do, Mrs Dawson, I'm delighted to meet you" and he held out his hand to her. She wobbled noticeably and whispered "my... you're not from around these parts are you?"

"No, I'm from London."

"England?" she queried as she took his hand.

"Yes, indeed."

"Are you staying long?"

"Only until Monday, then I have to go to Chicago on business."

"Oh, my, well you are a busy man...."

"I am, and now if you will excuse me I need to rest and have a cup of tea after a very long flight" he smiled.

"Oh, sure, but it's been nice meeting you, sir" she replied.

"Nice meeting you too, Mrs Dawson, I hope to have the pleasure again before I leave."

"Likewise, I'm sure" she replied and I grinned as Peter turned away and collected his bags from the trunk of my car. I nodded at Mrs Dawson who whispered "You're a very lucky girl, Helen, d'you know that?"

"I do, Mrs Dawson, bye now" I replied and then followed Peter up to the porch. I opened the front door and he followed me in.

"Is this your place?" he asked as he put his bags down.

"Yup."

"It's very nice, but are you sure about putting me up?"

"I'm sure."

"Well, you're very kind, but I think I'm imposing...."

"You impose all you like, honey, whilst I go and make you a nice cup of tea that you told Mrs Dawson you needed" I smiled.

"Yes, thanks, and she was a touch 'pushy' and inquisitive I must admit" he replied.

"A touch 'pushy', I'll have to remember that one!" and I laughed.

"Yes, please do" he smiled.

"Come on in, sit on the couch and take the weight off" I said with a smile.

"Thanks" and he did whilst I went out to the kitchen.

As we drank the tea and munched some cookies I told him what I had arranged over the weekend.

"After you've had a good soak in the tub and all your 'grubby' has been washed off" and I giggled at that, "it would be good for you to have a rest, because tonight I'm taking you to Rolfe's...."

"Who's he?"

"Rolfe's is a restaurant where the food is good and wholesome...."

"Oh, very nice."

"Then tomorrow morning I'd like to show you around Pops body repair shop and have you meet Mitch and the other guys."

"I'd like that, it will give me a chance to get the feel of things over here" he said and I thought 'put me on the list of things to feel, honey'.

"Okay, then after that I want you to meet my folks, we'll have lunch with them before coming back here to rest up, because we're off to a party Saturday night!"

"Oh, that's nice."

"Yup, it's my friend Karen's engagement party and we're going along with Rachel, my best friend, and her guy."

"I look forward to it" he smiled.

"Then Sunday morning we'll rest up before we go over to my folks for lunch again and then, if the weather's okay, I want to take you for a quick sail in my little boat."

"That would be really good" he smiled.

"Then back here for dinner and an early night so you're all fit to go to Chicago on Monday" I said with a smile.

"Well, I must say, you've thought of everything" he smiled.

"I try awful hard to cover all the bases" I replied.

"And you succeed."

"Now, if you've finished your tea, I'll show you your room and then you can slip into the tub and scrub the 'grubby' off!" I giggled again.

That night I wore the blue dress that I had worn when we first danced together and Peter looked neat in a dark blue blazer, white shirt, light blue tie and grey pants. He was tall, slim and distinguished with his wavy hair and glasses, I thought he sure looked like Michael Caine. At Rolfe's the waitress was all over him when she heard his English accent and she did ask at the start of the meal if he was the actor. He said he wasn't but I don't think she believed him because from then on she had a funny, dreamy look on her face. The T-bone steaks were good, Peter couldn't finish his and only managed a small ice cream for sweet - he said the portions were just too much for him and I guess the British just aren't used to the amount we serve up in restaurants.

All through the meal Peter was relaxed and charming and it was only when we got back home and I asked how Miss Italian was that he changed and told me he didn't know and didn't want to talk about her. I realised straight away that she'd dumped him, probably for the old guy she was translating for, and Peter was really cut up about it. So, here was my chance to get laid without any moral opposition to overcome and I felt good about that. I planned to let him rest tonight and then tomorrow, after Karen's party, I hoped he'd be in the mood to see to me. After a quick goodnight kiss we went to our rooms and crashed out for the night.

CHAPTER 13

HELEN HAS THE LAST WORD

Peter thinks I should finish off our story and I agreed, after all, a girl has got to have the last word. So, at the office the next morning I introduced Peter to Naomi, who was mightily impressed with him, before taking him out into the works and showing him around. He and Mitch got on well and Peter was in his element when he went into the paintshop and started talking to the guys in there. He obviously knew a lot about paint and the guys asked him questions about vehicle painting in Britain as well as talking over the problems with colour matching, especially metallic colours. It seemed as if he didn't want to leave and I had to remind him about lunch with my folks.

Mom, Pops and Melodie were happy to meet Peter and they were knocked out by his accent and his politeness. Mom looked dewy eyed at him when he spoke and Pops just kept nodding with a silly smile. Melodie never stopped asking questions about London and the Queen, and I was glad when we sat down to lunch so that Peter could have a break from it all. After we had finished eating and Peter told Mom that her cooking was 'simply superb', Pops whisked him off into the other room for 'man's' talk.

"He's the first Englishman I've met, so, tell me, are they all as charming as him?" Mom asked when we were alone.

"Pretty much" I replied.

"And I guess they must make good husbands...."

"Yup, I think they do, but don't go getting any ideas, Mom, he's married at the moment and I think he's got the next wife all lined up after the divorce."

"You think?"

"I'm not sure, he may be having a little trouble with her" I replied.

"Well find out and let me know" said Mom.

"Okay" I laughed.

"A man like Peter is worth trying to catch and you're not getting any younger you know...."

"Thanks Mom, I do have plans…."
"Good."

I had to drag Peter away from my folks in the afternoon so we could get ready for Karen's party. I'd fixed up with Rachel that we'd pick her and Guy up at about seven for the drive over to Baltimore and I needed plenty of time to get ready. I planned to wear the red dress I'd bought in Kensington and get all dolled up and then some, because I knew Karen would look like a million dollars and I wanted to be up level with her and knock Peter sideways at the same time. A girl's gotta do what a girl's gotta do when she's setting up a man trap! At last I was ready to go and when Mister Reserved saw me come down stairs I watched him melt and his blue eyes widen.

"Hello, hello" he said very slowly.

"Am I okay to go out, sir?" I asked.

"Well, quite frankly, I think I'd rather stay in…." he smiled and I thought 'oh, yes!'.

We arrived at Rachel's apartment just after seven and Guy was already there looking very smart in a white Tuxedo. Rachel was wearing a dark blue dress with a low neckline showing off her boobs and cleavage to maximum effect. After the introductions, Peter's accent and easy charm left Rachel dewy eyed, as if she couldn't believe what was going on around her, and Guy smiling at everything Peter said. We set off to Baltimore in Guy's Pontiac, he said it was because he couldn't drink as he was on duty at the hospital at six the next morning. That meant he would have to leave the party at around midnight to get back for some rest and that suited me perfectly as I didn't want to be too late to bed.

We found Ralph's apartment quite easily and on entering his luxury pad, Karen rushed over to meet us. She looked like an 'A' list celebrity, with her blonde hair put up, make up just perfect and wearing a long black dress with a plunging V neckline that showed off her cleavage. She wore a large diamond pendant around her neck with matching ear rings and smiled as soon as she saw us. She was dragging a tall, good looking man with dark hair, streaked with grey, dressed in a Tuxedo, behind her.

"Hi, you guys" she gushed and kissed me and then Rachel. We

smiled and all said 'hello' to her.

"Well, here he is, so, everybody, meet Ralph, my fiancé...." Karen held up her hand to him and I noticed the large diamond in the engagement ring. After all the introductions, we were offered champagne and we toasted the happy couple. There were quite a lot of distinguished looking people there and I guessed they were either attorneys or friends of Ralph's. I noticed how some of them looked down at Rachel in her wheelchair and I didn't like it, I felt kinda protective of my friend. Peter and Guy saw their expressions too, and it always surprises me how folks seem to think that if someone's in a wheelchair, they're stupid or something. Guy and Peter were like knights in shining armour, charming and protective all evening, standing close to Rachel and involving her in every conversation whilst Guy kept resting his hand gently on her shoulder. The most moving moment came when Guy was telling Karen and Ralph, surrounded by guests, about sailing with Rachel in 'Lady be Good'.

"She's a forty eight footer and needs two crew at the helm" he said and I could see he was making an impression on the men as well as the women.

"So, Rachel and I have to steer her together, like this...." and he took Rachel's hands and pulled her from her wheelchair and stood behind her with his arms around her waist and said "show them how we do it, honey." Rachel smiled and took the imaginary wheel in her hands and slowly turned from side to side and my eyes grew moist. I thought 'what a wonderful person he is'.

"It's fortunate that you've got such a lovely woman to help you, Guy, in England the crew on my uncle's boat all look like pirates from the Caribbean!" said Peter and everybody laughed. He is just so cute that I could eat him all up and I made up my mind for certain to do that later. I gazed at Rachel's smiling face and thought how happy she looked and I'd forgotten how tall she was. Then, having got her standing up, Guy moved to her side and with his arm around her waist, supported her against himself. Then Peter moved instinctively closer to Rachel's other side, to be there in case she fell away from Guy. I almost cried and then noticed how the other guests attitude changed towards Rachel when they saw her, tall and looking lovely, supported by two very handsome men.

At last it was time to leave and with kisses and huggies we all said goodbye to Karen and Ralph before driving back to Atlantic City.

We'd just got through my front door when Peter grabbed my shoulder and turned me around before giving me a long, sweet kiss that left me breathless.

"Wow, not so reserved after midnight I notice" I said.

"You are very lovely" he whispered.

"So are you, honey" I replied.

"I'm a little lost for words" he whispered.

"That's okay, honey, let me do all the talking" I replied and he smiled.

"Right……"

"I'll pour us a Jack Daniels whilst you get cosy on the couch and we'll drink slowly to the future and then you can take me up to bed because it's showtime!" He laughed and gave me a quick kiss and said "I do love live shows."

"Oh, so do I, honey" I replied with a smile and went over to pour the drinks. We sat and talked for a short while before I took his hand and led him up to my bedroom where I slipped off my dress and stepped out of it leaving me wearing my lace panties with the red roses and my stockings and garters. I put my hands on my hips and asked "what d'you think?"

"Simply wonderful" he smiled. I slipped the lace panties down and kicked them away and asked "is this better?"

"Absolutely…."

"Good, so come and get it cowboy!" And he did! He had me down on the bed and was smothering me in kisses within a few moments. It was gorgeous and I felt really worked up as he stopped to get undressed and then he was on top of me and I felt him pushing at me before I opened up. He made love slowly and gently and it was not long before I had a good hard, sharp come. He felt me tighten and at the right moment speeded up and let himself go deep inside. I kept saying "oh, my God" as my heart slowed down.

"This is too good for the common people" he smiled.

"Peter, honey, it was almost too good for me" I whispered.

"That's the proof that you're not a common person then, but a

Princess...." he smiled and kissed me gently and passionately as I melted, because no one has ever called me a Princess before and at that moment I was sure something magical happened between us.

We slept entwined in each other's arms and awoke to the phone ringing next to the bed.

"Hi, Helen" said a chirpy voice I recognised.

"Hi, Rachel."

"You sound sleepy, did I wake you?"

"You did, honey, but it doesn't matter...."

"So, guess what?"

"I don't know, I give in this early in the morning...."

"Guy's went to the hospital from here...."

"Good for him...." I replied lamely.

"No, you don't get it, he stayed with me...."

"Oh, honey, you mean?" I perked up.

"I do, and it was heaven just heaven and to feel him deep inside...."

"Okay, honey, spare me the details this early, I get the picture...."

"I'm just outa my mind over him...."

"I'm sure you are...."

"And did you make out with Peter... and was it good?"

"He's lying right beside me so you can ask him yourself...."

"Oh, great, he's such a nice guy...."

"He sure is...."

"Hey, we're two lucky babes...."

"We are...."

"Call me sometime later when we can have a quality time talk...."

"Okay, honey, bye now."

Sunday lunch at Mom and Pops was easy and relaxed as Peter charmed the pants off them once again. Mom dewy eyed and Pops nodding and smiling as they listened to the run down on Karen's party, told English style. After we had finished with coffee, Pops took Peter into the other room for more 'man's talk', leaving me with Mom and Melodie.

"What's going on, Mom?" I asked when we were alone.

"Your Pops has got some ideas about the business and wants to talk them through with Peter."

"Oh, yeah?" I said in a suspicious tone.

"He's such a nice guy and Pops says he's the sort of...."

"Why doesn't Pops include me in these discussions?" I interrupted.

"He will, honey, as soon as he's got his ideas fixed in his mind."

"I'm not happy about this" I said when Melodie interrupted by asking "Mom, are you going to marry Peter?" Why do kids say these things? They're worse than parents!

"I don't know, baby" I replied quickly.

"She only hopes so at the moment" said Mom and I had to smile.

"I've told you Mom, he's already married and he's got...."

"I know, Helen, but these things have a habit of turning the right way and can be fixed" she interrupted.

"Yup, and I believe things when they happen, not until."

"Well, you wouldn't have believed Rachel would date that dishy Doctor of hers, would you now?"

"Nope, I guess not" I replied.

"So, okay then, hear what I say and if you're taking Peter sailing you'd better rescue him from Pops before it gets too late."

We drove quickly down to Cape May in the afternoon sunshine and I chatted all the way to Mister Not So Reserved. Peter told me that he wanted to come and see me on his way back from Chicago on the Friday, which was the fourteenth of June and stay until the Sunday. I was so happy about that and said I'd meet him at the airport again. He said he'd try and fix it with Freddie boy so that he would be over here in time to go to Karen's wedding on the nineteenth of July, and I was really made up over that. I felt as if my life was beginning to straighten out a little and I wondered if I would ever see Eric again.

The 'Princess' took us out on the gently rolling ocean and I relaxed completely in the company of this lovely English guy. We talked and laughed as the 'Princess' splashed through the waves and Peter said that we should try the Doctor Guy Williams method of steering and I agreed, so he stood behind me with his arms around my waist, as I held on to the wheel. He kissed my neck every time the spray broke over the bow. We were soon a little wet and oh so randy. He suggested that we should 'go below' and do things to each other but I told him he'd have to wait until tonight in the shower! He said he'd enjoy getting wet with hot water instead of cold sea water and having me naked instead of being all wrapped like an Indian papoose, so I promised him that it was a date.

After our shower and a little love making, I fixed dinner for us and when we had finished we settled down in front of the log fire and drank Jack Daniels and talked until we were ready for bed. We made love gently but passionately once again and then fell asleep. As I closed my eyes I just didn't want this to ever end but I knew that Peter had to fly out to Chicago in the morning. I kissed him hard as we said goodbye at the airport and I knew that the days would drag until he returned on the fourteenth. He promised to phone every night and he kept his promise.

On the Wednesday afternoon we had the meet at the office with Matt Franklin and Reece.

Pops started by telling him that there was no possibility of any form of employment let alone a partnership deal. Reece looked more unhappy as the facts were laid out in front of him and he turned a shade of green when Matt told him that if he carried on pushing then he would find himself looking at a writ for harassment. Reece got the picture and left without a word and I hoped to God that other than seeing Melodie from time to time, I wouldn't be bothered with the loser. To think I almost got married to the guy!

Peter arrived back from Chicago on the fourteenth and stayed until the Monday before flying back to London. We had a great time together and got along so well that I felt that at last I had met someone pretty special, and then I thought of Eric. He hadn't bothered to show up, even when I was having a lunch break in the park and feeding the fat birds. What was that guy all about? Had I imagined him? Naomi said she couldn't remember seeing him and that worried me, but I remembered that Mrs Dawson said she had seen a tall guy hanging around and I made up my mind to ask her next time I saw her. So, I guess Eric was history now and I had to hope that Peter didn't get hooked up again with Miss Italian.

The weekend that Peter was with me, and spending too much time with my folks, Rachel had gone up to New England to meet Guy's parents. His Pops is a neurosurgeon, operating on the rich and brainless, and according to Rachel, a very nice person as well as being seriously wealthy. His Mom is a very laid back, sweet lady, who hoped that she'd be a grandmother before she got any older, and she made a great fuss of Rachel. Just when things couldn't get any better for my friend, Richard, Guy's brother, showed up on a few days leave! He told Rachel that he was so pleased to meet her and have a lovely woman about the place that wasn't making eyes at him. She said that having two gorgeous men around for the whole weekend making a fuss of her was almost too much to handle, but she managed! When I heard all this I was getting as excited as Rachel and hoped against hope that Guy wouldn't let her down and if he did, he'd make it so gentle for her, but, as Mrs Dawson says 'you never know what's around the corner'.

I arrived back from work a little earlier than usual one evening and saw my neighbour watering her roses so I decided to ask her about Eric.

"Hi, Mrs Dawson" I called out as I got out of my car.

"Oh, hello, Helen…."

"The roses look good" I said and she took the hint for a chat, put down her hose and came over to the fence.

"Yes, they're coming on just fine…."

"Good…."

"I must say, that young man of yours…."

"Peter" I nodded.

"He's a very nice person and I see he's been staying with you quite a lot recently…."

"Yup, he has…."

"Do I hear wedding bells in the distance?"

"Don't think so, Mrs Dawson, he's a very busy man…."

"No man is too busy to get married" she interrupted.

"Well, I don't know about that" I replied.

"I do…."

"And that reminds me, d'you remember the tall guy that you

saw sometime ago?"

"Who was that, dear?" she replied and my neck began to tingle again.

"You said you saw a strange guy looking through my window...."

"There's lots of strange people around here, I don't recall anybody in particular" she said and my tingle got a little worse.

"You said he was dressed in leather and kinda looked like a guy that went sailing...."

"Did I?"

"Yes...."

"Well, if you say so, dear, but I really can't recall, now, I'm glad you like my roses, I planted them out last Fall and they're just beginning to come on so well, don't you think?"

"I do" I replied as my neck carried on tingling. I made some lame excuse to leave her and went inside to pour a Jack Daniels. I was confused now more than ever, had I imagined Eric? And if I hadn't, why didn't he show up?

Things got a whole lot better when Peter phoned and said he'd arranged with Freddie boy to fly out to Atlantic City on the twelfth of July, going on to Chicago on Monday the fourteenth and then coming back on the eighteenth in time for Karen's wedding on the nineteenth. I was so happy and everyone was pleased that Mister Reserved was going to be over for the big day. Mom and Pops kept giving me funny looks and I knew what they were thinking but I was trying to be sensible about the situation and keep both feet on the ground, although I did drift up now and then when I thought about him.

I spent another great weekend with Peter before he went to Chicago and other than dinner at Rolfe's and the usual visits to my folks we also took Melodie sailing. My daughter and Peter certainly hit it off and I was surprised at that because usually Melodie is a bit melodramatic when she meets guys. After Peter left for Chicago on the Monday the week rushed by and only long calls from Rachel and Karen, both up in the air over the wedding, disturbed my TV dinners. Everything was in place for the Saturday and when Peter got back on the Friday we had a night in and dinner by the fire followed by early bed.

Guy and Rachel picked us up at midday on the Saturday for the drive over to the Hilton in Baltimore. We were all dressed up and ready to make a good show of it all. I'd never seen Rachel so excited and she beamed with pleasure all the time and laughed at everything Guy and Peter said the whole way over to Baltimore. Karen looked stunning in a cream silk dress and Ralph looked a dream at the ceremony that was held in the Kennedy Suite, which had to be seen to be believed. Karen had spared no expense and from her silk dress to the flowers and the full sit down lunch, everything was perfect and so obviously expensive. When the dancing started to a five piece band and we'd had a little too much Champagne, Karen came over to our table and kissed all of us.

"So, how's the Atlantic City delegation?" she asked.

"We're all good" I replied.

"Happy to hear it" she replied.

"You look quite incredibly beautiful" said Peter.

"Why, thank you, sir" said Karen and she smiled.

"You really do" said Guy and Karen bobbed her head to him.

"So which of you two guys are gonna dance with me first?"

"I will, as soon as I've had a dance with Helen" said Peter.

"And I'll just hold Rachel's hand and watch" added Guy.

"Oh, no, honey, dance with Karen, please…." said Rachel.

"Are you sure?" he asked.

"Of course, honey, give her a whirl, I want her to know what it's like to handle your body before her wedding night!" said Rachel.

"Oh, my God!" said Karen and we all laughed. I realised that the two men in our lives were just the best and at that moment I thought of Eric and hoped I'd never see him again. And I hoped Peter would never set eyes on Miss Italian, not ever. We danced, laughed, got a little silly and eventually left the party in the early hours and drove home. It was a great event and I felt happier than I'd been for a long while. Peter and I made love gently and with a lot of feeling before we fell asleep.

Sunday flew by and after a long lunch with my folks, Peter and I relaxed back home with Melodie. The more I was with him the more I fell in love with him and I dare not say how I felt in case I frightened him away. Then, when Melodie had gone up to bed and we were alone, sipping a good measure of Jack Daniels, he said

"I've booked my summer holiday...."

"Oh, yes" I interrupted, hoping it was good news.

"And I'd like to spend it with you, if that's alright" he smiled and I just flung my arms round his neck and kissed him hard and deep.

"I'll take that as a 'yes' then" he smiled when we broke.

"You betcha" I grinned and kissed him again.

"Good."

"So, when's your vacation?"

"Last two weeks in August."

"I'll tell Pops, he'll run things whilst we're away somewhere...."

"Really?"

"Yup, so where d'you wanna go?"

"I really don't mind, as long as we're all together...."

"You know, Mister, I'm beginning to like you a helluva lot" I smiled.

"That's nice because it's mutual...." he replied and kissed me.

On Monday morning we said 'goodbye' at the airport before Peter flew back to London and I knew the time would drag until the sixteenth of August when he'd arrive back for two weeks vacation with me and my girl. It was late afternoon when Pops called the office and said that I was to come over for dinner and a serious talk about the business. When we'd all finished up, Pops sat at the table and began his serious talk.

"I realise, honey, that the business is growing fast, almost too damned fast, and you need help...."

"I sure do" I interrupted.

"And I've been giving it all a lot of thought...."

"Good."

"I've spoken to Mitch and I've talked it over with your Mom...." I looked at Mom and she smiled sweetly and I guessed what was coming next.

"Go on, Pops."

"How would you feel if I asked Peter to join the business?" he asked with a smile and I was pleased that I had guessed right.

"Absolutely fine, Pops" I smiled.

"Okay, that's what I'll do then."

"So tell me, is he going to be a partner?" I asked.

"Well, I'll have to discuss it all with Matt first, as I've got to make sure that you're secure and always have the last word on everything...."

"Huh! That's usual, so no problem there, Joe" said Mom and I pulled a silly face at that, but inside, I was so happy and hoped that Pops would make Peter an offer he couldn't refuse.

"That's great, Pops, have you asked Peter if he's interested?"

"Not yet, honey, I just wanted to get everything clear before I did."

"That's good, and you'll be able to ask him when he comes over for his summer vacation on the sixteenth of August."

"Wow! It couldn't be better" smiled Pops and Mom looked pleased.

"So you are going to marry him then" said Melodie.

"Perhaps" I replied.

"Oh, Mom, you're so indecisive" she replied and we all laughed.

The rest of the week was very busy at work and Pops had to come in and help out. Thursday night, after a long soak in the tub, I called Rachel.

"Hi, honey, how are you?"

"I'm so good you wouldn't believe it!" she replied.

"Go on...."

"I was just about to call you and tell you the news" she said excitedly.

"What, honey?"

"Guy's taking me up to see his folks again this weekend...."

"Wow, are you the flavour of the month or what?"

"Oh, yes, you can say that again...."

"This is getting serious...."

"It sure is, he's been round to see me twice this week... and stayed all night to meet my needs!" she giggled.

"You little...."

"I know, and it's so lovely with a man you love" she said happily.

"It is, so, wedding bells?"

"Don't hold your breathe, but it's looking good from here...."

Peter often called from London and it seemed as if he was counting the days down to his vacation and getting more excited about it the closer it got. I was certainly missing him and so it seemed were Melodie and my folks. Work slowed a little and we were all glad of that. I took longer lunch breaks and sat in the park eating the usual deli rolls, wondering if Eric would show up, but he didn't. Rachel and Guy were seeing each other very regularly now and spending time out on his yacht or dining their way through some of the local, expensive restaurants. I really hoped and expected something to happen and I was getting impatient for her. In the evenings I started to plan a route to go north for our vacation. I thought Peter would enjoy a drive up through New England to Canada and back, staying at motels and occasionally at somewhere more expensive. Melodie helped me out with suggestions of places we should visit that she just knew Peter would like. She had really taken to him and I wondered how he felt about all of us, and what hold Miss Italian still had over him. I felt that I did love this gentle, unassuming, charming guy and made up my mind to ask him to marry me at the end of our vacation. When you're sure about somebody, you have to ask, especially when the guy in question is a reserved Englishman. God only knows how they built an empire!

Peter arrived on the sixteenth and I was there with Melodie to meet him at the airport. After an age in immigration he finally came through into Arrivals and we rushed up to meet him with a big American welcome from both of us. When the kissing and huggies had finally finished he said "take me home for a nice cup of tea!" He said 'home' and my heart skipped a beat.

"Sure, then I guess you'll want a shower to clean all the 'grubbies' off" I laughed.

"What's 'grubbies' Mom?" asked Melodie.

"Something that Peter gets after a long flight" I replied and we all laughed. As we pulled into the driveway, Mrs Dawson spotted us and was by the fence as usual.

"Back again I see" she said as we got out of the Chevy.

"Yes, Mrs Dawson, this time on holiday" smiled Peter.

"My, my, a vacation, well something around here must be attracting you back….."

"Your roses are the attraction, Mrs Dawson" I interrupted.

"Well, if that's the case, I think I'll plant a few more in the Fall……" she smiled. We laughed and went into the house.

I hoped that Peter would be happy about my ideas for our vacation drive up to Canada and when Melodie and I showed him our route and told him all about it he just smiled.

"That's wonderful, I'm sure we'll all have a great time" he said. He was so easy and laid back that I thought of proposing before we set off, but decided against it for the moment. But I might make my move half way through the vacation, if the time was right. I thought it was important to get that settled, one way or the other, before Pops made the job offer. I made him promise to keep that back until the end of the vacation and he agreed. I had wondered whether Peter would really be interested in coming to the States to live, as it meant leaving his job, his home and hopefully, Miss Italian. I hadn't asked him about his divorce and guessed that he'd tell me when he was good and ready. We spent the rest of the day quietly and had lunch with Mom and Pops on the Saturday before setting off on our vacation on the Sunday morning.

I drove up the coast road to Newark and then joined the Freeway to miss out New York and went on up north towards Kingston. We talked, laughed and Peter sang silly songs that amused Melodie no end. The scenery was full and green with the summer and when we stopped at Diners or Big Mac's for a bite and a break, the scent of the trees was all around us. I was so relaxed and happy and hoped that this feeling deep inside would remain with me always. I got to thinking that if Peter wasn't interested in me or Pops offer of a job, then I'd always remember this vacation and be content with that, so I made the most of it and things just got better. We stopped, for the first night, at the Woodgate Motel at Kingston, over looking the Hudson River. It was really beautiful and we were all pretty impressed by the surroundings. After dinner we went for a long walk by the river, holding hands, and talking about our visit to Wallingford on the Thames. Peter kept giving me little kisses on my cheek until Melodie told him to save it for later. As we were all sharing the same room, Peter had to be Mister Reserved in bed whilst I got a little frustrated, well, when a girl is getting used to being well knocked up by the guy in her life, she doesn't want to break the habit, especially on vacation.

It took us two days of leisurely driving through Albany then Syracuse before we hit Buffalo and Niagara Falls. I'd only been to the Falls once before when I was a kid and I'd forgotten just how beautiful they are. We all gazed at the fantastic view for a while before Melodie wandered off to another view point close by. Peter put his arm around my shoulder and I looked up at him.

"America is a great country" he said.

"It sure is…."

"Full of nice people" he smiled.

"True…."

"And some of those people are very nice indeed."

"You think so?" I smiled.

"I know so…."

"Go on…."

"One in particular is very special…."

"Really?"

"Helen, I really love you and I want you to marry me…."

"Oh my God, yes, oh, so 'yes' you wouldn't believe!" I whispered and he kissed me so hard that I almost fainted. Melodie came running back when she saw us holding each other tightly. I smiled at her and said "Peter's asked me to marry him."

"Thank goodness we've got that out of the way at last, now we can relax and get on with the vacation!" she replied and we laughed. We celebrated by booking into the Falls Hotel, in adjoining rooms, and having a dinner to die for. I called Mom and Pops from our room and told them the news and they were delighted, then I called Rachel and Karen, who were so happy for us both. We made love nearly all night and were pretty tired at breakfast. From then on the vacation just took off in a pink cloud of happiness. Melodie announced that she'd prefer to call Peter by his name rather than 'Pops' as that sounded too old for him. We left Niagara and went on up to Rochester and spent a day there overlooking Lake Ontario before heading up to Vermont and New Hampshire. I thought that life doesn't get any better than this, so

238

enjoy.

The days just melted into one long, easy and happy stream of life as we drove out to Maine and the Atlantic coast. We finished up at Portland overlooking the grey green ocean before setting off back to Atlantic City. When we arrived back home on the Saturday afternoon I saw Mrs Dawson in her garden and called over to her and told her the news. She smiled and told me that she had an idea all along by the way Peter looked at me. She was happy for us and when I invited her to the wedding she was all choked up. We went to Mom and Pops for dinner and after a lot of laughter and too much wedding planning from Mom, Pops made Peter the job offer. He was really surprised but accepted straight away and I asked myself again 'does it get any better than this?' Well it does, and it seems that really good things come suddenly. When I got into the office on the Monday, after I said goodbye to Peter at the airport before he flew back to London to make all his arrangements to leave England for good, my phone rang and Naomi patched Rachel through.

"Hi, honey" I said.

"Helen, you'll never guess, Guy has asked me to marry him!" she said excitedly.

"Oh, babe, I'm so happy for you, I really am...."

"Thanks, he asked me when we were sailing yesterday and as he stayed last night I haven't had a chance to call until now... can you believe it all?"

"Nope, not really" I replied.

"Neither can I...."

"Have you fixed your wedding day?"

"Nope, not yet, but I guess that it will be sometime in October...."

"Great...."

"Guy wants us to get married up in New England...."

"It's so beautiful there in the Fall" I said.

"Yup, and I'm so excited, well I guess I won't sleep now until the wedding!"

"Sure you will" I laughed.

"Now, Helen, you've gotta help me with everything...."

"Sure, honey, I'll be with you all the way" I replied.

"And I want you to be my maid of honour and Melodie, my

bridesmaid."

"Oh, that so sweet."

"Now, that's all my news for the moment, so, promise you'll drop by after work tonight for quality time together."

"Okay, I will."

"Before you hang up, just give me the latest on Peter."

"He went off this morning to fix up everything back home, he's quitting his job and...."

"What about his divorce?" she interrupted.

"He says it should be through by the end of September and he's sold his house...."

"Hey, you could get married in October too" she said.

"Possibly, but I'll wait and see, remember he's gotta get passed immigration first, so there could be a hang up there" I replied.

"Don't you worry, he'll make it through okay" she replied.

"Yup, hope so."

"Sure, and now we've both found our guys, who'd a believed it a coupla months ago?"

"Not me."

"Hey, and isn't it strange that that Eric guy has disappeared?"

"Yup, I'm beginning to think I imagined him outa desperation" I replied and the back of my neck tingled as I saw his handsome face in my mind.

"A line man, married with a coupla kids more likely" she said.

"Probably, anyhow, I must go and I'll see you after work."

"Okay, honey, look forward to it."

From then on the days seem to rush by as I juggled with work, the arrangements for Rachel's wedding, buying the dress and my plans for when Peter came out to Atlantic City for good. I went sailing in the 'Princess' as often as I could and relaxed with my thoughts and hopes for the future. My folks and Melodie were getting excited as the time for Rachel's wedding and Peter's arrival got closer, but I tried to keep calm just in case anything went wrong. I did wonder if Peter had asked me to marry him on the rebound from Miss Italian and I couldn't quite get that clear in my mind. He said that he would come over for Rachel's wedding, no matter what, and I was pleased about that, as I wanted my fiancé by my side on the big day. Well, if Eric was an angel he

240

certainly fixed it for us, as Peter got his clearance to come over for good on October the twenty third, just a week ahead of Rachel's wedding. I was so happy that when Melodie and I met him at the airport, we just kissed and hugged for an age. At home we sat and talked through everything and set our date for November the twenty ninth, so we could be settled down by Christmas.

Pops came to work with Peter and showed him around for a few days after covering all the details of his new job. On Friday morning we all set off to drive up to New England for Rachel's wedding. We went to Guy's home in Fall River, just south of Boston, to meet with his folks and say 'hi' before booking into the Grosvenor Hotel where Rachel and her folks were staying. The excitement was almost too much and I began to think that I'd be glad when it was all over. On the Saturday we were all dressed at last and ready to go and my Mom as well as Rachel's were still flapping around us as we prepared to leave for the church. Rachel looked fabulous in a white silk dress with the prettiest little lace hat and veil you ever did see. Melodie and I had light blue matching dresses and everybody said we looked cute. Peter and Pops kept on smiling and both Moms had tears in their eyes and so did Rachel's Dad. He was so proud of his girl that words couldn't say how he felt.

We three had a surprise for everyone that we'd planned at Rachel's request and I was sure it would bring a few tears at the church. We arrived outside the church and helped Rachel into her wheelchair before her Pops pushed her up to the steps in front of the door. I could see the folks inside and hear the organ playing softly as we got Rachel out of her chair and her Pops carried her up the steps and then stood her down. I brought a walking stick and smiled as I gave it to her and she gave me a wink. She was determined to walk down the aisle and held on tight to her Pop's arm and I stood to the other side of her and held her arm as she moved forward, one slow step at a time towards her handsome husband to be, standing with his brother before the altar. It took an age to get down the aisle but I didn't care and the organist just kept on playing 'here comes the bride' as we slowly made our way past the tearful guests.

I was so happy and proud of my lovely friend who at last was going to be married to the man of her choice, who simply adored her. Folks say that some marriages are made in heaven and this was certainly one of them. Pops gave his daughter's arm to Guy who had tears in his eyes as he held his lovely girl close to him. I stood tight up and held her arm to support her as the ceremony began before handing her bouquet back to Melodie, who smiled.

Well by the time the service was over there wasn't a dry eye in the church, and then after Guy had kissed his bride long and hard he picked her up as if she was the lightest feather in the world and carried her back down the aisle as the whole church erupted in applause. I followed on with Richard and Melodie and we all arrived outside on the steps as the cameras began to click. Both tearful Moms arrived and kissed us all and my Mom held back for only a moment before she joined in as well. Karen and Ralph, both with tears in their eyes, kissed Rachel before making a fuss of Guy.

From then on it just got better and the reception back at Guy's folks place was absolutely fabulous. A large marquee had been set up on the huge back lawn and everything from the dance band to the food was just so. We drank Möet Chandon champagne, ate until we were full to bursting and danced until the early hours. Rachel and Guy were going to spend their first night there, what was left of it, before going of on honeymoon to Acapulco. We all couldn't be happier.

As soon as we arrived back home and had sobered up a little, I started, with Mom, to make my wedding plans. The end of November was not that far away and I had to make tracks pretty fast. Running the business with Peter's help was a lot easier and I was surprised how quickly he settled into it all, but I guess when it comes to fixing up wrecked autos, it's the same the world over. His know how on colour matching and efficient spray painting really impressed Mitch and the guys in the paintshop as well as increasing our speed of vehicle through put. Pops was right as usual, Peter was a great asset to the business, and he just charmed the customers to bits, especially the women. I made a mental note to keep an eye on one or two of them who seemed to be having scrapes a little too often and appearing at the works for Peter to give an estimate for their vehicles. I was just concerned that they didn't ask him to check out their bodywork at the same time!

Everything seemed to be going well for the wedding day, Pops booked the Atlantic Suite at the Marine Hotel for the ceremony and reception and he said that he wanted it to be a grand occasion, no expense spared. I asked Karen and Rachel to be maids of honour along with Melodie as bridesmaid. Peter asked Guy to be his best man and Doctor Gorgeous said he was delighted to be asked. Peter booked a hotel in Bermuda for our honeymoon and I knew that we'd have a romantic and relaxed time there together.

I was now pretty excited about everything and decided a week before the wedding that we needed a days break from it all and if the weather was settled, we should take a sail in the 'Princess' before the winter set in. As it happened, the Sunday before our wedding was a bright, clear day with little wind and we rushed off to Cape May leaving Melodie with my folks and planning to have dinner with them all when we got back. We arrived at the car park by the jetty and unloaded my sports bag with all the food and set off towards the 'Princess' moored half way along. Suddenly, coming in the opposite direction, was a tall figure with blonde hair that I knew so well and my heart froze as my neck tingled. What would Peter say about this guy who I had felt so strongly about and had 'urges' for? I didn't want to upset Peter and panicked about what to say or do! We all arrived by the 'Princess' at the same moment and as we stopped, Eric smiled at us.

"Hello" he said and before I could say a word, Peter asked "what the devil are you doing here, Eric?" I was amazed to hear that and said to Peter "d'you know this guy?"

"Yes, he pops up from time to time, he says his name is Eric Bloodaxe, and he's more of a bloody nuisance than anything, but I think he's harmless...." At that Eric put his hands on his hips and let out a roar of laughter.

"You're the first person who's ever called me harmless" he said through his laughter before looking at me with those bright, twinkling blue eyes and asking "what do you think, Helen?" Before I could answer, Peter looked at me and asked in a surprised voice "d'you know this fella?"

"Yup, I'm afraid so" I replied.

"Well that's a surprise...." said Peter with concern.

"Stop right there for a moment, both of you, and get aboard the

'Princess'" said Eric.

"Why?" asked Peter.

"Because I want to speak to you and there's no better place for a Viking to talk than on a boat when the wind is light and the sea is calm" Eric replied sternly.

"Right" said Peter and nodded to me. We all clambered aboard and cast off from the mooring. Once beyond the harbour entrance I raised the mainsail and swung the 'Princess' round on to a southerly course, keeping the coast well in view. We settled down and waited to hear what Eric had to say, and my heart was beating overtime, hoping he wouldn't say anything that would upset Peter.

"This is very pleasant" said Eric as he looked across at the green coastline.

"Sure is" I replied nervously.

"Well, Eric?" asked Peter after a long pause when the only sound was from the water breaking under the bow of my little boat. Eric looked at both of us, sitting close together, my hand holding the wheel and Peter's arm around my shoulder.

"I have seen you both a number of times over the last months....." he began and both Peter and I were surprised at that. What on God's earth was this guy all about? I asked myself.

"And I have told you that I was here to guide you to a happy outcome to your complicated lives...."

"Complicated? You can say that again" Peter interrupted.

"But I have found it very difficult because you both have a free will and no matter how hard I tried on several occasions to bring you together, you both wandered off like lost sheep" said Eric and I smiled.

"I can believe that" I said.

"You can have no idea how difficult it has been for me to arrange things for your benefit...."

"Such as?" asked Peter.

"I don't want to have to go through everything but for a few examples, there was your meeting in the lift...."

"You're telling us that you fixed that?" I asked.

"Yes, and before that your Father's accident at work to make sure you went to Paris...."

"What?" I demanded.

"And the life wrecker who took Sophia away from you" said

Eric and Peter looked stunned and I felt warm inside because I had been right, Miss Italian had dumped him for the old guy.

"I don't believe this" said Peter.

"I'm telling you the truth, now listen to me carefully, I know you will find this difficult, but I have been appointed as your guardian angel and I will be with you both for the rest of your lives, looking out for you and your family and friends...."

"You're kidding...." I interrupted.

"We're not allowed to 'kid'" he replied seriously.

"Go on" said Peter.

"I have had words with others who have made good things possible for your friends Rachel and Karen, because their happiness affects both of you and I will make sure that I will try and guide them also, now, after today, you will never see me again, but I will always be close and all you have to do is think of me and ask for my help and the thoughts that come into your head will be my guidance for you."

"I really don't believe this" said Peter.

"That's up to you, now, as you two were my very first mission as an angel, I was given permission to appear before you in an attempt to make the whole thing successful in a short time, and I doubt whether I will ever be able to do this again" Eric said in a serious tone.

"So now what?" I asked.

"You are both happy together and you'll stay that way after you're married next Saturday and then when you are away in Bermuda....."

"How d'you know about that?" asked Peter.

"He's a line man with the phone company and he listens in to all our calls" I said smugly and Eric laughed, his blue eyes sparkling.

"And you will always be happy and have a child, a boy, who, along with Melodie will do well in the future and they will be a delight to you both" he smiled and I began to get a little nervous again.

"What else?" asked Peter.

"Nothing more, but enjoy each day together and get the pleasure of life from your children, family and friends" said Eric.

"And that's it?" Peter asked.

"Yes, because that's the true secret of life and it's all you need to ever know" Eric smiled.

"Wow, it's that simple, huh?" I asked sarcastically.

"Yes, now, as much as I enjoy sailing and your company, I must return as I have other matters to attend to" said Eric with a gentle smile.

"Okay" I replied as I began to swing the wheel to bring the 'Princess' round a hundred and eighty to return to Cape May. When we arrived back at the jetty and moored up, Eric gave me a gentle kiss and shook Peter's hand before just whispering 'goodbye' and walking off towards the car park to disappear behind the boats on the hard standing. Peter looked at me and said "well, did I just imagine all that or what?"

"I've no idea, honey, I really have no idea" I replied.

Peter's mother came over from England before we got married on the Saturday following and flew off to Bermuda for a fabulous honeymoon. We sun bathed, danced, dined, drank and made love to excess and boy, did we enjoy it! When we were back home our life together settled down into work, which we both loved, and a great social life with Rachel and Guy, Karen and Ralph. We all spent time on 'Lady Be Good' sailing up and down in Chesapeake Bay, enjoying Guy's cooking and drinking his best wines. All our husbands got on very well together and became great friends. Ralph bought a small ranch and bred horses near Ohio and we spent some great times there.

Two most wonderful things happened the next year when Guy's dad operated on Rachel and she was able to walk a little with sticks; and I became pregnant. I had just given birth to little Oliver when Rachel announced she was pregnant! Well, we were all overjoyed. I thought it couldn't get any better than that, but it did - as Melodie and Oliver grew up they became a constant delight to us. Mom and Pops spoilt them but they remained good kids and did well at High School and then at University. Melodie went into Television reporting and Oliver joined the Navy and became a Flight Deck Officer on the Nimitz Carrier. Rachel and Guy's son, Tony, grew up to be as tall and good looking as his Pops and went into medicine. Karen and Ralph mellowed, just got richer whilst staying adorable and they spoil all our kids like you can't imagine.

The years have flowed on by and Peter and I have become so comfortable with each other that are like a couple of soft, comfy shoes and our lives just seem to get better and better.

We never did see Eric again but we both often think of him and wonder whether we imagined him and if we didn't, we wonder if it is true that he's an angel and has guided us through difficult times to a very happy and contented life. We both like to think so.

Find out what Eric did with the difficult young woman in:

ERIC AND THE DIVORCEE.

THE FRENCH COLLECTION

AMUSING AND EROTIC TITLES FOR ADULTS

MARSEILLE TAXI by Peter Child

This is a tantalising revelation of the twilight existence of Michel Ronay, a Marseille Taxi driver. Every moment of his life is crowded with incident. Compromised by the lecherous women of Marseille, chased by the Police, harassed by the underworld and encouraged by gays, his life is a non stop roller coaster. Stay with him in his Taxi and feel the heat of the Marseille streets, smell the smells and then have a bath with someone to cleanse your body and mind from the experience.

ISBN : 0-9540910-1-9

AUGUST IN GRAMBOIS By Peter Child

Michel Ronay, a Taxi driver, leaves his tiring work driving through the hot, dusty streets of Marseille and heads for the cool tranquillity of his villa in Grambois for the whole month of August. With his second wife, Monique, her mother, two aunts and Frederik, his stepson, Michel prepares to enjoy a holiday relaxing in the peace and quiet of Provence, so what could possibly disturb him in the ample bosom of his family? His many mistresses perhaps? Or Edward Salvator? Or Jacques and Antone? Or Gerrard? Or....

ISBN : 0-9540910-2-7

CHRISTMAS IN MARSEILLE By Peter Child

Follow Michel Ronay, a Taxi driver around the cold, bright sunlit streets of Marseille in the frantic run up to Christmas. Laugh with him when he discovers that all his wife's family are coming to stay, cry with him when the Police involve him in undercover work that goes wrong, sympathise with him when his mistresses find out about one another. His life is just a frantic kaleidoscope of drink, sex and the fear of being found out. You will never get in a Taxi again without thinking of Michel Ronay.

ISBN : 0-9540910-3-5

CATASTROPHE IN LE TOUQUET By Peter Child

Michel Ronay escapes from the hustle and bustle of Marseille to Le Touquet, where he plans to start a new and prosperous life with his fiancé, Josette. After making business arrangements with his cousin, Henri, everything is set for a relaxed and wonderful future, until he meets Madame Christiane. Monique, Michel's wife, Monsieur Robardes, a solicitor and Henri are not at all amused by what happens in Le Touquet and Josette wonders if she should ever have bothered to leave Marseille in the first place.

ISBN : 0-9540910-5-1

To order the above titles contact Benbow Publications at www.benbowpublications.co.uk

Printed in the United Kingdom
by Lightning Source UK Ltd.
127385UK00001B/35/A